Y0-BQU-837

"Will you marry me?" John asked. "Don't think about it; just marry me and we'll straighten it all out afterwards."

"But I thought you and Myree . . ." Kim hesitated, and then she thought:

Me in the back room out of sight—doing the cooking when taking time off from drawing, typing, and tagging—probably somewhere between the soup and the frozen vegetables! And meantime—Myree in the front room! Oh, no you don't, Dr. John Andrews! No, you don't . . . !

NOBODY READS JUST ONE LUCY WALKER

- #1 The Other Girl
- #2 Heaven Is Here
- #3 The Distant Hills
- #4 Sweet and Faraway
- #5 The Call of the Pines
- #6 Come Home, Dear
- #7 Love in a Cloud
- #8 Follow Your Star
- #9 Home at Sundown
- #10 Reaching for the Stars
- #11 A Man Called Masters
- #12 The Stranger from the North
- #13 The River Is Down
- #14 The One Who Kisses
- #15 The Man from Outback
- #16 Down in the Forest
- #17 The Moonshiner
- #18 Wife to Order
- #19 The Ranger in the Hills
- #20 Shining River
- #21 Six for Heaven
- #22 The Gone-away Man
- #23 Kingdom of the Heart
- #24 The Loving Heart
- #25 Master of Ransome
- #26 Joyday for Jodi
- #27 The Bell Branch
- #28 The Mountain That Went to the Sea
- #29 Ribbons in Her Hair
- #30 Monday in Summer
- #31 Pepper Tree Bay
- #32 Girl Alone
- #33 Runaway Girl

Published by Ballantine Books

HOME AT SUNDOWN

Lucy Walker

BALLANTINE BOOKS • NEW YORK

Copyright © 1968 by Lucy Walker

All rights reserved. Published in the United States by Ballantine Books, a division of Random House, Inc., New York.

ISBN 0-345-25235-7-125

Manufactured in the United States of America

First Ballantine Books Edition: January, 1971
Sixth Printing: July, 1976

CHAPTER ONE

Kimberley Jessica Wentworth tucked a stray wisp of hair under her ribbon band. She shifted her weight from one foot to the other, then marshalled into order the pile of books she carried under her arm. She was called 'Kim' for short, and this suited her appearance better than the cumbersome name wished down on her by her parents.

'Hullo! I mean—*Excuse me!*' Her voice was polite—barely—for after all, this was the third time of speaking. The man had ignored her two previous efforts.

He was bending over a nest of small plants, pressing down the earth on the newly set roots. In spite of the delicacy and urgency of this exercise he allowed his head to turn—just that much.

He saw the shoes first. They were white with blue heels and straps: obviously new. The girl was pleased with this attention to what she wore on her feet, for these shoes were the very latest thing and the only high fashion note about her whole appearance—except, perhaps, the very short skirt. But then everyone wore those!

The man's eyes—very penetrating—moved up from the shoes, took in the smooth tanned skin of a nice pair of legs knees that weren't knobbly, and a plain cream-coloured skirt Then they came upwards to a pixyish, puzzled face. This face was lit by a pair of wide-set grey eyes, and crowned with a sweep of dark hair held in place by a wide ribbon band.

Any other man but this would have thought she was a sweetie.

He, however, was busy with more important things. At least his expression implied this without any doubt.

He appeared *not to see* any charm in the candour of the grey eyes, nor in their quite unique expression of youthful wonder.

The pupils of his own eyes were pin-point because as he looked over his shoulder at the girl he was looking into morning sunshine in more senses than one.

'Did you speak to me?' he asked coldly.

'I did say "Good morning" the first time,' Kim explained

patiently. 'The second time I said "Hullo". And the third time I said—well, what I just said a minute ago—"*Excuse me*". Or something like that!'

She changed the books to her left arm and her weight back to her right foot.

'If you are looking for the Botanical section—which on certain days is open to the public——' he continued coldly, 'it is four hundred yards across the track to your right. You did not read the notice board?'

'I've been to that section. I was looking for Dr Andrews. He's a botanist attached to this Institute at the Mount. They said he was somewhere around. Probably down here.' She sighed.

'You're the only person in sight,' she added. 'So please could you tell me where I will find him?'

'Dr Andrews is not available to members of the public at anybody's whim.' He was very aloof. 'I advise you to go away, and come back on the Public's Open Day.'

Kim moved her head fractionally to one side and asked, *too gently*——

'Are you his guardian? I mean, I thought you were the plant man, or the head gardener, or something.'

He dusted the earth from his hands, then stood up, straightening himself. He was so tall he towered over Kim. So she looked down instead of up. She noticed his work boots were very dusty. They hadn't been cleaned for a long, long time.

'What is wrong with being a gardener?' he asked.

She looked up at him again. There was still that look of built-in wonder in her eyes. Someone, other than this man, might have scented danger. At least, *persistence*.

'Nothing,' she said. 'Did you think there was? The gardener has the best job. He works with the wild-flowers in this special section, doesn't he?'

'I think you'd better state your business young lady or you'll have someone coming down from the office to run you out. This section is "Private". There is a notice board behind you saying so.'

Kim ignored this last, and went straight to her point again.

'*I want to see Dr Andrews*,' she explained, extra patiently. 'There was an advertisement by C.O.C.R. in the week-end paper. They want an Assistant to the botanist at the Mount. That's here, isn't it? It said "Typing qualifications necessary, some botanical experience advisable but not so necessary Immediate appointment to suitable applicant for a twelve-week Expedition for plant collecting in the Outback Apply to the Director of the Mount, or Dr Andrews, immediately."' She had just enough breath to finish the last word.

'You seem to have it off very pat?'

'I do. I know someone interested in the job.'

'Then you should tell your "someone" to apply by letter, or *in person*, to the main office. Now, if you'll excuse me——'

He turned back to his work, crouching down with bent knees as he did so. He began to remove a young plant from a seedling box.

'In the Botany Department down at Crawley they don't pack plants tightly like that,' Kim advised him leaning over his shoulder to watch him work.

This time he was not only exasperated, he was angry. He stood up again turned round and stared at her with dark blue eyes that sparkled ice.

'Are you a University student?' he demanded. 'I would have thought you were too young. A *school girl?*'

'I'm not a University student, but I do know the department at Crawley——' Kim began.

'Oh yes. They have open day for the senior schools once a year! I'm aware of that. How old are you? Sixteen?'

'Nineteen.' Kim corrected him politely. She suspected he didn't believe her, but then no one ever did.

This matter of looking too young was a day-to-day problem for Kim. Everyone thought she was young—because by a mistake on nature's part, she looked it. She was tired of her mother, father, two older sisters—and sometimes her brother Jeff—treating her as if she was a child; a mere school girl. Now this man too!

She wanted to go away from them all. Right away. Preferably where there were plants to be looked after. She liked that part of her job in the glasshouses at Crawley Botany Department. Actually she had been appointed as a typist. Then it was discovered she could tag the plants accurately and that her penmanship was as remarkable as it was fine and delicate. Ralph Sinclair, one of the younger research men, had put her on to flower-drawings, and discovered her real value. She now spent more than half her time with a drawing pen in her hand.

It had been wonderful in a way, except she had been overloaded. She was too soft-hearted to say 'no' every time someone wanted drawings done. Specially Ralph Sinclair. He monopolised her time, praised her drawings, gave her more and more work to do, but never once looked at her, *except by accident*. He was so dedicated to his doctorate thesis that he saw in Kim only a steady hand and a deep love of wild plants and flowers.

He took her, as a person, for granted. So Kim wanted to get away from him too!

This job being advertised by C.O.C.R.—short for the hefty title *Council for Organic Chemical Research*—would be just the berries. Twelve weeks on an expedition into the outback as Technical Assistant to the botanist! A plant-search! What heaven! Besides, if her drawings were as good as she thought them herself, C.O.C.R. might end up taking her on for keeps as a Technical Assistant: even send her to work at the State Gardens or to be seconded to the Mount permanently. Well, why not dream?

Kim had never wanted anything more badly in her life than she wanted this job.

'The advertisement said—"Apply to Dr Andrews",' she said again.

'Then you tell your friend to do just that. *By letter* for preference. You are aware Dr Andrews does not care to take *girls* on expeditions?'

The way he said 'girls' nettled Kim, though she took care to hide it.

She shook her head soberly. 'If it hadn't been for a girl you wouldn't be here——' she remarked, ever so gently.

'I beg your pardon?'

'Your mother must have been a girl once.'

She was pleased with that one!

He'd be more than thirty, she guessed. He'd be very good looking if his hair weren't ruffled, and he didn't have streaks of earth on his square impressive forehead. He was really very impressive altogether, but she didn't care to admit that just now.

'Would you mind leaving these gardens at once. *They are not for the Public,*' he commanded. 'I happen to be busy.' He swung round, bent down over his work again and began to dust soil from the roots of a specimen he had just taken from a box. His back said she no longer existed.

'*Leschenaultia!*' Kim remarked, identifying the plant in his hand. 'It won't survive more than two seasons there, you know. Too many minerals in the soil on this side of the Mount.'

He stopped shaking the roots, and slowly turned round again.

'We have a three-foot depth of Darling Range soil top-dressing this particular area,' he said flatly—talking at a small girl again. 'Would you mind letting me go about my legitimate business? And you go about yours?'

'Every plant-man ought to know that you might dig in fresh earth but you won't stop the rain seeping down from the back slopes, picking up minerals as it comes.' She shook her head sadly. 'It's the seepage that does it. Your *Leschenaultia* could die. That is unless you have magic in your fingers. Some do, you know——'

He did not answer her.

She transferred her books from one arm to the other again, and turned her back on him.

'I shall find Dr Andrews for myself——' was her parting remark, not admitting defeat. Anyway—if she sought out the Mount's Director he'd only send her back to the Botanist. She'd skip that step!

Kim shook back her hair and began climbing the steep slope to the track. Beyond this track was a green sward of grass and beyond the grass was a stand of trees hiding the Botanist's herbarium from the rude stare of the Public's gaze.

By the time she had reached the trees she changed her mind about looking for Dr Andrews just now. If he didn't *care to take girls* he had better not know she was a girl till he had given her the job. Then she could sue him—or something—if he tried to take it away from her when he found out. Sex discrimination wasn't allowed in the Government's C.O.C.R. institutions.

She didn't have a name like Kimberley Jessica Wentworth for nothing. Wentworths were worth where they went. That was a family tradition. Her grandfather Kimberley had been a strong character. Very persistent.

Her name was always cut short to Kim and more than once when she had sent a postcard for drawing materials, the answer had come back addressed to Mr Kim Wentworth. That 'Mr Kim' might be of help now!

Deep in thought she went home instead of going in further search of the elusive Dr Andrews. There, in her box of a room—part of the sleep-out—she drafted a 'brilliant' application for the job of Temporary Technical Assistant to the Chief Botanist, C.O.C.R. Expedition. In perfect writing too. She signed the application Kim Wentworth. That might make that 'Mister' pay dividends for once. She added a loose page of the pen and ink plant-drawings which she had done for Ralph Sinclair at Crawley. She had accurately labelled, in tiny print, each and every part of the plants in the drawings.

An hour later—after three cups of tea for extra courage—she went down to the University, waited till Ralph Sinclair was at his most absent-minded and busiest, then asked him to dictate a reference for her.

'Do it yourself, dear girl. You can see I'm up to my microscopic eyes in *Knuzea pulchella*——'

This was exactly the answer Kim hoped for: indeed half-expected. She wrote herself the best reference ever. It would have stunned even Ralph, if he had had time to read it. He signed it absently. Then suddenly realised that all this rot Kim had been talking really meant she was likely to leave the Department.

'What will I do if you go?' He all but wrung his hands. If they'd been free of the lovely grey and scarclet *pulchella* flower he would have done just that. 'Who's going to do the drawings?'

'You'll have to do them yourself, I expect,' Kim said regretfully. 'On the other hand, there's Myree Bolton. She already has her first degree. With a mass of distinctions too. She can draw, but I don't know about typing——'

'Myree Bolton? You mean the girl doing Honours? The one with the pile of curls on top of her head? The campus beauty? Of course, of course! Do go and find her at once Kim, my love. She must begin work immediately——'

The 'my love' hurt Kim more than ever, specially as Ralph

was already putting his eye to the microscope again. He was enchanted at the prospect of having the campus beauty working with him, was he? He had already forgotten that Kim was actually likely to part from him.

She decided he could go find Myree Bolton for himself.

She reached the door and looked back. A shadow of young, fleeting sorrow passed over her face. She had worked so hard for him; been the smallest bit in love with him—and now, at her going, he thought only of the pulchella flower and Myree Bolton's pile of golden curls!

'Ah well! Such is my life!'

She thought it all very sad.

In the typist's room she borrowed an envelope from the cupboard. She now folded her application, together with her brilliant testimonial, into the envelope; stamped and addressed this, then posted it in the Department's outward mail-box. After all, a University out-stamp on the envelope could do the application more good than not. If Dr Andrews was at all observant he would see that this letter came from higher realms before he even opened it. Kim felt a little smug at her own perspicacity. She was going to get that job with whatever ammunition she found at hand.

Half an hour later she swung open the wire gate of her home. It was after midday by this time. She looked at the flowering apple hibiscus on her right, then the budding boronia growing in a wild patch on the left by the picket fence.

How she had had to stand over that patch to prevent would-be waterers in her family from letting the mineral-weighted tap-water touch the tiny plants in the long dry summer!

She walked round the back of the house and looked at the water-tank her brother Jeff had obligingly erected to store the earlier winter rain-water as it flowed generously down the iron roof of the garage.

Her boronia had survived, when no one else's had! She had used rain-water *only*.

'All that trouble for plants that size,' Celia, her sister, had said caustically. 'Boronia only flowers for one month in the year anyway! Meantime we have to put up with that hideous tank in the back yard.'

Thinking of this remark, Kim opened the door of the garage. The van was there. *Her* van. Not that anyone else in the family conceded it was her van at all. They had long forgotten its history. Specially Celia, whose memory was always choosily short.

Kimberley Jessica Wentworth came from a family of foresters. Her father worked with the Forestry Department south of the river. Her brother Jeff was forestry adviser in the karri forest down south. Celia and Diana worked as experts in the Botanical Gardens. There hadn't been any money left in the family to give Kim a professional training. So she had become a typist.

'She's only a child anyway,' Celia had declared. 'She doesn't know one plant from another, and never will. She's for ever drawing them. That doesn't rear plants, or test soils——'

'Maybe we could have her taught Commercial Art,' Jeff had suggested, sorry a little that his infant sister was the only member of the family *not* to have a higher qualification.

'Draw toothpaste ads and do sign-writing! Ought to be money in that,' Diane, the cool one, had agreed. Diane, like Celia, was obsessed by the shortage of money with which to buy fine clothes and a motor car—though she didn't care to show it. Everyone in the family lived beyond his or her means. It was their way of life.

Kim had overheard this family conversation but did not feel her destiny lay in toothpaste ads. She became a typist instead. Foresters and botanists needed typists at headquarters, and so did the University at Crawley. Maybe—if she couldn't become a trained expert—she could do the next best thing. Work alongside such people who *were* botanists.

Two years ago, when Kim was seventeen, her godmother had died and left her four hundred dollars. The family had whooped with joy. Now they could have a car. Four hundred dollars was a nice deposit on a good used car. Only Jeff showed some conscience about taking the young sister's money this way.

'You can't do that,' he pointed out. 'The money stays in trust till she's twenty-one.'

'We can borrow it,' Celia said airily.

'Everyone can put in something from now till she's twenty-one,' Diane added. 'Then she can have her wretched four hundred dollars back.' Their bird-brained mother was the

Trustee for the money, and there'd be no trouble in twisting mother's arm!

Everyone in the family looked at the seventeen-year-old girl with a degree of antagonism. Why should she be the capitalist of the family? What had she ever done to earn four hundred dollars? Besides she'd get the benefit of car rides, wouldn't she? Who cared about a stupid thing like a Trustee's Act, anyway?

'You could use it to send her to the Institute to get a qualification,' Jeff suggested half-heartedly.

'Four hundred dollars? Poof!' Celia said flatly. 'It wouldn't get her through First Year.'

'What we need is a few comforts,' Diane pointed out coldly. 'Everyone else has a car——'

Jeff had shifted ground but stuck a little to his principles.

'Then buy a van with windows and bed benches. I can rig a work table in it; put in a small fridge and a butane gas stove. That way we can all—including Kim—use it for outings. We can take week-end runs down to the karri forest——' He had grinned at his silent youngest sister who had much more spirit in her than anyone in the family realised.

'I'd like a van,' Kim said at last—after long thought. She had done some elementary calculations while this conversation had gone on over her head.

In one year I'll be eighteen—she had thought. *I'll get a driver's licence bang on that birthday. When I get that licence I'll show them who owns that van!*

That was two years two months ago. The van was far from new, but still going well—due mainly to Kim's own care of it: and a friendly mechanic down the street.

Meantime she had become a typist, managed to get a typist's job at the University—where mostly she did Ralph Sinclair's pen drawings for him—and saved all her money At least all that was possible without looking too *too* shabby.

'That child wears dresses years out of date,' Celia complained to their mother. 'For goodness' sake keep her out of sight when my friends come around.'

They *all* referred to Kim as *that child*, as if she'd never grown up. Kim had long ago decided her sisters were too old to be important. Twenty-six and twenty-seven respectively was the same thing as being middle-aged to Kim.

Jeff—the oldest of the family—was different.

'Bratto!' he once said thoughtfully. 'Come the day you really grow up, you get out on your own. What with that eternal drawing of yours, you've probably got as much in you as any of us. You were just born too late.'

This day, two months after Kim's nineteenth birthday, she opened the double door of the garage and climbed into her van. She began industriously checking over its contents. Fridge was okay, and working. Some butane gas was left for the little stove: but more was needed. Sleeping bags were tucked under the bench, and the bush rugs folded on top of them. The curtains over the window could do with a freshening wash but they'd have to wait now.

She had put her pile of books and her dangle-bag on the back seat and she now fished in her money purse for the ring that carried the front door key, the office key and a car key. She looked at her brand new cheque book—something she had never had before. For two years she had saved, and now had opened a current account. A cheque book was necessary if caught without cash in the outback.

But she wouldn't be caught that way! If Dr Andrews didn't take her with him then she could work as a cook or a governess, or something—on a station. *She was going outback—in* or *out* of the Expedition team. She was *going*—as Jeff had advised her long ago. Meantime she had *her* van. She had somewhere to live.

Those who didn't *try* didn't get!

Kim backed the van down the drive, swung out to the right and managed to avoid knocking down Celia who was coming in at that moment, and who stood protesting. This, Kim chose not to hear because she felt she didn't have to explain to a protesting sister what she was doing *with her own van.*

She parked outside the gates of the Botanical section at the Mount and walked first up the made road, then across the grass to the track leading to the potting sheds and the office.

Lunch hour would be well over by now, so this would be a good time to attack!

She swung open the main door and found herself staring straight into the navy blue eyes of *that man*—the one from down in the special garden!

Wouldn't it!

He had the expression of someone looking at a child worse than tiresome. This made Kim's blood temperature rise five points.

'I didn't know they let the field workers come into the office,' she said by way of reprisal for that look. His hands were earth-stained as he raised one to light a cigarette. His all-weather desert-boots were dusty as ever. Otherwise he was good to look at—quite devastating, in fact—but Kim didn't allow herself to dwell on this. Her sisters' boy friends were always good to look at. And they'd all been hateful. They treated her, Kim, as an amusing but contrary *infant*.

Two young women in white coats turned round from peering into a seed tray, and stared at the intruder with incredulous expressions. So did a man sitting behind an office table at the far end of the long sunlit room.

They all stared at her.

For once Kim did not mind. At least she thought she did not mind. She'd think about it all later. Maybe when she was far outback: or maybe to-night when her head was on her pillow and she wanted to cry—because everyone looked at her *that way*.

But—as a matter of principle—she never did cry!

She was being rude to *that man*, of course. She was sorry and wished she could take the words back, but it was too late. Besides it was the condescending expression on his face! It was a cold look meant to freeze.

He let a faintly ironic glance waver round the long room from one worker's face to another.

'It's not Thursday, Public Day, is it? *Or is it?*' he asked.

He turned back to Kim.

'Schools' visits are made in groups,' he paused, then added clearly, '*Mondays and Thursdays only*.'

'I'm not a school girl,' Kim stood on her dignity. 'I'm nineteen. I did mention that before. I've brought a message for Dr Andrews.'

The two women at the seed trays, and the man at the desk, looked first at her in surprise, then at *that man*.

There was something explosive in the air.

'Would you please tell Dr. Andrews that he will receive an application from a very outstanding person for the Technical Assistantship advertised by C.O.C.R. last week-end. He will receive it to-morrow morning. The advertisement said the

Expedition would be starting from Manutarra. That's up north, isn't it! The applicant will be there when Dr Andrews and his party arrive.' She had to take in a new breath to finish. 'The applicant will have a personal van and will be fully equipped for the Expedition.' She thought she sounded rather like a catalogue: but that was how she meant to sound.

The older man at the desk had the dead-pannest face Kim had ever seen.

'What makes you think Dr Andrews will approve this applicant?' he asked at length. 'We haven't received other applications yet.' The two girls in white coats seemed suddenly to be sharing a silent joke.

'You won't receive any other worthwhile applications either.' Kim was half sad for him, half patient sweetness.

'You see,' she continued with gentle reasonableness. 'Only students take on the short-term field-work jobs. And it just happens that Final Examinations are looming for all except the Honours students. There are several of *them*—the Honours students, I mean. But they need to get on with their own research topics at this time of the year. They haven't time to go four hundred miles to Manutarra as a starting point.'

In the silence that followed, Kim took time off to banish a slightly miserable thought of Myree Bolton, the golden-haired Honours student, doing Ralph Sinclair's drawings for him. *She'd* have time to go anywhere at any price because she had *money*.

The tall lean man in the dusty desert-boots said not one word. He smoked his cigarette and looked out through the glass doors as if Kim didn't exist.

'She's right, you know,' the desk man said, looking at the dusty-booted one. 'The only type we, or C.O.C.R. is likely to get at this time of the year is an out-of-work drongo. I never heard of any of that sort being able to type, tag and keep intricate records, let alone be able to get to the jump-off point.'

'Who is this outstanding person of whom you speak?' the enemy asked sceptically, looking directly at Kim again.

'That is Dr Andrews' concern,' she replied with careful dignity, head high. 'I believe he will be in charge.' The monkey in her was delighted at thus being able to punish him for wiping her off as an unimportant school girl. 'Would you be so kind as to tell Dr Andrews—when anyone *does find him*

—that a very good application—in fact a brilliant one—is on its way? I'm afraid I must go now. I have some shopping to do.'

There was such a staggered silence in the room that Kim's aplomb missed a beat for quite half a minute. The enemy was looking at her too steadily. It made Kim feel uncertain for the first time.

'You seem to know a great deal about another person's application,' he said.

'I do. I typed the reference. I'm a typist, you see. I did mention that before.'

She collected her assurance about her like a cloak, nodded her head severally, one nod for each person in the room, then turned and pushed open the glass door.

Such a pity! she thought, *because he really is so good to look at. Celia would make a dash for him if she ever saw him! Still——*

She let the door swing-to behind her.

She heard a prolonged '*Phew . . ew!* as she went out into the sunshine.

Then she heard laughter.

They were actually laughing at her.

For one searing moment she was desperately hurt. She kicked the grass with her proud new shoes as she went towards the track. But she didn't *cry*.

They were laughing at her!

She couldn't quite see the shadows of the lemon-scented gums as they lay like delicate black lace across the road to the gate. She couldn't see the diamonds dancing on the water where the peacock blue of the river lay in a dreaming afternoon silence at the foot of the Mount. It was the *laughter* that really hurt.

Kim looked up and saw her van parked by the gate, and her spirits lifted. This was something of her very own.

Outback she would wear working overalls: the ones with a wide pocket across the front of the bib like the men wore when they were on field work. She was going right now to town to buy herself some like Jeff's. If she didn't get the job at Manutarra she would get one in Geraldton. That would be over three hundred miles from her family. Anyway she was going anywhere that was a long way away. From Ralph

Sinclair too—because he never looked at her in a 'seeing way' at all. Besides she had always wanted to go outback! Badly!

She climbed into the drive seat of the van, started up the engine and swung the vehicle round. Then she sped down the hill towards the city.

'Two long-legged pairs of working khakis; two short-legged pairs.' She made her shopping list up as she drove. 'Two cylinders of butane gas; a First Aid Kit; two cases of Universal Outback Provisions: oh, and send a telegram to the roadhouse at Manutarra, and *don't* send one to Mr Ralph Sinclair to say good-bye.'

And a hat!

'Can't go without a hat on my head. Not in the outback!'

Kim lifted her chin bravely at this last decision. The thought of a hat was like hoisting an escape pennant into a new life. She'd wear it—as from when she bought it. Cockily too! Over one eye—just to show the family she really meant business.

She had always wanted to go to the outback. It was some of the enchantment of this particular advertisement.

So! With this nice punchable, idiotic hat she would look the part! If not this job—then some other, as long as it was north of Twenty-six!

CHAPTER TWO

Four days later Kim drove away in the soft splendour of early morning. She had set out from home at dawn.

Marchagee would be a good place to stop for a snack, she decided. That would be a hundred and sixty miles on. How fast could she go, and stay out of the Traffic Court for speeding?

Well, not so fast because she kept being beguiled by the wild-flowers all around; and the winding road up the Bindoon Hill.

The colours of bush, flowers, and trees, were glorious because it was spring. Green overshadowed the creeks. Gravel tracks wound under avenues of gum trees leading to the homesteads. A few miles on came acres of wild-flowers. Leschenaultia, flannel flower, pink myrtle, wax flowers, grass lilies, blue-lady orchids, and golden prickly wattle. A blaze of petal colours sang on every side. And sang in Kim's heart too. She had run away at last!

'Now, if I could stop and paint by one of those creeks—maybe I could do some trees! White gums, wandoo, blackboy, jarrah, zamia palms!'

Oh! The heavenliness of *Escape*!

Kim had to banish thoughts of dallying. After all she had yet four hundred miles to go to Manutarra, the rendezvous for the members of the Expedition. She understood very well this jump-off place had been selected because some botanists would be coming from the north and some from the east. A place had to be picked that was central to them all.

Moora, Nambon, Watheroo. She read the magic words on the sign posts as she and her van rattled past. Hours raced past too, because sometimes she stopped to make her own sketching records for the sheer love of putting on paper the things she saw.

There was no time to stop at Marchagee, the halfway house. She'd leave eating till she came to Three Springs. She was slimming anyway.

Mingenew! A turn-off here between sheep-white paddocks and glorious golden wattle groves. Mile upon mile of them. Clumps of mulga lined the tracks too.

On, on all day Kim travelled, stopping for petrol refills at lonely wayside roadhouses: making snap drawings while her van was being checked. She bought a few sandwiches and two bottles of milk. They would have to suffice, for she'd many many more miles to go yet.

She turned off the road to a gravel track, heading north-east, and left behind the hazy yellow seas of wattle. She had set sundown as the D-hour for arriving at the meeting point.

The roadhouse at Manutarra, nearly four hundred miles north-east, was planted down on the fringe of the outback. It was a modern building set around a square courtyard in which two shade-giving gum trees grew. A hundred yards down the road was the only other sign of life in an empty grass-plain world—the store which was also the Post Office and petrol station.

The low scrub, minnie-richie mostly, did not move in the

windless air. Neither did the leaves in the two gum trees; nor anyone in the store or the roadhouse. It could have been a world asleep—except for the thrumming from the engine-house.

Kim pushed open the glass door of the entrance, then let it swing-to behind her.

A vase of everlastings stood on the reception counter. Nothing but the generator outside stirred or made a sound: and no one came even when she rat-tatted on the counter.

Back at the store where she had filled her tank with petrol, the man had told her she would not find Stephens, the manager, at the roadhouse. He had just gone through with his wife on his way to the air-field to pick up the papers and stores.

'If you're booked in, your key will be tied to a tag on the counter, Miss. That's the way he works it. You'll be okay.'

'Will the roadhouse be okay?' Kim asked uncertainly. 'Suppose I accidentally set fire to it—or something?'

'You won't. No one ever does.' He was dustily philosophical. 'Walk round behind the counter and take yourself a bottle of milk from the fridge. You can make tea in your room. The gadgetry's all there. The staff never comes into the front part except at meal time. They don't service the counter. Union rules, and all that——'

Kim found things to be exactly as the man at the store had said. The establishment seemed empty of people. Only the faint odour of cooking told her that somewhere in the nether places there must be a cook—and perhaps a waitress or two. Off duty, no doubt!

There was a whole row of keys lying on the counter. Each bore a tag with a name on it. They were the keys for the people booked in who had not yet arrived. Her own name leapt out of the row as she looked at it. The tag read—added to her name—such instructions as *Room 7. Take milk from the fridge. If anything else from store-shelf put chit in box on counter. Letter in your room.*

Kim went back to her van, drove it into the courtyard and parked it nose-on to the strip of cement walk outside Number 7. All the doors round the courtyard were painted in bright colours. In the middle was a shady plot of ground, thanks to the two gum trees.

She turned the key in the door of her room.

First she put the milk in the mini-fridge under the work table, then took the hot water jug from the cupboard, and the sugar bag and tea bag provided by the management. She set the jug to boil.

She stared with pretended courage at the letter lying waiting for her on the table.

'Friend or foe? To be or not to be? I've won the job, or I haven't! If not, well heigh-ho for farther north!'

She picked up the letter, then fearing it might contain something as nasty as an adder, dropped it. She had an odd feeling there was something wrong with it.

'Tea first. No one ever ran away from a mad selfish family without first having a cup of tea to reinforce.'

Within a minute the water-jug boiled. Kim put two tea bags in the pot and poured the boiling water on them. She had brought in from her van the packet of sandwiches from the store at the turn-off. She sat back in a cane chair, poured the tea, and nibbled a sandwich.

The odd feeling of something wrong with that letter came over her again. Not the inside of the letter, but the *outside*. She looked at the postmark. *Perth*. The counter-mark was 'Private Mail Bag, Manutarra'. That was all right. In the bottom left hand corner was neatly printed——

C.O.C.R. *Botany Department. South West Division.*

If not claimed please return within 7 days.

Then the penny dropped!

It was addressed to *Miss* Wentworth.

Of course! *Miss* had been on her key-tag too!

They'd found out! She'd meant them to read 'Kim' for a man's name—on account of them not wanting *girls* on expeditions.

She tore the envelope open, and a single sheet of paper fell from it.

It read——

Council for Organic Chemical Research (Botany Department)
South West Division

Dear Madam,

You are hereby appointed Temporary Technical Assistant to

Dr John Andrews, C.O.C.R. (Botany Extension Services) for the duration of the Plant Collecting Expedition beginning from Manutarra, Sept. 3rd of this year. You are required to report to Dr Andrews not later than the *evening* of Sept. 2nd.

Your remuneration will be under Clause Four of the Technical Officers Award of this Branch. Details will be forwarded to your home address.

Yours faithfully,

George Stanton (Chief Clerk, C.O.C.R.)

Kim read it again. Then again.

She wanted to jump up and dance, yet somehow, for some silly reason, she was nearer tears. Till this moment she hadn't really believed in success.

She'd actually won *the job*! The letter hadn't contained an adder, but a bouquet!

'Kim, my girl,' she told herself. 'It's Dr Andrews—whoever he might be—who's going to worry about my being a girl now. The Clerk of Records appointed me. It was all done from Head Office! I wonder how they knew I was a "Miss", and not a "Mister"? C.O.C.R. must have booked me in here at the roadhouse, as my telegram did too. Why hadn't I noticed?'

From outside came the sound of vehicles pulling up. She lit a cigarette and stared disbelievingly at her own image in the mirror. She couldn't even *think* because she was so relieved; and so happy too.

Then came a sharp rap at the door.

Kim had left the key in the lock so, still only half with-it, she called 'Come in!'

In came a girl; tall, slender, *very pretty*, and with a lovely cap of real golden curls on the top of her head. This was the ice-queen with fury fires within, for sure! She really looked it!

Kim's legs came down from the chair with a clang.

'Myree Bolton!' she said. 'How did you get here?'

'I was booked in by C.O.C.R. You're the typist from the Research Section at Crawley aren't you? What's your name? Sorry but I never really knew.'

'Kim Wentworth,' Kim said more dazed than ever. 'You were supposed to take my place at Crawley. I mean—that is

—not *typing*. Oh no—except for plant names on tags—but to draw the plants, section by section. Ralph Sinclair's work, you know——'

'What rot!' The elegant slender girl was disdainful. 'I'm doing an Honours Degree, and I don't type. I was booked by our Department to join this Expedition as graduate-botanist in order to study the topic for my thesis.'

'Oh? So the Expedition *was* taking girls after all? Are there any more like you?'

'No. The Botany lot agreed to my coming at the last moment.'

She was more supercilious than ever as she went on. 'Someone high up put a special case for me. Professor Watts, I expect. After all, I do have to have a topic. No topic—no thesis. Of course Dr Andrews would have asked for me. I'm sure of that. He knows me quite well.'

She put significant overtones to that 'quite well'. Very meaningful.

Kim's legs went up on the chair again and she laughed with a whoop of glee.

'How I wish that dusty-booted man at that same Mount could see us! "*No girls*", he said. Very flat and very final too. Wait till we get back!'

'*What man?*' Myree opened her carry-all and began taking up the best places on the table under the mirror, for her cosmetics. She was fractionally interested, that was all.

'Oh, no one you would know. A sort-of plant man. A very superior type. Probably an expert.'

Myree was busy distributing her things in careful order. 'You still haven't said *what kind of a man*. He seems to have made enough impact to provide you with impulses to revenge. A woman scorned?'

Kim's legs wavered between coming down from the chair, or not. They decided not.

'Thank you for calling me a "woman". You're the first ever. He's one of the staff men who tried to warn me off the Mount because it wasn't visiting day for "school girls".'

Myree turned round and looked at Kim as if she were a plant specimen.

'You haven't developed much of a figure yet, have you? Not in the right places, I mean. Of course, I've only seen you from a distance round the Department. Rumour amongst the others had it that you were addicted to Ralph Sinclair. Is this other man on the Expedition?'

Myree was subtly interested, in her cool way.

'Certainly not,' Kim said firmly. 'He's a very rude man. Quite offensive, in fact——'

'Because he thought you were too young to be interesting?'

Kim wished she had Myree's eyebrows. They were exquisitely shaped with a nice little bend at the outer end that gave them a very prideful expression.

'True,' she said casually. 'At least he said I was too young. He doesn't have very good manners.'

'Sounds interesting to me. I like frank people. I hope he *does* come.'

'With all your brains why not concentrate on Dr Andrews? My brother said he'd heard he was a bachelor. Of course, he could be absent-minded and selfish like . . . Oh, well, never mind like *who*.'

'Like Ralph Sinclair? So that was the trouble was it? I guessed right. But why run so far? My dear child, a scientist should marry a scientist. After all they have to live together, haven't they? You're only a typist——'

'True again. Oh dash! Look what I've done——'

Kim stood up and shook herself. She had knocked the ash tray from the arm-rest with her elbow and spilt ash on her dress. She tried to rub the debris away.

'I only have one other dress with me,' she said disconsolately. 'My bag's full of shirts, slacks, shorts and working overalls.'

Thinking hard of other things, Kim was making the ash smudges on her dress worse as she tried to rub them off.

'You should sponge it!' Myree advised. 'It's only synthetic material, isn't it? A rinse on that place won't show. It'll soon dry. You ought to know that——"

'I wasn't thinking——' Kim said. She escaped to the tiny bathroom with its shower recess. She was so entranced by this lovely ablutions adjunct that she promptly forgot the supercilious manner with which Myree had given her advice. She first sponged her dress, then turned on the other taps, not only of the wash basin, but of the shower recess—just to see if they really worked. She examined the little cakes of soap left in the soap-rests, then pulled the chain of the cistern to make sure that worked too.

She examined her face in the mirror over the basin.

'It's really me!' she declared. 'Actually I've been in a trance ever since I arrived. I hadn't quite, *quite* believed I'd get the job. I don't even mind about Myree——'

Half an hour later the girls showered, then changed their dresses for dinner.

Myree was very glamorous now in a beautiful blue dress. It was short-short, but her knees were camouflaged with dream-like tights.

She had looked at Kim's dress and noticed the seams were not quite straight. It was a *made-over*!

What a bother to have to share with——

Myree pulled herself up and revised her thoughts. Kim may not be a scientist, but just how useful could a typist be? Well, come to think of it—*very*!

Myree sat on the window bed—on the principle that possession of the best bed was nine points of the law—and as if she was in no hurry for dinner. She watched the other girl put a last pat to her not-very-docile hair. Then she opened a text book, and began to leaf through it.

'Let's go over to the dining-room,' Kim suggested. 'I'm ravenous—in spite of three cups of tea and a sandwich——'

'It's not polite to rush the dining-room right on the tick of the clock. We should at least *appear to be ladies*.' Myree replied, not looking up.

Kim sat down on a chair and watched Myree turn the pages of her book. She took in the fact that Myree was monopolising the window bed as if it were her own. Much educated by her two sisters, she deduced the fact that Myree really wanted to make an *entrance* in that dining-room.

'Be in last, and make sure we're seen?' Kim asked equably.

Myree examined the other girl's face, but made no reply. There had to be a catch to this question of Kim's. It was too, too frank to be taken at its face value. In the silence, heavy footsteps could be heard outside. They belonged to men walking across the courtyard towards the dining-room. For half an hour there had been the repetitive sound of cars, caravans and even heavier vehicles drawing up.

'What is this Dr Andrews like?' Kim asked, breaking the icy silence. 'I suppose you do know him?'

'Oh yes, I've done quite a lot of my field work at the Mount.' Myree sounded bored but in a way that did not mislead the other girl.

'Let's go,' Kim said standing up with determination. She was hungry, and she was not going to be Myree's docile subject about everything. 'By the time we've both looked in the mirror, unlocked the door, then locked it up again—*and* decided who is going to mind the key—ten more minutes will be up. I'm *hungry*!'

Myree closed her book with meticulous care so as not to crease a page, then put it with equal care on the bedside table. She had placed it square-on so that the bottom edge was exactly parallel with the edge of the table. This had the compulsive effect of making Kim straighten her brush and comb and shut the drawer tight where she had put her cosmetics.

She wondered what Myree would have thought of the padding oozing from the old sofa at home, and the fact nobody could ever find which knife was where, in what kitchen drawer. Or where *anything* was for that matter.

They walked side by side round the cement path that led in to the glass doors of the dining-room.

As Myree pushed open this door Kim gave an ecstatic sigh.

'Air-conditioning too. How gorgeous!'

'Don't you have it at home?' asked the other girl; supercilious again.

Kim stopped still and looked about her. She took in the fact that most of the people in the dining-room were men. Some were sitting at tables, others were standing in a group talking together. There were one or two women with heat-tired eyes sitting with sun-weathered eagle-eyed men. Station people.

Standing by three adjacent tables in one corner were men who had an air of quickening purpose about them. This was the Expedition party!

Two, more senior men, stood talking a little apart. They had their backs to the girls as they entered, yet—by the way they stood, their impressive air—Kim guessed these were the leaders of the party. They had authority stamped over their well-set shoulders and their long straight backs.

One of them turned. He had bright smiling brown eyes, an easy expression and an unruly mop of hair. Kim felt a wonderful sense of relief. If this was Dr Andrews, and she hoped he was, all was going to be well. He looked an absolute pet.

Then the other man turned round.

He was tall, barely smiling, assured. He was different from everyone else in the room because of the subtle air of distinction about him.

It was her enemy from the Mount!

Kim felt cold all over. Myree, however, was walking towards him. In a very taking way too! Her backside wobbled beguilingly.

Kim stole another glance at him. He was tall and rangy, with a knock-out personality, and was dressed immaculately in khaki. He had a strange direct look in his dark depthy eyes, as he glanced past Myree at Kim. He obviously still had most aggressive tendencies where *she* was concerned.

Perhaps he had only come to bring the specimen cases, or the microscopes, or something. To-morrow he would be driving one of those Land-Rovers back down south. Jolly good luck to that too!

Kim brushed her hair away from her forehead and quickly turned to the other man, the nice one. He was coming towards her.

This could be Dr. Andrews. That's why he was smiling at her—being the host, as it were. He wasn't as tall as the other man, but he was tall enough and he had a fine friendly manner. He hadn't minded girls coming at all. It had all been a myth. He liked them. He wore his liking in his welcoming eyes.

Myree, meantime, was giving her most brilliant ice-queen smile to the enemy. What a let-down poor Myree was in for! In a minute she would probably get the snub of all snubs. Kim couldn't bear to wait for it, and in any event here was Dr Andrews speaking to *her*, the mere Technical Assistant.

'How do you do?' he said, smiling. His pleasant brown eyes had a twinkle in them. 'I hope you had a good trip up. A long drive, I'm afraid. You must have a lot of courage to come all that distance in one day. By yourself too.'

Kim said, 'How-do-you-do' and 'Yes, thank you she had had a very good trip up. She'd made a few drawings as she'd come along. She'd record them properly later when she had time. No, she hadn't minded being alone, even for ten hours. Her botanical observations, you see——'

Well, she told herself. *I do have to make some kind of an impression! Considering Myree's academic attainments it's only fair——*

When she stopped explaining herself she saw a rather blank look had come into the man's eyes.

'Are you Dr Andrews?' she asked, imagining she was summoning up the kind of assured smile Diane and Celia wore so often. 'I haven't told you *my* name. I'm . . .'

'Kim Wentworth,' he finished for her, the smile coming back. It was almost a grin. 'We know Myree Bolton, of course. She did some preliminary research work with us at the Mount some months ago. She was interested in a special "find" we made out on the Sandy Desert last year.'

Myree was ten paces away talking very eagerly to *that man.* Kim chose not to notice this too much.

'We had to check your reference with Ralph Sinclair at Crawley, of course,' her welcomer went on saying. 'That's how we knew you were a "Miss" and not a "Mister".' His grin deepened in quite a big way.

Kim blinked. He hadn't minded her being a girl then? Why had they given her such a wrong impression of him at the Mount?

Of course they would check her reference! Why hadn't she thought of that?

'There's a table over there. Shall we sit down?' he was saying. He looked round, then added—'We're all here now. We might as well have dinner.'

As they moved towards the table he added a resounding postscript to his remarks. 'I'm not Dr Andrews, by the way. You've promoted me, I'm afraid. I'm George Crossman, the organic chemist with the Expedition. That is Dr Andrews over there talking to Myree Bolton.'

'Oh no!'

Kim stood quite still, dazed by the thunderbolt he had thrown at her head.

'I beg your pardon?' George Crossman said, but not sure he had heard right.

Kim wasn't listening to him.

That man was Dr Andrews? She'd been rude to him—

well, not quite unforgivably because after all he had called her a school girl, and he had *meant* to be rude to her.

The chair, with George Crossman holding it, was still waiting. Kim sat down on it not very gracefully.

'Thank you.' Her voice had a frog in it. Her ears were muffled and the only thing she could hear was the laughter that had followed when she had gone to the office at the Mount. Those superior-looking females in white coats, and the man at the desk! They'd all *laughed at her*!

George Crossman, sitting opposite her now, was saying pleasant nothings about the decorations in the dining-room, but Kim did not hear him.

She would never forgive him—Dr Andrews—of course. She was tired of being laughed at. Her family had been doing it ever since she was born.

'Yes thank you,' she said absently to the waitress who was standing beside her, holding out the menu. 'I'll have the kangaroo-tail soup. Then roast chicken.'

CHAPTER THREE

George Crossman watched Kim's face with amusement. Here, he thought, was a naïve but interesting young person. Kim recognised the signs of his summing-up from long and hazardous experiences with her sister's friends.

'About Dr Andrews?' she asked innocently. 'Is he——?'

'Not to worry!' George interrupted her. 'John always has that stone-wall effect on people when they first meet him. You have to get to know him. He's really a splendid chap. Look at Myree for instance. She met him up at the Mount last year. I think she took quite a shine to him—only that's between you and me, of course.'

The flick of Kim's eyelashes indicated she did not particularly want to look at Myree just now. Nor at Dr Andrews. She knew, without looking, that the two were talking to one another with great interest. Also, as they did so, they had moved towards the group of younger men by the corner table, obviously intent on joining them for the meal.

'Well . . .' Kim said slowly. 'Well . . . what I really wanted to know was this. Does the fact of having *brains* forgive one for being female? Like Myree for instance? *He* was quite flattening *to me* about not taking girls on an expedition. I came across him when I went up to the Mount with my application. I didn't know who he was. Now he shows all the signs of welcoming Myree.'

'Yes I know. I heard about his attitude at that time. It was quite a talking point at the Mount.' George Crossman's eyes were twinkling more than ever.

'Please don't tell me about it,' Kim begged. 'You see I *know what happened*. What I don't know is why he—I mean, why Dr Andrews—changed his mind. That is—about *my* coming——'

George's expression was suddenly wry but still amused.

'Nobody knew who owned the name on the application but it was the only one that came in that was good enough,' he said. 'Experience in typing, tagging and pen drawing—*just everything*! An excellent reference too——'

'I know that,' Kim said, now a little shame-faced. 'One day I'll tell you why it was so jolly good. Brilliant in fact. You think it was, don't you?'

'Sparkling with diamonds of rhetoric. No one knew Ralph Sinclair was so good at English composition.' He smiled broadly. 'Shall I go on?'

'Please do. I'm ever so good at listening to things about myself. I have a largish family who have seen to that.'

'For an out-of-season application it was almost too good to be true, so John Andrews said—after C.O.C.R. had raised no objection—"Check the damn' thing with Ralph Sinclair and if it's okay accept the applicant." He did add—"We don't have any alternative offer as good."'

'Did he really say that?' It was Kim's turn to raise her eyebrows. 'All in one breath too?'

'My, oh my, Miss Wentworth! You really don't like him do you?'

'Call me Kim, please. Did Ralph Sinclair say I really was everything that was in the reference?'

'Everything and more. That is, when he wasn't almost in tears because you'd left him. He was using words not allowed in reputable dictionaries because we were taking you from him. That was enough for us—even though we did discover from him that Mr Kim Wentworth was Miss Kimberley Wentworth, no less.'

'Oh, I forgot to mention to Ralph that I'd temporarily changed my sex. On paper only,' said Kim.

'Well, to cut a long story short,' George went on. 'We informed headquarters at C.O.C.R. that the application they approved was from a "female". They said "If it's good go ahead and accept. The C.O.C.R. does not discriminate between sexes as a matter of policy." We told John Andrews about the applicant being a female *afterwards*.'

'Was he very angry?'

'Blistering.'

Kim smiled. 'Good!' she said with satisfaction.

George Crossman looked startled.

'I like to have an enemy around,' Kim explained. 'I'm used to it. A whole family of enemies, in fact. That is, except my brother Jeff and he isn't always peaceable. It's actually most beneficial to have a foe. It saves me treading on the cat or mutilating my beautiful plants when I'm frustrated. I just fume with fury against *people* instead.'

'Please put me on the same side of the fence as your brother. I prefer to stay peaceable.'

Kim smiled at him cheerfully. 'It's nice to have a friend as well. You really landed me this job, didn't you?'

'Not across John Andrews' dead body. But certainly behind his back.'

'Thank you,' Kim said warmly. 'I love you from now on. Purely in a platonic way, of course. You do understand how I feel, don't you?'

'Quite.' He was more amused than ever but by this time was hiding it. He was beguiled by the curious expression of mixed wonder and seriousness in the girl's very candid eyes. 'Now you know,' he went on, 'why Myree Bolton was later allowed to join the Expedition. One female was disaster but two females might balance out any very dreadful consequences of that disaster. Besides——'

'I know. Don't tell me,' Kim begged. 'She has *brains*, and Dr Andrew forgives anyone for being the wrong sex if she has brains.'

'Exactly.'

Myree also has a pretty face, beautiful clothes and a fanciful figure—Kim thought, taking a side look between lowered eyelids at Dr Andrews and Myree Bolton seemingly getting on very well together over at the far table. Two eager young brain-boxes made up the rest of their party. Six men of various ages were at the third table. There was yet another group at a fourth table. These were probably the men who'd come from the north: or the Eastern States.

Kim suddenly opened her eyes wider. Then frowned.

The young man facing her. She'd seen him before somewhere. Or had she? The tiny sprouting of a young Galahad's beard was confusing of course. It was a light gingery one, barely discernible. His eyes had a sort-of red-in-the-brown colour! And the too easy manner? If only he shaved clean she was sure she would remember.

She thought and thought, forgetting to say 'Thank you' to George Crossman when he passed the salt.

George watched with growing interest. His eyes didn't twinkle just now. They were more serious. 'Those wide dark-fringed eyes,' he was thinking. 'And the cheerful smile that hides a streak of stubbornness! Original too, or she would never have braved an application that had inevitably to be found out. She *meant* to come.'

Kim shrugged her shoulders.

'What does that philosophic shrugging gesture mean?' he asked courteously.

'Oh, just giving up a riddle that probably isn't a riddle at all. I was trying to remember the young man with the attempt at a beard, and the brown eyes, over by the wall. Maybe I've seen someone like him. There are thousands of students round and about Crawley——'

George Crossman turned round and looked at the far table. 'The chap sitting opposite John Andrews? He's Stephen Cole. I doubt if you've met him before. He's come across from Sydney to join this Expedition. The whole two thousand miles of it. He works in a private herbarium over there in the east. Some tycoon owns it. Seems this tycoon is building himself a status symbol in the form of Private Botanical Gardens.'

'I didn't know the C.O.C.R. accepted people from private institutions.'

Kim's interest in the young man was waning. Tycoons were a foreign people to her—except in books and newspapers.

'This chap does have *some* qualifications,' George Crossman continued speaking of the young man thoughtfully. 'Seems he's only one subject short of finishing his degree. His boss not only paid his way, but put in a contribution to the Expedition expenses. Did you ever hear of a research organisation, always short of funds, turning down a munificent gift cheque?'

'No,' Kim agreed, wrestling with a wing of brush turkey that was masquerading as roast chicken on her plate. 'Hence Mr red-head Cole?'

'Hence Mr Cole!'

'And that's where Dr Andrews' principles about outsiders went down the drain?'

George Crossman looked a little more serious.

'It's clear you don't know John Andrews. Stop disliking him in advance, Kim, and to the peril of your digestion. When you know him you might change your mind. All the other men are highly qualified. In any case C.O.C.R. probably wished this particular member on him. *They* got the cheque. Not John.'

Kim smiled. It was the half inimical, half naïve smile she had practised so often in the bathroom mirror at home. One day she hoped to perfect it and wear it as purely inimical.

'When I do forgive him, I'll let you be the first to know,' she said. 'That's a promise.'

'They're all getting up,' George Crossman said when the meal was finished. He pushed back his chair and stood up himself. 'The others arranged before dinner to meet in Barney Sage's room. It's Number Fifteen, I *think*, but am not sure of the number, so check will you? We always have a Night-Before-Starting-Party. The last of frivolity till we get back to civilisation.'

'Is *everyone* invited?' Kim asked uncertainly.

'Of course. That reminds me. I'd better check the caravans and see they're okay for gear. John seems too taken up with My Fair Lady Bolten at the moment. Will you excuse me, Kim? I'll see you later——'

'Of course,' Kim stood up too. 'I want to go to the desk and send a message to my brother if it's possible. He'll tell the rest of the family I'm safely here——'

'It's Outpost-radio from this area. You'll have to get the

manager to fix it for you. Don't forget every word rings round the whole north-west—so can't be private. Okay?'

'Okay!'

Kim went towards the door hoping that the manager was back from the airfield.

Funny how she wanted to run away from her family; and swore she never wanted to see them again. Now she was here, she wanted to send them a telegram. She supposed she was perhaps fond of them after all. Also she wanted to thank Jeff for the ten dollars he had given her as a parting present.

The others in the Expedition were streaming out past the desk, through the main entrance, to the courtyard. Dr Andrews passed her, deep in conversation with Myree.

The impact I make on some people! Kim thought, glancing sideways at them. *Like a cloud hitting a sunbeam. I just don't.*

She waited by the desk, but no one came. Minutes went by and she rat-tatted with her fingernails on the counter again. There was no bell in sight.

Everyone else had left the dining-room by now. Even the station people and their wives had gone. The two waitresses had disappeared into the nether regions to have their own meal, and there wasn't any manager. He was not yet back from distant airfields.

Kim went outside and looked round the semi-lighted courtyard.

Five caravans, three Land-Rovers, a jeep, her own van and the right number of dust-smothered overlanding cars with tow-bars at the back and kangaroo bars in front, stood before various suit doors. There was no car with a Manutarra registration number that might credibly belong to the roadhouse manager. So he hadn't come back yet. No manager, therefore no one to operate the radio-telephone!

Ah well, to-morrow morning then——

She was disappointed. To offset this feeling she went round the cement walk to her own room with an air so bright it told nobody—because nobody was about—she hadn't a care in the world. Myree had left the key in the door but she was not there either. 'Gone to the party in a hurry!' Kim thought. 'Not so lady-like after all!'

She washed her hands, did up her face a little and smoothed her hair somewhat. Then she set out round the cement walk.

Number Fifteen was on the far side of the courtyard but her

knock on the door brought only one of the wiry leathery tired-eyed station-owners to open it.

'I'm so sorry,' Kim apologised. 'I was looking for the rest of my party. I was told Number Fifteen——'

'You mean that lot with the Botanical Expedition? I saw them around bringing some bottles and cans of drink, and other stuff, from one of the caravans. I've no idea which suite they went to.'

'Not to worry,' Kim said smiling. 'I'll find it.'

The cement-brick walls of the roadhouse were built to withstand the cyclones that brushed across the north-west coast in the Wet. They were thick and impenetrable and were anchored to the walk, as the roof was anchored to the walls. So they were sound-proof. There was nothing that Kim could hear from any door. No one had thought to leave a door open for her——

Well, be fair! They couldn't! The roadhouse had its own generator so the suites were air-conditioned, and for that doors had to be kept closed.

She knocked at another door and this time a station-owner's wife came.

'Your friends could be in any one of the suites on the other side of the courtyard,' she said. 'But aren't you too young for this kind of bedroom party?'

Kim felt as if a shutter had closed before her with a clang.

Too young!

Was she as damn' childish-looking as all that?

No one had come to see where she was, not even her room-mate Myree. Not even the friendly, kind, organic chemist, George Crossman.

Too young!

Kim had felt dreadful lots of times in her life. In self defence she had built a not-to-care manner as she faced the world. Deep inside her a still, small voice told her she was only making things worse. At these times she resolved that still, small voices were only invented to be smothered.

But now? This minute? Standing alone in the courtyard with the gently rising east wind curling the fringes of dying grass, touching the leaves of the two gum trees, she felt more dreadful than she had ever felt before.

Left out!

Too young! Or just her absence not noticed?

She bit her lip and went back to Number Seven. She fished in her dangle-bag for the key and let herself in.

Not even George Crossman? And he'd seemed so nice! He had asked her to sit down with him for dinner. She had thought . . .

He had only been discovering that she was a not-very-interesting person, after all! A mere *bratto*, as Jeff would have said.

'A proper little *chit*,' Celia would have remarked.

Kim sat on the bed and kicked off her shoes. She was pleased with herself for automatically sitting on the bed near the window—the one Myree intended to take from her. In a few minutes, when she was over feeling so dreadful, she would get up and put Myree's things and Myree's beastly reference book over on the other table. The one by the bed next to the far wall. That would tell Myree something anyway—*all worms* were not to be trodden underfoot. The least of them would some day turn.

She had had such a wonderful hope of escape: such a heavenly dream of adventure in the outback! She had meant to be a new person. Once in those working overalls, and the steering wheel of her own van under her hands . . .

She lay back on the pillow and closed her eyes.

She wouldn't cry, of course. She never cried. Absolutely on principle! But it did hurt that George Crossman . . .

She'd taken a special shine to him——

She wouldn't think about him. She'd think about the youngish man with the pretence of a beard, and the red-brown eyes. Where had she seen someone like him? Even with her few short peeks at him she had seen he had a sort-of ready charm. It had seemed familiar. Or hadn't it?

There came an imperative knock on the door. Very commanding.

Kim's eyelids flew open, but she lay still on the bed and thought, 'It's not Myree, because the key is in the lock. Could it be George Crossman? Or just the beastly roadhouse manager who has come back from the nether reaches of the bitumen?'

The knock came again. This time even more insistent. It was meant to be heard.

Kim swung her legs off the bed. The rest of her followed automatically. The knock had a sort-of 'Open up!' command about it.

Actually she was fighting off going to that door. She couldn't bear to be disappointed—because in spite of what she was saying to herself there flickered a tiny hope that she had been invited after all.

A third knock quite startled her. Well, she'd open it. If she didn't straighten her hair she wouldn't be disappointed if it was only the manager, or one of the maids——

Kim opened the door.

Her grey eyes widened. She wished wildly she had swished a comb through her hair after all.

It was Dr Andrews.

He had one hand flat on the door jamb and was leaning against it. He was the picture of controlled patience.

'Are you hiding out? We've been waiting for you for half an hour.'

'For *me*?' Kim sounded incredulous. 'Why *me*? I mean, are you sure?'

'You're a member of the Expedition aren't you? We're having a party over in Sage's suite. George Crossman said he told you——'

'I couldn't find it,' Kim said lamely. 'The suite, I mean——'

'It's Twenty-five. Not so easy to find because it's the one tucked in the corner on the far side. An afterthought when they built the place.'

He stopped leaning on the door jamb and straightened up.

'Well, are you coming?' he asked. 'As a matter of fact that's an order. I always give a few last-minute instructions on these night-before gatherings.' His eyebrows went up fractionally, and he seemed really to look her over, as if he'd never seen her before. Kim resented this but refused to allow herself to show such feelings. Besides he was the boss, and had *come for her*!

'You wouldn't be feeling ill?' he asked. He looked irritated at the possibility.

'I'm never ill,' Kim said firmly.

'Good. Well, are you ready? Let's go!'

'I'd like to . . . well . . . to comb my hair. It's quite two hours since I looked at my lipstick.'

'Then get to it, young lady. I'll wait.'

'Oh no. Don't do that. I'll find my way now I know the right number.'

He took a cigarette out of a packet from his shirt pocket and lit it leisurely.

'I said I'll wait.' Unexpectedly his voice was almost, but not quite, gentle. It was dark outside but the light through Kim's open door shed the kind of glow that made the expression on his face softer. It warmed the ice out of his eyes anyway.

'I won't be a minute,' she said quickly. 'One swish with the comb. One slash with the lipstick.'

'And one dash of powder I suggest. There's a shine on your nose.'

Kim could hardly believe her ears. She didn't care about the shine on her nose. And powder as such was 'out' anyway. It was the way he said it. Not unkindly. Not a bit unkindly.

'I'll sit on the cement wall and finish my cigarette. Four minutes? Right?'

'Right,' said Kim. And suddenly she smiled. It was a smile that could have pierced the heart of prison walls, but Dr Andrews had turned away.

'Not four minutes. Three,' Kim added, as she fled in behind the door, now left ajar to give him light. She had to juggle with her cosmetics tidied away in the drawer—because of Myree—and wait for the beastly neon light over the mirror to stop flickering and start lighting up properly.

Someone had come for her! And that someone was Dr Andrews!

She hadn't been left out, after all!

CHAPTER FOUR

It was a wonderful party. Kim had never been to one like it before. Beer cans, ginger beer cans, and bitter-lemon bottles stood everywhere in Barney Sage's room. There were packets of cheese biscuits, cartons of salted peanuts, and even some defrosted crayfish-tails nested on lettuce in between wedges of cucumber and tomato pieces. These were set out on an upturned carton. On the top of another carton, also in cradles of lettuce, there were chicken pieces that really tasted like chicken, and not brush turkey. There was one enormous beautifully iced fruit cake sitting in pride of place on Barney Sage's pillow.

Every expedition had a professional cook, of course. Kim recognised this fact, and it gave her quite a wollop of joy to see him, the cook, also taking pride of place and monopolising the best chair.

When she arrived with Dr Andrews there had been a hail from all.

'Here she is!'

'Come on in, Kim! Where've you been since sundown?'

'Come and sit over here, chick. The best cushion on the best part of the floor has been waiting for you!'

So they had missed her! They had been waiting for her, and wanted her. She hadn't been forgotten at all.

Now she very nearly did cry—which would have been quite unique for Kim.

Someone pressed a frothing glass in her hand and another ushered her to the cushion on the floor.

Then, quite pointedly, the young man with the red-brown eyes and too easy but charming smile, weaved his way between others sitting about. He sank down beside her.

'You're mine for the evening,' he said. 'I saw George Crossman monopolising you at dinner——'

'Oh, but he was very nice,' Kim insisted. 'Besides I hadn't met any of the others. Except Myree, of course. And——'

She could hardly tell him how she had come to meet Dr Andrews at the Mount.

The young man was smiling right into her eyes.

'Where have you been all my life?' he asked. 'Now don't reply till I give you the classic answer to that question. You should take one swig of your shandy and say—"Waiting for you".'

Kim took her swig of shandy and looked over the rim of her glass at Stephen Cole.

Funny, she thought. *It isn't just the colour of his eyes! It's something that's in them—something . . .*

The young man really had a delightful manner: so companionable. Was it possible that some people could be *too nice*? Or that she had been mistaken earlier?

Kim was almost sure that she had met him before, or seen

him. Or known something about him. She racked her brains as she listened to him talk.

Well, if not him, then someone like him! Well, not to worry for now. This party was too much like fun to be thinking of anything else.

John Andrews had followed Kim into the room. When the others welcomed her he excused himself, quite perfunctorily, and went across the floor to join two earnest, very brainy-looking young men—down from the far north to join the Expedition at Manutarra. They had just appealed to Myree Bolton for a verdict on some scientific point. George Crossman was missing.

'Gone to straighten up the roadhouse staff about being on the ball at five-thirty in the morning,' Stephen Cole explained to Kim. 'Breakfast at six. Since every member of the party has arrived—including those chaps from the north—John Andrews says we can make a seven o'clock start instead of eight o'clock as per former schedule. He's a devil for slogging, is our Dr Andrews. I hope you have your working breeches with you, Kim?'

'I have. Brand new ones to stand up to the extra wear and tear. Three short and two long. The last just for the look of it: or if it turns cold. It can drop forty degrees at night out on the desert fringes, can't it?'

'Depends how far we're going.' Suddenly, to Kim's acute ear there was a subtle change in his voice. He did not look at her but flicked a tiny speck from the froth on the top of his drink with the nail of his little finger. 'Do you know the exact route, by any chance?'

Kim did not know, and said so. She had a queer feeling that even if she had known she would not have admitted it. Which was silly.

George Crossman came in at last.

'Oh, there you are, infant!' He greeted Kim with a smile. 'Someone told me you were lost.'

'Not any more.' She didn't mind for the first time in her life being called 'infant'. 'Dr Andrews came and found me,' she explained.

Her eyes flew round the room to where he sat.

He was still talking in a very absorbed way to Myree. His head was turned up because he was sitting on the floor, his knees encircled by one arm; and Myree was leaning over the back of the chair—*too far over*, because her dress was low cut.

Well, thought Kim. *Now I've really seen something. A female talking down to an anti-female. Yet he's not really that. I wish I hadn't been such a donkey that day I went to the Mount.*

George Crossman set about ousting the tawny-haired young man from monopolising Kim. Soon she found herself once more being charmed by George's easy friendly manner. He broke the ice between her and all the others in the party. She had never felt so gay in all her life before. The release from her family, and from general frustration, was so wonderful she could have *cried* with happiness. Here was a group to which *she belonged*. In her own right.

Two hours later Dr Andrews signalled that the party was over.

'Early start to-morrow,' he said hefting himself suddenly from his seat on the floor. He seemed to Kim longer and leaner, more tenacious-looking, now. Everyone in the room sensed this subtle change.

A silence fell. Now the adventure would begin—as from this minute.

'You heard me?' Dr Andrews said with a smile. There was authority in his manner. 'Early start. Breakfast is arranged and we leave at seven. Now for the rules. Lift a hand those who have been on similar expeditions before.'

He glanced round the room as several hands were raised. He smiled at Myree's raised hand. 'I mean long expeditions lasting over a period of more than four weeks.'

Myree withdrew her hand but without embarrassment. She flashed a smile at the boss instead.

'I have travelled far *in books*,' she said. 'Your books.' Her beautiful eyebrows arched as she spoke.

Kim's eyes widened. So he wrote scientific books about plants too? And she had called him the plant man, or the gardener! Who, she wondered, had done his drawings? Would they have been better than hers?

'For information to the newcomers,' Dr Andrews was saying. His eyes rested on Kim, not expecting her to know anything about expeditions at all, 'we travel in pairs, either when in transports or when on foot. No partner in a pair will let the other partner out of sight. Right?'

'Right!' The assent and the understanding came from all round the room.

'It's easy to get lost,' Dr Andrews said more easily. 'I'll merely add the fact we are travelling in some regions virtually unmapped. Tracks, but not roads.' He paused to let that sink in. Then went on—'I'll give few rules, but all must be obeyed implicitly. When leaving the transports each partner must *carry a water-bag and must wear a hat*. I won't insult your collective intelligence by telling you why. We'll be moving into semi-desert regions. We are looking, in particular, for uncatalogued specimens.'

'What about prospectors, and aborigines, John?' Barney Sage asked.

'Coming to that now. Both types can be of great help to us. Apart from knowing the terrain and the water-holes, long-time prospectors and their kind know the herbal qualities of the plants in their hunting grounds. They learn them from the aborigines. Don't forget that some of the most valuable drugs to society came from botanical expeditions amongst African tribes, Mexican herb dealers etc. The fever bark tree gave the world *Cinchona calisaya* and so quinine. The blue gum trees of Australia *eucalyptus*. That's your field, George ——'

John Andrews looked across the room at George Crossman.

'You're the organic chemist. So I'm pairing you off with Charles Barke here, for the obvious reason that he too is an organic chemist. You'll take Number One caravan as it is fully equipped for a testing laboratory.' He went on, detailing the place in vehicles, of others in the party.

He let his glance slide round the room.

'Miss Wentworth and Stephen Cole will pair off for the first short stint. I may switch that later. Kim will act as recorder, tagging and drawing specimens as required by any member of the party. Your van will stand up to it, Kim?'

'Yes, I brought my service card from the garage and the R.A.C. report with me.'

There was a tiny croak in her voice as she spoke. She was unexpectedly nervous at speaking out in such a group. For the first time she was a little awed by all these brain-boxes around her. Funny, she'd never felt like this at Crawley. She was a little disappointed that she wasn't to be paired with George Crossman. With him she felt she would have been safe from ridicule because she was the only one, bar the cook and the motor mechanic, who wasn't a scientist.

John Andrews continued his instructions. Out of her disappointment at not being with George Crossman, Kim surfaced to hear his last remarks.

'I'll lead off naturally. Miss Bolton will come with me as we're both working in the same field——'

'Who's the lucky one in your outfit, Boss? *You?*' The young man speaking was too facetious. The moment the words were out of his mouth he knew he'd dropped a clanger. He looked alarmed.

Myree arched her pretty eyebrows—liking the implication—but John Andrews barely smiled. He ignored the interjection.

Stephen Cole had edged his way back to a seat by Kim and he prodded her gently with his elbow.

'Myree's promoted already,' he whispered with a grin. 'I bet she worked it. She monopolised the boss all evening.'

Kim did not answer. For one thing she wasn't going to make the same crude mistake as the facetious young man who now looked utterly dejected. For another, she was busy thinking——

From now on Myree would probably have nearly everything her own way. She had a built-in knack for getting the best of all—even the bed by the window. Kim sighed regretfully.

'I think that's all for to-night,' John Andrews was saying. 'There'll be final check-overs in the morning. Oh, there is one thing more.' His face relaxed and something like a grin appeared. 'As from now, it will be Christian names only. This goes for everyone.' The smile deepened as he added, 'I hope there aren't too many Johns, Bills and Jacks in the party. Could lead to confusion.'

Very clever, Kim thought, not wanting to be pleased with John Andrews any more, ever. *A smart way of letting everyone know he's to be called by his Christian name too. No handles like Dr etcetera, etcetera.*

Oh dear! Why wasn't she born smart too?

She watched him slide down to his former seat on the floor

next to Myree. Myree, for her part very vivacious, began speaking to him at once. In an undertone too. All very private. She must have said something amusing because John Andrews' face flashed with another quick, open, shining smile. It changed his whole personality for that short second.

He must have liked very much whatever it was Myree had said to him.

Kim sighed for the second time.

Ten minutes later John Andrews was on his feet again. He put his hand under Myree's arm to help her up.

'We finish up for the night, John?' George Crossman asked. He was second in command and therefore expected to do the closing up.

'Yes. Party's over. Don't forget all! Up and ready to depart shortly after sunrise.'

John and Myree went through the door leaving a pool of silence behind them.

'He brings Kim, but takes Myree,' Stephen Cole remarked thoughtfully, unafraid of speaking out now the great man had gone.

'*Taking* is better than *bringing*,' Charles Barke also was unafraid in John's absence. He laughed at his own remark. Only George Crossman appeared to be deaf. He was making his way to the door alone.

'Well, that clears the field for me,' Stephen said jumping up. 'Just shows luck comes my way sometimes. Come on Kim. I'm taking you home. Round the courtyard by moonlight three times. Then maybe a halt under those two nice shadow-giving gums.' He bent down and put his hand under her arm. 'Up with you, Petso. It's you and me for the door, and what spots of wicked dark we can find for ourselves outside.' He said this last loud enough for all to hear.

He let his gaze wander with calculated idleness around the group. 'Let everyone think what he wills!' he added meaningly.

Maybe he was only trying to be funny!

Kim sat in the drive seat of her van, resting her elbows on the steering wheel.

The courtyard of the roadhouse was a sight to behold. The sun was not so long risen and the frail morning light with its hint of heat, and the pungent scent of the wild-flowers, filled Kim with a sense of exhilaration. Of excitement too! She was really on her way!

'Well, when do we start?' Stephen Cole asked. He was sitting beside her in the van. 'What's the boss waiting for?'

'We call him "John" now. Remember?' Kim was only half listening. She was in a wonderland of happiness. She was no longer a lone one.

'That's what Life is really about, you know,' she continued her thought aloud.

'Really is about *what*? A hot kiss in the moonlight, like last night for instance?'

As Stephen had stolen the kiss, Kim ignored this remark.

'One adventure after another, of course. Some passable, some beastly: and some like now.'

Stephen gave her a side glance from his too-bright brown eyes.

'You are a one, aren't you?' he said. 'Always saying something odd. What's only passable? You mean kissing? Everyone does it nowadays.'

Kim nodded her head thoughtfully as she looked at the line of transports. 'My family always treated me as the odd one. Way-out, or whatever——'

'I'll tell you what you're not going to be—for long anyway.' His tone was half bantering, half serious.

'Yes. You tell me,' Kim said, not so absently.

'We might do a spot of moon-lighting when the others tuck in—but you're sure not going to be the *driver* for long. That's what I'm telling you, pretty one. *I'm the one that has to have the power in his hands*. I'm the man of the party. You getting the message okay?'

'It's my van,' Kim said briefly.

'So it is. All the same, I never heard of a man being passenger while a girl drives. Makes me look like a—well, like a——'

Kim really attended now. She tilted her head a little sideways as she looked at him, and asked——

'Well, you raised the subject. What do you look like? And why shouldn't you look like what you are? I look as I am, I suppose.'

'You, dear girl, look like a lost chicken in a brood-nest of brains. *Inexperienced!* However, you'll learn. As for me?'

Yes, as for you? Kim wondered, but did not say this aloud Why did he give her an odd feeling of familiarity? Besides, she hadn't really liked being kissed last night. Of course it was necessary to have *experience*, she reflected. That had been her mood about kisses anyway.

'I'm a botanist collecting for one of the richest men in Australia. He owns the choicest of herbariums,' Stephen went on firmly. 'He happens to be a very powerful man in industry. My Mr Mathews is just that, and if——'

'In what industry?' Kim asked, not really curious. Her eyes had gone to the figure of John Andrews walking down the line, speaking a few words to the drivers as he gave each a paper. She was so absorbed she didn't notice the change in Stephen Cole's expression, nor the fact he did not finish what he was saying. On the contrary, he seemed deliberately to take a sudden pull on himself.

He noticed her concentration on the approaching John Andrews and gave himself up to a new line of thought. Kim's charms for instance. Specially those eyes. There was something special about them. The way she *looked* at one—as if a little faraway about it. Then so ingenuous about being kissed!

John Andrews had reached the Rover immediately in front of Kim's van. He said his few words as he handed over the piece of paper to the driver—pointing out something special to note on it. Then he came down the gravel stretch to Kim.

'We've already said "Good morning", haven't we?' he asked. This was very civil but not factual, Kim thought. He had twice passed her between the suites and the breakfast room without noticing her. He'd had his thinking-cap on, she supposed. She had an uneasy feeling he had special occult powers, and did not approve—merely as a matter of principle—her longish walk with Stephen last night.

John Andrews' eyes moved from Kim to Stephen Cole sitting beside her. 'You both know the rendezvous? No temptations to stop and pick up some doubtfully unique specimen you might happen to see on the way. We're not out picking bouquets of wild-flowers.' He allowed himself a half-smile as his eyes came back to Kim, but he passed the piece of paper—a map section—across her to Stephen in the passenger seat.

'You'd better be navigator, Stephen,' he added. 'Your driver will need all her attention for the road. Excuse me, Kim——' He leaned across her as he pointed with a pencil to a spot on the map. 'You follow this track here for roughly fifty miles. We have morning tea break there. The turn-off is bull dust and sand track. You can't miss it. There's the proverbial black stump twenty yards this side of it. Follow on a hundred and four miles by the speedometer and watch out for a group of three ant hills standing side by side. They call them the Three Aces. Turn left from there and pick up a gravel track that will bring you to Paper-Bark Water-hole. That's the rendezvous for lunch. Right?'

'Right!' Stephen sounded very responsible, almost as if the leader had just directed him to take a thirty-thousand ton passenger liner through the Suez Canal. John Andrews' attention came back to Kim.

'Are you any good at map-reading Kim?'

'Quite as good as at plant reading,' she said cheerfully. 'I can trace the steroid nucleus——'

His eyebrows went up as she added. '*Seventeen carbon atoms, and number eleven is in ring C. They have other atoms in side chains always attached to*——'

'*exposed points and between the rings*,' he finished for her. 'Splendid. I see they taught you something while you were doing the drawing for Sinclair down at Crawley. In that case, after the morning tea break you can hand over the driving to Stephen. You do the navigating from there on. It's rough country and will need both judgment and strong hands on the steering wheel.'

Stephen's face broke into a grin.

'Of course! he said. 'I really should take over from now——'

'It's my van,' Kim said flatly, firmly, and not to be budged.

So! Once again they were back to the Little Girl theme and someone else was to take over her van. She was no longer inclined to forgive John for having passed her twice this morning; and not noticed her.

'Well, young lady.' John Andrews' manner was strictly non-commital. 'As from the start of this Expedition *all* vehicles are my responsibility. Including yours.' The eyes, dark blue with the early morning sun shining in them and making his pupils narrow to pin-points, were too mild not to be hiding something. Kim was not to be deceived.

One thing for sure. In this heat it won't be ice particles! She decided.

'When do we really make a start?' Stephen asked. 'Not to worry about Kim, John. We'll get along fine. She's really a nice willing chick when you get to know her as well as I do —*already*.' The meaning in his voice was unmistakeable.

'I'm quite sure of that,' John Andrews said dryly and turned to take the last map section, and the track-finding information, to the driver of the end vehicle in the line.

Kim eyed Stephen balefully.

'Just how well do you know me?' she demanded. 'Half an hour in the moonlight and——'

'I was merely patting down his feathers, sweetie. Yours too. Take Lesson Number One from one who knows. It never pays to rub fire sticks with the tribal head. He'll inevitably make smoke first. There's always other methods of getting one's *own way*.'

'For instance?'

'The roundabout course.' Stephen spoke as one who had long acquired wisdom. It sat ludicrously on his tufty red-headed self. '*I know*. Take it from me.'

'I have a feeling you do know,' Kim said thoughtfully.

'*From experience!*'

The other transports in front were starting up their engines. Kim drowned any reply Stephen might have made by pulling the starter button and throttling up the engine. The roar could have been heard across the Gibson Desert.

Stephen threw back his head and laughed. When the noise subsided he patted Kim's left hand where it gripped the steering wheel.

'You're quite a one, aren't you?' he said not for the first time since sun-up. He seemed to have made up his mind, for all time, that she was a pleasing *joke*.

CHAPTER FIVE

John Andrews had walked back along the line of caravans and Land-Rovers, opened the drive door of his own jeep and hefted himself in. He started up, swung the vehicle around the U shape of the courtyard, lifted his hand as a sign to the rest of the cavalcade to follow, then drove out past the main entrance, on to the dusty bush-shaded road, and headed east into the sun. Beyond John's very impressive profile Kim caught a glimpse of Myree's face. She was talking, with much animation, to John. Stephen found this noteworthy too.

'Like someone said last night,' he remarked philosophically, 'A rose is where you find it.' He leaned out of the window to watch John's jeep—with Myree as a more than willing passenger—disappear in a dust cloud.

'Roses don't grow in the bush,' Kim said.

'Meaning?' Stephen demanded.

'Whatever Myree is, she's not a rose. A cornstalk maybe, when you consider the colour of her hair. A very pretty waving-in-the-wind cornstalk.'

The car in front had moved off so Kim followed suit.

'You know something, Kim?' Stephen asked. 'I think I'm going to enjoy this trip. I might even let you drive a mile or two past the morning-tea break. John Andrews regardless.'

The way was long—mile after mile after mile of it. It became hot and dusty, but the bush flowers were everywhere. They turned the vast stretch of empty forsaken land into a sweetly scented heaven. Kim wished she could get out and look at some of them! These were the last outposts of golden wattle and morning iris. Then came swathes of pink wax flower, and touches of flame grevilleas. The world was full of colours. A wild unguarded land of brush, tree and wild-flowers as far as the eye could see!

They drove slowly at first, as each car did, to let the one in front clear well away. This was to avoid the dust thrown up from the car wheels.

Myree has the best of it always, Kim thought without envy.

Even last night. I let her have the bed near the window after all. I thought it would do my character good. I wonder what she and John talked about so late—later than me by an hour!

'I'm just plain weak,' she said aloud. 'No spine.'

'Good,' Stephen remarked with an air of anticipation. 'Don't blame me, only yourself, if in the next twelve weeks I wind you round and round my little finger.'

'I won't,' promised Kim. 'Furthermore, to prove it—about my being weak, I mean—you can take over the driving as from now. I know just how beastly you must feel letting a mere girl act as a chauffeur for you.'

She braked to a stop and climbed over Stephen as he slid under her across the seat, into her place.

Just too too easy! Stephen thought. *This little jaunt would be a piece of apple cake.* Kim the typist, recorder, tagger and artist was already in the hollow of his hand. In any case, and irrespective of the secret part of the mission there could be some fun on the side——

'About Ralph Sinclair, and all those drawings you did for him, Kim——' he said as he started up and edged the van back into the middle of the track.

'Well, what about them?'

'They were for his doctorate thesis, weren't they?'

'They were to help him with his doctorate,' Kim said vaguely. Her thoughts were still with the sea of wild-flowers. She was sure the mauve patch way over to their right was the first stretch of the *mulla mullas*. If only she could get out to *see*. And red-centred hibiscus! Who'd have thought banksias would grow so far north as this? They had unusual brown and yellow in the flower——

'Exactly,' Stephen said after a long pause. The subtle tone of satisfaction in his voice brought Kim's mind back from the wild-flowers to the man beside her.

'What do you mean—*exactly*?' she enquired.

'Darling child, a doctorate is a high level piece of *original* research. Right? *He ought to do his own drawings*. Or oughtn't he?'

'I said my drawings were to *help* him. So does a piece of paper and a computer and a microscope help him. Tools only. You can't even build a house without tools.'

Stephen glanced sideways at her. He met her startled questioning eyes. She didn't see any wild-flowers now. Only

Stephen's glowing brown eyes. Her heart missed a beat because there was something unidentifiable in those eyes.

'*Tools*, of course!' Stephen agreed. 'I'll tell you something, Kim. Don't tell any of the botanists in this party about your work for Ralph. I wouldn't like to hear of him having his thesis set aside because someone *helped* him.'

'What rot you do talk,' Kim said scornfully. 'Everyone gets helped. People get helped by going to lectures, or having a seminar with a senior tutor.'

'How right you are, my darling girl. But don't say I didn't warn you. Hold your hat on, Petso. I'm going to step up the speed or we'll be giving our dust to the man behind.'

Kim's heart, bound by loyalty if not by a certain kind of love to Ralph Sinclair, felt as if it had had a small hole punctured in it. A barb of worry.

Stephen had to be wrong, of course. In fact he was wrong. Staff members helped with the drawings in major publications. It was routine copying work and had nothing to do with creative or original research.

Stephen was a funny one even to think of it. It could almost be an accusation!

'I'll make a bargain with you,' she said quietly. 'I won't talk about my last job, if you don't go making jokes like that about who does what drawings and for whom.'

'Done,' said Stephen with a grin. 'A bargain and a promise. You help me with my work here and I won't spill the beans on Ralph.'

Spill the beans on Ralph? There could almost be foreboding in the thought. A sort-of moral blackmail?

'But I'm here to help everyone—I mean, you and the others too.'

'Of course you are, Petso. But you and I have a special bargain. Yes?'

Kim stared at his profile.

'Yes——' she said very carefully: thoughtfully. 'You and I will have an extra special bargain.'

Stephen took his foot off the accelerator and the van slowed down, almost to a stop. He held the steering wheel with his right hand and let his left arm slip lightly round Kim. He leaned sideways and kissed her full on the lips. He glanced down the track; then for a fleeting moment back into Kim's eyes.

'We're going to have fun, you and I, sweetheart,' he said. 'Lots and lots of it. That was a swifty of a kiss but a nice one, now wasn't it?'

'Yes, Stephen, but if you don't put your foot hard on the pedal we're going to blind those behind us with a dust cloud.'

'So much wisdom in so small a head!' He laughed, then straightened up, pushed his foot hard down on the accelerator and shot the van ahead at full speed.

He'd won! He'd proved what he had suspected—Kim was love-addicted to Ralph. She would do as she was asked in order to save Ralph's skin. Or was it a doctorate?

Sharp on ten o'clock they stopped for Thermos tea and a chance to stretch their legs in the scrub. The others in front were already on the move.

'Fifteen minutes only,' Stephen said.

'I know. If I die of thirst in the desert, take out my heart and you'll find "Dr Andrews' Ten Rules" written on it.'

Stephen laughed. Kim saw him push his fingers through that wiry springy hair of his, then stroke the ridiculous wisp of shaggy hair on his chin—allegedly a beard. She wished he didn't have red-brown eyes, otherwise she might get to like him—in spite of that pointless conversation about her work with Ralph Sinclair. Stephen had a certain smooth charm, but was really very considerate and attentive. All the same—well—she could but *wait and see*!

She wandered over the patches of red gravel between the stunted wattle and the here-and-there clumps of spindly bush. Lovely delicate pink and white everlastings grew in mats making a patchwork quilt of the land.

'We'd better go, Kim,' Stephen said as she came back to the van. 'Those fellows behind might start shooting.'

'Um. But not too fast!'

She climbed into the passenger seat again so that Stephen could drive. '*We* don't want the dust from the car in front either.'

'Confound all the dust, 'fore and aft,' Stephen remarked as he hoisted himself up behind the wheel.

Kim, in the passenger seat, decided it was nice just to sit and look and daydream.

How old, old, old was this land! What was it waiting for in its vast weird silence? It touched her heart in a sad yet proud sort of way.

Stephen drove and Kim daydreamed.

Shortly after one o'clock—only four minutes late—they arrived at the luncheon rendezvous.

The line of caravans and transports looked so strange sitting out there on the empty plain—empty of all but the monumental ant hills and a long grove of paper-bark trees near the water-hole.

John Andrews came down the line to meet them as they braked to a stop.

'All go well?' he asked leaning one elbow on the window. 'I see you're the driver, Stephen!'

'Everything absolutely to schedule: morning tea break and all,' Stephen replied promptly. 'The others are not far behind. I saw their dust cloud as we came up the incline about five miles back.' He paused, smiled at the leader. 'Of course I'm driving! Can't have the child wearing out too soon, can we?'

This about the child, Kim thought, *is an old, old tale: begun roughly one hour after I was born.*

She remained silent while John made his enquiries, and Stephen gave the replies. Then she opened the van door.

'Stiff?' John asked thoughtfully, looking past Stephen to the girl.

'I'm not ever stiff,' Kim shook her head as she stepped down from the van. 'You see—I don't think I told you before—my father and my brother are foresters. I'm used to driving long distances with them. Hundreds of miles in fact. In this van too—over the ranges, and through the forests—down in the Warren area.'

'Hundreds of miles?' he asked, mocking her as if he thought this a childish exaggeration.

'Spread over the years,' she explained carefully. 'Since I was about three.'

'Have you ever climbed one of those tall karris?' he asked curiously.

'Yes.' She lifted her chin decisively. 'Two hundred and twenty feet of a king karri at Pemberton, amongst others.'

A shadow of thought seemed to weave its way behind his eyes.

Kim bet herself *he'd* never climbed a king karri. Not that he couldn't, of course——

Now there'll be no more nonsense about the helpless child! She hoped.

She summoned up a smile to put him at his ease. That would jolt him! She guessed nobody had ever found it necessary to put Dr Andrews at his ease before.

'I'd better go and find the others——' she began, then paused thoughtfully. 'Do you give Stephen the instructions about filling the radiator? Or do I? The engine does get a bit hot And, of course, the van'll need a petrol refuel.'

'Certainly, I give all instructions about all the transports,' John Andrews said gravely. Kim bestowed another smile on him, then she pushed her brown ranger-hat back on her head at a casual but intriguing angle, and strolled off in the direction of the paper-barks, and the signs of temporary human habitation under their shade. Her back said she hadn't a care in the world. Well, not a *real* one.

John Andrews put his hands in his pockets and watched her go. Then his eyes met Stephen Cole's over the bonnet of the car.

'Fill it up with water and petrol,' he said abruptly. 'Check the oil and the temperature gauge. Report to me when finished. You heard the girl?'

Stephen grinned.

'Well she is rather child-like you know! Needs a man around—and that sort of thing.'

That girl—John Andrews found himself wondering. Then, catching himself at it, stopped. The cook had said there was a crack in the engine block of the kitchen caravan. He'd better get the mechanic on to that straight away.

That girl—And the way she wore that hat!

He pulled his thoughts up short and thrust his own jungle hat to the back of his head as he came to a halt. He watched the last Rover rolling in in its own dust cloud. He stood with his feet slightly apart and his hands tucked in the belt of his shorts. Lunch would be on time, God be praised!

The jaunty way she had pushed that hat to that absurd angle, then sauntered off——

'Confound the girl,' he said aloud, addressing a short-tailed goanna that waffled its way across the track at that moment.

His thoughts strayed to Myree Bolton. There was a girl with brains! She'd get a First in her Honours. A very good conversationalist. Strange how blue-stockings had gone out with the suffragettes. And beautiful women had come in with the opening of college doors to them.

The Land-Rover was braking to a skidding halt in front of him.

'You treat your tyres like that, my friend,' he said bluntly to the driver, 'and you'll about-turn and go back whence you came.'

'Oh-ho, what cooks?' the driver asked out of the corner of his mouth to his partner. 'Someone's dropped the fat in John Andrews' fire. He's on the sizzle.'

The camp that first night was all-heaven to Kim.

A great shoulder of rock had in some age long past thrust itself up out of the red Australian heart. The underground water seeped through into a pool large enough for a swim, and beautiful enough for an artist to think about giving up the rest of his life to it.

Myree Bolton, knowing about these things beforehand, had brought a swim suit. It was the very latest: a bikini with gold and cream stripes: very body-revealing. Kim had to make do with a bra and shorts and a sleeveless cotton blouse over the bra.

'I look like Orphan-Annie in comparison with you, Myree ——' she said ruefully.

'My dear girl. You look exactly like yourself!' Myree said without pity: very supercilious.

It consoled Kim to see that the men didn't have swim togs either. They made do with the dusty shorts they'd worn during the day.

Once in the water Kim forgot to envy Myree. It was fun splashing and being splashed by the others—all full of high spirits.

John Andrews, though seeming most of the time to be one of them, kept that little social distance that was necessary between the Leader and the Rest. He didn't splash or be splashed but he swam as strongly and freely as the others, then clambered on to a large red rock to smoke a cigarette and look on.

Kim, too imaginative for her own safety, could suddenly

see how he blended with that rugged outcrop behind him. She hadn't thought of him that way before.

She was swimming on her back, her head lifted in order to see better.

He looked like a man carved in stone. His profile of straight lines was part of the rock line too. He was alone, liking it that way—as the last man left by the last tribe must have learned to be long ago.

A 'coo-ee' came from Kim's left and she rolled over in the water to see what went on.

Myree was standing on a flat rock on the far side of the pool. The fading glow in the sky caught and silhouetted her figure. She stood, one arm lifted high to attract attention, her head thrown back and all the smooth slim curves of her figure beautifully outlined.

'John!' Myree called across the pool. 'Dare I dive? Is it deep enough here?'

He signalled with his hand that it would be safe. Myree dived superbly. She didn't come up for a long time. Then Kim saw that she was swimming underwater to the rock where John sat.

Her wet head emerged below him and one shining arm came out of the water asking to be caught so she could be hauled up on to the rock beside him.

'I could have climbed up without help,' Kim thought. 'I guess I must have had practice climbing that king karri down in the forest. Maybe I'll teach Myree some day!'

She swam forward in the water, one arm after the other, paddle-kicking her feet, till she reached the camp side of the pool. She clambered out, shook herself like a shaggy dog, then made for the canvas shelter stretched over her van and which made a shade veranda around it.

'Hey, Kim!' Stephen Cole called. 'Your turn to help the cook serve. You'd better scramble. I'll give a hand too.'

This was the first night in sleeping bags under the stars.

In the small hours of the morning the east wind came whispering out of the desert and Kim sat up to pull an extra cover over her feet. That wind could be heard talking to itself as it came nearer and nearer, blowing over a thousand miles of desert and bush and scrub, bringing with it the scent of the shrubs and rare flowers the party had yet to find. About midday to-morrow it would turn into a hot and searing wind. For the present it simply told Kim she needed a cover.

Over on the far side of the deadening coals of the camp-fire she saw a figure sitting up, one arm wrapped around his knees, the other lifting the glowing tip of a cigarette from time to time. He was alone. It was John Andrews.

Kim lay back, her arm under her head so she could see across the faint glow of the camp-fire. She supposed a leader's job must be worrying. Perhaps he had to stay awake at night to do his thinking and his planning——

A little finger of compunction touched her heart. She felt inclined once more to forgive him for having been so ungallant when she first had met him. She might even forgive him for turning out to be Dr Andrews himself.

After all, he can't help being himself. Now can he? She felt sad, and did not know why.

Kim turned her head into her arm. Then, listening to the wind, she fell asleep.

Thereafter the time passed in a daze of activity.

The Expedition had, within a few days, reached its major base—far into the outback. Each evening as the plant-searchers returned to camp with their finds, George Crossman came out of his caravan-laboratory specially to meet Kim. In his half-amused, half-affectionate way he managed to prise her free of Stephen Cole's company, for some of the time.

The joys and discoveries and exclamations of surprise—sometimes of disappointment when a specimen was rejected—constituted the only topics of conversation round the evening camp-fire.

The Expedition was so far inland now that the seas of pink and white everlastings had been left many miles behind. So were the violet covered poverty-bushes, many of the hakeas. Long gone were the sprawls of heavenly blue leschenaultia Kim had seen all the way up to the Greenough River on her way to Manutarra.

Now, in place of those more luscious glories, were the semi-desert flowers. The crimson sturt pea lay here and there like splashes of red paint on the ground. Flame coloured grevillea bushes showed their brilliant flowers round the corners of rocky outcrops. The illyarrie tree sprouted its amazing variety of flower and nut from twisted tree trunks. The rose-pink of the spiked feather flower peeked in unexpected places where even the prickle-leaved variety of wattle had not dared to grow.

By day Kim was flat out busy tagging specimens, drawing others, and recording all that were brought in for classification.

On the fifth night of their stay at the main Base, Kim sat by the camp-fire leaning against George Crossman's shoulder while others nearby talked of their plant finds. She stared into the coals while she listened without much interest to her beautiful flowers being called by such freakish names as *Eucalytpus erythrocorys,* or *Verticordia spicata.*

She couldn't pronounce the names anyway. She had already confessed this shortcoming to George.

'Don't try,' he said, kindly. 'Don't lose your own ideas in the face of science—if you're not a scientist, Kim. Let a flower be a flower for its *interest*, not for the sake of a generic name.'

John Andrews overheard these last words as he slid down to a seat on the rug edge next to George.

'You'll have to learn to *spell* them from here on, Kim,' he said, intruding without apology. 'Several of us have *special* specimens we want recorded: and sectional drawings made of them too. They'll take priority over the other specimens you've been working on. Remember, all information about them is *confidential*. Right?'

'Of course,' she said, sitting up and taking notice. They were on to something *new*. She felt the thrill of discovery down her spine.

John looked across Kim to George Crossman.

'How about a table and drawing space in your caravan George?' he asked.

'I have a folding table in my own van,' Kim said quickly 'I can put it out under the canvas shelter for work—so long as there's no wind to blow papers about——'

George Crossman made a humorous grimace.

'You see? She doesn't want my company.' He glanced at Kim, a teasing twinkle in his eyes. 'I think she prefers Stephen Cole breathing down her neck while she draws——'

'He does not breathe down my neck,' Kim said promptly.

'He's merely interested in what my hand does. He finds it absorbing to watch someone drawing——' she broke off suddenly. John Andrews' eyes were fixed on her. There was an odd expression in them.

'Some of these new records must be kept confidential,' he repeated, his voice compelling attention.

'Of course,' Kim agreed. 'They'll be clearly marked——' It was her turn to break off. What was John thinking at the back of that camouflaged mind of his? Did he suspect she was irresponsible, or something?

She felt indignant with him all over again.

There was quite a weighted silence, then John turned to George Crossman as if he had second thoughts. Or a new idea.

'It might be just as well for Kim to work under the shelter for a day or two,' he agreed. 'In any case it would be more useful if Myree worked in your lab with you, George. She would like an organic analysis of some special *Hibbertia miniata*. It's rare and there could be something of interest in it for you too.'

'*Miniata?* It's all but died out. A lucky find for Myree!'

'She's observant,' John said bluntly. 'And very particular about details. Myree misses nothing.'

Kim thought he said this last with satisfaction. One botanist enamoured of another botanist's find?

She stared into the fire coals and let John and George talk on about their work. She was thinking of dear darling Ralph Sinclair and the almost holy smile he used to wear on his face when he found something in the dissections that was new or unexpected. Her own face, as memory stirred her, wore a sudden tender look of which she was unaware. What had made her think of Ralph? Something about Stephen Cole breathing down her neck—holding over her head that silent blackmail threat that Ralph might have his thesis set aside if *someone* suggested too much of the work had been done by another!

In one mood this threat of Stephen's made Kim want to laugh. In another mood it made her uneasy. It would be so simple to set up a *rumour*—— A research worker might never live down a rumour—however false it was in fact.

Poor darling Ralph!

Then, on the other hand, Kim thought, she wasn't playing

fair to Stephen. He had only been joking about the drawings she had done for Ralph, of course. He was being marvellously kind to her. He sharpened her pencils, washed her brushes and cleaned her fine nibs. She liked him for his thoughtfulness. It showed quite an interesting and generous side of his nature.

John Andrews' voice broke in on her thoughts. He was still talking to George.

'. . . so, in that case I'll revise my plans and take Kim in the jeep with me for this next part of the trip. That will leave your lab clear for Myree. As I'm collecting the living specimens I can get my descriptions typed and some drawings of the locality while on the hunt. Kim can then be passed on to the next wanting her skills. Probably Myree or Charles. We'll leave in two days' time.'

Kim blinked. She wished she had listened to that cross-talk instead of fire-dreaming of Ralph's non-existent problems, and of Stephen's helpfulness.

In two days' time she was going somewhere with John Andrews! For heaven's sake! She hoped there wouldn't be fireworks.

Then her heart dropped again at the thought he might be taking her to keep his eye on her. Those confidential records!

He mightn't like her much, but he should at least *trust* her.

'Well, that will be all for now, Kim,' John Andrews said as he drew in his long legs, and stood up. 'You'll need to pack a kit as well as your drawing materials. I have a portable typewriter and all the specimen cases necessary. We'll be away three to five days at least.'

Why hadn't she listened indeed? And *why* was he taking her with him on *second thoughts*, not first ones? Because she could keep records and draw? And Myree couldn't?

'Tea-o!' one of the men called from the other side of the fire. The billy was being lifted from the coals with a stick thrust through the handle. 'Ten minutes for late supper——' the voice went on. 'Fifteen minutes for ablutions. Lights out at nine-thirty! Come and get it, boys and girls!'

'Coming!' Barney and Stephen Cole called in unison. They made their way through the shadows to where Kim was sitting. George Crossman, on Kim's far side, seemed to regard Stephen's arrival with some annoyance.

'We're making an early start before the heat turns on, Kim,' George said, a rough note in his voice. 'Five a.m. is the starting time. It might be a good thing to let Stephen say good night to himself—*for a change*.'

Was he, or was he not, joking?

George had actually implied——?

Well, how dare he!

Alas, there were too many people around, including Stephen, to ask George what he meant. Instead Kim accepted a mug of tea from his hand—very meekly. George, she guessed, did not know that when meekness sat on her brow she was brooding at her most dangerous. Stephen enquiring into the private life of her immortal soul was difficult enough to contend with. All the same—she was puzzled.

CHAPTER SIX

Three days later the Expedition split up into separate parties. One group—the chemists, the cook, the mechanic and Myree, remained at Base with George Crossman in charge. Two of the Land-Rovers with members aboard made off in a south-easterly direction. Another party including Barny Sage and Stephen headed due north to search new territory.

John Andrews, with Kim's help, began to prepare his jeep and pack in supplies. This was to be a long jaunt east in search of a plant species of which he had found evidence on a previous expedition.

As they sealed in the last containers, cartons of tinned food and the sleeping bags, he told her he had first known of this species from a group of aborigines who had some in their possession.

'Didn't you ask them to give you one of the plants?' Kim asked, pushing her hat to an appropriate angle to register impression.

John's eye was quite withering as he glanced down at her.

'They were in possession of a dried form of chemical which I surmised could only be taken from that type of plant,' he said, explaining to a child. 'That, Kim, is *evidence only*. Not the plant: though I had found some of the same family but different species on an earlier expedition.'

'Oh,' she said deflated. 'I must remember that evidence is *not* a plant, but a *plant* is evidence. Have I got it right?'

John fixed down the back flap of the jeep in a banging kind of a way. Then he seemed to relent, smiling at her half-ruefully. Kim interpreted this change as evidence—as of an adult being sorry he had *smacked* a child.

'I'm sorry I have to monopolise your services for the time being, Kim,' he said, shoving his own hat to the back of his head and looking—not at her—but at some distant vision a few thousand miles away over the horizon. 'That evidence could lead to—well, never mind that! If I find the source, namely the plant-species, I will need drawings of the growing specimen in its environment. Its immediate background—habitat—all that sort of thing. On-the-spot records. This sort of work is the reason for your being with the Expedition.'

'Oh quite,' Kim said cheerfully. 'Actually I'm excited. I hope when we find it it will make us as rich as Stephen's millionaire boss——'

John's eyes came back from distant views and fixed her with something either exasperated or baleful. She wasn't sure which. One thing she did know—she meant him to feel that way. Just to punish him.

Then she sighed, changed the angle of her hat and said meekly,

'Shall I get in now? I think we've packed everything. There's nothing left on the ground anyway.'

Why did she always use two left feet wherever she trod?

John's answer was to open the passenger door for her, then walk round the bonnet and heft himself into the drive seat. He sat, his hands on the steering wheel, as if thinking. Then he looked down at her.

She was quite small, almost hiding under the brim of that ridiculous hat, *as if away from him*. He wondered was she nervous of him? Or . . . well . . . or what?

'Are you all right, Kim?' he asked.

Her eyes widened in surprise.

'Yes, of course. I'm always all right. Nothing ever happens to me that isn't absolutely and altogether all right. At least I *make* it come out that way.'

This was bravado. Half her wrong words and all her wrong laughs had come as a sort-of defence mechanism.

She looked away from him, suddenly alarmed at the scrutiny in his eyes.

She wanted really to shed her old self. Well—for the time being anyway. How could she tell him that underneath the pep talks she didn't quite believe in herself at all? Well, not all the time anyway! Was he reading that in her face?

She thought she was generally pretty good at faking expressions so she'd fake one right now. 'Obliging obedience' was the most suitable.

John started up the engine and drove out on to the track.

'We follow this route for about thirty-five miles,' he said after a silence. 'Then we cut off across the bush in a south-easterly direction. I've a surveyor's map for the further hundred miles after that. We're breaking little-known territory. We cross a narrow tongue of the Gibson Desert. A sand plain. Then I anticipate finding shrubland again.'

Kim nodded.

'If you'll give me the map, I'll navigate.'

He glanced down at her, surprised at her confidence.

'You can do that accurately?'

He'd asked that question once before! Kim shifted her hat from one angle to another.

'Quite accurately,' she said cheerfully. 'Those trips in the ranges and forest, you know. Remember?'

John Andrews drove on, a thoughtful expression on his face. Then he braked the jeep to a stop. He took the map out of the door pocket, unfolded it and pointed to the area they were now crossing.

'I believe you!' he said categorically. 'Now follow this. That's the main Base marked X.' He moved his finger along a meandering line. 'We're about at this spot now. The road we're taking for the *last* hundred miles is an old disused station track. An abandoned station, I'm afraid. However, we leave the track here——' He moved his finger farther along the line.

'And after that?'

'We'll take a reckoning by my watch and the sun; then check it against the compass in my working bag. I want to get into the sand-plain country round about *here*. It's desert fringe mostly.' This time he made a circling movement with his finger. 'We'll make camp and see what we can find thereabouts.'

'Do we have a two-way walkie-talkie?' Kim asked.

'Yes, but after we turn off the main track it will be useless. We'd need a modern 25 watt transceiver unit and a radio base to make any effective communication. That, I'm afraid, the Council for Organic Chemical Research cannot afford. You don't know any millionaires, Kim? The kind likely to make munificent funds to anything as irrelevant to society as a Botanical Garden?'

'We might ask Stephen Cole to put in a good word for us with his boss. Stephen's boss only keeps a herbarium as a status symbol.'

Kim's remark had an unexpected effect on John Andrews. He smiled as if struck by something amusing. It was a beautiful slow smile that took possession of his mouth, then his eyes, practically against his will.

'Why are you laughing at the idea?' Kim asked with a touch of her old truculence. 'If you don't ask you don't get. The worst that could happen is that he could say "no". We'd be just the same as we are now. The best——'

'The best is that he could say "yes" and dig deep in his coffers? I wasn't thinking of the nature of his answer at all. It was something you said——'

His eyes slid round and looked at her, one eyebrow flicked up. Then he went back to driving the car as if the conversation was now over.

Kim furrowed her brows. *What had she said?*

She went over the words in her mind—'We might ask Stephen Cole to put in a good word for us.'

He guessed what was puzzling her.

'It was the "we" and the "us",' he suggested helpfully.

Kim flushed, then sat bolt upright assembling as much dignity as she could.

'*We* might ask Stephen Cole to put in a good word for *Us*.'

She had identified herself with him, and with his beastly Botanical Garden adjacent to the Mount! Well, it wasn't really beastly. It was just that he'd been——

He caught her eyes as he glanced at her again,

'War over?' he asked.

The stiff little braces that maintained her pride seemed unexpectedly to turn to foam rubber.

'War's over!' she agreed. *With reservations. The peace treaty hasn't actually been signed by pen on paper.*

His foot pressed firmly on the accelerator and the jeep swept on over a smoother piece of track.

'It was quite lively while it lasted wasn't it?' he asked easily, the smile still hovering somewhere in the near-distance of his face. 'The war, I mean. It's gone on quite a time——'

'Well—don't ever call me a school girl again,' Kim advised. 'You did that day at the Mount, you know.'

'I won't.' His face was dead serious now. 'You can climb king karris, do superb plant drawings. And right this moment are navigator for a hazardous trip. Do you realise—in your important role of reading that map—you could lose us in a waterless desert? Or turn us over on crumbling breakaway country? Worse, have me drive outland instead of inland? What would become of *our* Botanical Garden in such a case?'

'It would go down the side of the Mount and into the river,' Kim said with equal gravity.

'So please keep your mind on the map, and I'll keep my mind on following your directions. We leave the track in a few minutes. After that, both our lives are in your hands.' He paused quite a long time, then glanced at her once again. His smile was really kind this time. 'Would I put that responsibility in the hands of a school girl?'

Kim shook her head.

'You've too many brains by far to do anything so foolish,' she said ruefully. 'And talking about "brains" why didn't you bring Myree—just to make sure you'd be safe? She can draw, you know—She's so *particular*——'

There was quite a silence.

'I thought of it,' he said at length. 'But then I owed it to Professor Watts to see she had her thesis project under way. Alas, I bowed to duty!'

So that was it! Kim was disappointed in spite of their armistice. Funny how there was always a let-down round the corner!

He would like to have Myree with him but he gave Myree up selflessly so she could get on with bringing her past work up to date!

Oh well! Such is life as it was and always had been!

Still—come to think of it—second best was better than no best at all! At least she was here, and an armistice was on!

They drove all that day. They went an incredible distance because of John's fast pace. It was all of three hundred miles.

Kim navigated accurately for they arrived safely at the sundown camp for which John was heading. It was the old abandoned station homestead.

'Doesn't it look dreadful?' Kim said sadly. The sorrow for things fallen, lost and gone was in her voice. John had stopped the jeep and they sat for several minutes looking at the shambles of an old house, the heaps of ant-eaten timber slats; the rusted galvanised iron sheets that had once been the out-houses. 'To think that perhaps once it was someone's home,' she said. 'Someone *lived* here——'

'So very empty!' John Andrews reflected. Kim's acute ear caught a note of regret in his voice too.

'I wonder why they went away? Why didn't they sell it?'

'Not enough water-holes in the area to sustain it in time of drought,' he said. 'This is drought area you know. Bang on the desert fringe. And the salt has come through. It's barely subsistence land. Let's say they tried—and it didn't come off.'

'I guess that must be the reason.' Kim thought about all the endeavour wasted. The appalling hardships. The loss.

'Well——' John gathered his thoughts back to the present, and started to unfold himself to get out of the car. 'They left one bounty behind,' he added. 'A camp-out for wanderers and prospectors. Also a drinking well of bore water, as I discovered last trip. Once we're inside that old homestead you'll see evidences of passers-by who are grateful for shelter and water supplies.'

Kim pulled the handle of the door and dropped to the ground.

She pushed her dusty hat to the back of her head and dug her hands in her pockets while she gazed at the shambles around. Falling fence posts, rusted wire, bush undergrowth taking over again!

She turned back to the homestead to see two of the quaintest men she had ever imagined emerge from the open doorway of the ruin. There was no real door, nor anything but bags and old timber slats to cover the windows.

These two wiry figures were wizened and weathered by the

shrivelling heat, and the alternate harsh cold, of a life on the track in the outback. They wore the shabbiest, most ancient, felt hats Kim had ever seen. She had a feeling these head-covers never left their heads, even when their owners slept. Their brown clothes were shabby and patched, but clean. The men were shaven too.

'What did I tell you?' John said as he began to unpack some of the gear for immediate use from the back of the jeep. 'We have company. A couple of old prospectors taking a civilised holiday in between long treks after the proverbial pot of gold.'

The two men ambled cheerfully towards them.

'What you reckon? We got company!' one said. 'You have any tinned stuff, mate? Any smokes? We can pay.'

They ignored Kim, she being small and young. They dealt only with bosses.

'I have both, and in reasonable plenty,' John said.

'You expect to meet us kind of blokes, eh?' the same one asked.

'Well, I've managed to have that pleasant experience before,' John remarked easily, lifting the two sleeping bags to the ground, then disappearing into the jeep's back while he dragged at a heavy carton. He did not explain that these were the people he actually kept a look-out for. Prospectors who lived all their lives in the remotest outback! They were mines of valuable information. They knew the country and often knew more of the fauna and flora than anyone else. Habitual wanderers over the face of the land were his best sources of knowledge.

'I'll give you a hand at that, mate,' the first man offered. 'Seems like this carton is the goods, eh? Crikey Bill, tin uv plum pudding! Who but a real gent would'a thought of that, this time uv the year?'

'As you said,' John replied. 'This is the goods! Tinned plum pudding and all!'

The carton contained an assortment of tinned fruits, puddings, biscuits, nuts, and boxes of tobacco and cigarette papers. Kim's eyes widened as she watched the lid torn aside.

'Come on, Bill!' the one who had been the talker said to his mate. 'Let's get these blokes in an' make 'em good an' comfy. Good job we did a clean-up uv the old joint. Made a fine wallop uv that kangaroo-tail stew too.'

Blokes! thought Kim. *Is that what I am? A bloke?*

Then she realised she had stuffed her hair up in the crown of her hat for coolness' sake. And, of course, she was wearing her working shorts. They saw her as a slim stripling of a boy,

She looked at John.

Who did the explaining?

John, busy with the carton and its contents, said nothing. Time enough later for explanations she supposed. And—well —it was a bit awkward. The two men were now using a vocabulary that was generally operative only between males of the species.

'We've made a decent kind uv a fire in the ol' stove,' the talking member of the pair went on. 'Kind uv need it. Temp drops thirty to forty degrees about three in t' morning.' He shouldered the precious carton, while Kim and John followed him into the old ruin. The veranda with its absent boards needed careful negotiation. Some fallen pieces of rusted iron sheeting were the only reminder of its roof. Kim stood inside the door and stared.

An odd floor board or two was missing from the far side. If there had been any paint it had disappeared long since. One wall was papered with old jute bags.

'My name's Peck,' the carton carrier explained. 'That's Bill out there. He don't talk unless he has to. That is, practically never. I do the talkin'. Them bags on the wall is to keep out the dust. The rest of it's fine an' dandy, eh?'

Kim blinked.

'Me an' Bill cleaned it up good and proper,' Peck went on. 'One thing we can't stand is a holiday in a dirty place.' He nodded his head round the room. 'She's not too bad, is she? Other rooms aren't no good. Too many holes in the walls. 'Cept maybe the ol' pantry. The east wind gets in. Dust a foot high. Say——' He looked Kim up and down. 'You an' your mate can have the bit uv floor on the side uv the fire. Me an' Bill will make do with this side for the duration. How long you be likely stayin'?'

Kim looked round for John. He was inside the doorway holding the sleeping bags, and had heard. He grinned in a way Kim had never dreamed him capable.

'Go on, Kim,' he said blandly. 'You tell them——'

He knew her voice would give her away. She could have hit him,

'I don't know——' she began haughtily.

'*Cripes!*' roared Peck. 'You hear that, Bill? We got a chick with us. *It's a she!* Screamin' galahs——!'

He pushed his hat on the back of his head and scratched his sparse thatch of hair.

'She your daughter, or something?' he asked John.

John failed to conceal the grin on his face as he glanced sideways at Kim—waiting for the explosion.

Kim had her own way of parrying that amusement.

'He looks quite old enough to be my father, of course,' she said, extra casually. 'I dare say you'll find some grey hairs when he removes his hat. If you look hard enough. As it happens—he is *not*!'

'Then what be you exactly?' Peck asked, gravely suspicious now. 'I don't hold with mixed parties unless—well—— Me an' Bill don't get mixed up with—— Well, we're kind-uv old-fashioned out here in the outback. We don't like no cause for *that* kinda trouble——'

Bill spoke for the first time. Light dawned with him very slowly.

'They're married maybe,' he suggested hopefully. 'Anyways it's up to us to look on it thetaways. No business of ours——'

'In that case,' Peck pronounced firmly. 'We'll accept you two's married an' no questions asked. So you two gets the bridal suite. It's the ol' pantry out back of what used to be the kitchen. There's room for two and two only, side to side, an' so long as neither of you kicks in yer sleep.'

'Oh, and why the pantry?' John asked, too cheerfully for Kim's peace of mind.

' 'S the only place that's got no holes in the roof,' said Peck succinctly.

Alarm began uneasily to dawn for Kim.

'What will I really do, John——?' she began.

'Well, you *would* come on the Expedition,' he said blandly. 'Now you know why a certain botanist you met on the Mount was anti young women in *any* expedition.'

Oh yes! she thought. *But he'd been happy to have Myree!*

CHAPTER SEVEN

For Kim—that was the night that was!

Lying in her sleeping bag, watching the last of the fire glowing in the old stove, she did a run down of the men she had met in her short adult life. To begin with—before she arrived at names and addresses—she had to think about this very situation. Were the knights of old quite as chivalrous as the itinerant wanderers of Australia's bushland? Likewise a certain botanist—though she was almost reluctant to admit this.

Peck and Bill had de-camped from the fire to the pantry themselves, when they discovered Kim was against the proposition of sleeping with John. The pantry didn't turn out to be quite so small as they had hinted earlier in the evening.

John had said he would sleep in one of the broken-down holes-in-the-wall rooms. This idea Peck and Bill debunked with vitriolic disdain.

'Those rooms has goannas and more'n one snake making their beds thereabouts,' Peck declared. 'You go an' take one look at 'em.' John had done precisely this. When he returned from his tour of inspection he had decided the back of the jeep was preferable.

At this stage in the evening's period of decision-making a bush rat had leapt, a small shadowy figure of a wallaby-type, through the open doorway. Kim had squealed.

'I only had a fright!' she declared in self defence when the men laughed at her. 'I'm not afraid of them—*really* ——'

'Not much miss!' Peck remarked. 'One of them on your face in the middle of the night and you'll screech for your boy friend's hand.'

The two old prospectors had not understood the scientific relationship between John and Kim. It was double aboriginese to them. John, knowing in advance this would be the case, had not laboured the point.

Kim, afraid of the worn cliché about protesting too much, had fallen silent.

'From here youse two is goin' right back of outback? So

you sez, anyway?' Peck pondered. 'Seems we can't fix morals fer other people here or there. Out there in the wild country no bush rats'll jump across you as you'll be side on to the camp-fire. Can't see why not here—— All the same, Bill, s'pose we betta give the chick an' her mate the best room an' the old stove.'

It was clear that since Peck and Bill were in the old abandoned homestead first it was their domain, and their principles concerning hospitality were at stake. The pick of the palace was on offer to the newcomers, and they now considered their gesture should be appreciated.

'Quite right, Peck,' John said, making the ultimate decision. 'Kim, you sleep that side of the stove, and I'll sleep this side. Invitation accepted, Peck. Our grateful thanks.'

'Well, why not?' thought Kim. 'That's what we'll be doing for the next week—as Peck says. We won't have a roof over our heads—that's the only difference.'

Decisions made, they ate kangaroo-tail stew, one tin of pineapple mixed with plum jam—this being the bushmen's idea of wild luxury—drank a lot of hot tea, swapped yarns of the outback, then parted company. Peck and Bill went to the pantry—after ablutions in the old trough in the back yard. Kim and John—after performing the same rites separately in the back yard—took to their sleeping bags, one on either side of the stove.

'Good night, Kim,' John said in a final sort of a way. She thought his voice indicated that he did *not* want to be called if a bush rat came scurrying or jumping through the doorless doorway.

'Good night, John,' Kim replied in what she called her 'civil' tone. She meant this to imply that, now knowing about bush rats, she was not likely to take fright. In any case she would prefer to call Peck or Bill first.

Under her breath she had added—*God bless!* Yet didn't know why she had done so.

She heard John turn over in his sleeping bag. Then silence. This was one real piece of knowledge she was learning about him—he slept well. When he turned out the kerosene lamp, he turned himself out too.

Breakfast next morning consisted of the rest of the kangaroo stew, and the last of the pineapple, and plum jam. It was soon over. Kim thought the most delectable part of the dawn meal was the damper Peck made in the coals of the brush root in the stove, and the hot black tea. She did not mention her predilection for the tea and damper, as she didn't care to reject the enthusiasm of the two prospectors for pineapple mixed to a squashy dough with plum jam.

John, in his early morning silent mood, repacked the stores in the jeep. First he removed yet another small carton containing cigarettes for Peck and Bill—as a mark of appreciation for their willingness to sleep in the pantry. Meantime, Kim played the housewife inside. She insisted, against the wishes of Peck and Bill, on sweeping and tidying the main room. They were of the opinion they could do better themselves but told John in private they 'didn't care to hurt the little lady's feelings'.

Kim, sensing this attitude of superiority about sweeping a derelict room in a ruined old house, made a magnificent job of her efforts. If there'd been anything other than a broom made of a sapling gum with its leafery still intact, she would have done better. And, of course, there wasn't any furniture to bother about: only cigarette butts on the floor and dead coals round the stove.

As a last farewell mark of pride, and a return to impishness, she picked up a piece of red ochre from the ground and wrote—very large—on the outside wall——

Kim Wentworth Was Here!

When John had gathered himself and his long legs into the jeep: apparently out of sight, she began to write again. Her head was just that much on the side, and the tip of her very pink tongue peeped from the corner of her mouth as she wrote——

So Was John.

The two prospectors waved their terrible hats, shouted more advice about the route, and bade them a whooping goodbye. At least Peck did the shouting and Bill did the waving.

'See you in Church!' was the last thing Peck was heard

to say as distance divided them. 'Proper thing to do, y'know!'

Kim took this as the joke she was sure Peck meant it to be. Unexpectedly John's face had a distant frozen expression. He was not amused any more. Moreover, in spite of the mounting heat and the drying quality of the east wind, his narrow eyes sparked icicles all over again. What had Peck been saying to him in private?

Five minutes later, as they drove over the sand-plain he seemed to have put the prospectors, and *all that*, behind him as he turned his mind to work again.

'When you have time, Kim, make at least one duplicate record of the terrain: also detailed drawings of the plants I hope to find. Myree will want copies. It's possible we may write up a report in collaboration. The research she has been doing on other plant-life leads up directly to this species.'

'Of course.'

He was thoughtful and the small muscle at the corner of his jaw appeared to Kim to be in fine working order. Her heart dropped.

They were back to zero again. And he was thinking of Myree!

Already, with that preoccupied look, and that jaw muscle beating a tattoo, he was mindfully in a deep and fascinating 'collaboration' with Myree. Kim could imagine the two heads—his strong-featured and dark close to Myree's beautiful golden curled one—bent over a microscope. Or maybe over the great botanical treatise they would write in partnership? And find fame!

John said nothing for a long time, for which Kim was grateful. It gave her time to put her feelings back in a strait-jacket. She didn't really want the armistice over, and the war on again.

The carpets of everlastings had been left behind many many miles ago. The scrub had changed to blue-grey in colour, sprinkled with the small ground-level prickly wattle, and here and there a brilliant flame-coloured grevillea struck a fire-light in the bush.

They passed unexpected, almost unreal, groves of the brown and yellow banksia that she had not known grew so far inland. Some hours later they came again upon sprawling creepers of the blood-red sturt pea with its uncanny black eye staring up to the pale hot sky.

'Oh I wish we could stop——' she began.

John gave her a look meant to settle such ambitions.

'And pick some flowers?' he was caustic. 'We are not on a picnic, Kim. We are in search of one very particular species.'

She shook her head sadly.

'Fame bought at such a price!' she remarked judicially. 'All facts and no beauty!'

Silence.

'Of course I know,' she went on, as if agreeing with some inner argument that might win favour with John. '*We must find that species*. Some for you and some for Myree. Very important. It's just that when one sees curious flowers growing madly in their natural state——'

'You think they're striking? And you'd like to spend valuable hours sitting down beside them and *looking* at them——'

'Don't you ever *look* at flowers?' Kim asked gently—still not wanting the war *on again*. 'Or are they just specimens to you—like they are to Myree?'

Darn! Why did she put that last bit in? Being meanie again.

'Myree would have had a scientific approach to the work,' he said, then added thoughtfully. 'There's some larger species of *hibbertia* over to the far right. Very unusual. She would have found this useful.'

'She would have had the correct scientific approach to it?'

'Quite.'

'She would have been very "particular" about detail?'

Silence!

Now I know, Kim thought darkly. *He and Myree would have been able to wallow in beastly scientific names. Whereas, I bet, if I told him that same flower is just plain 'Yellow Bush' instead of that hideous Latin name he gives it, he would throw me out of the jeep here and now, and let me walk for it.*

Even as this last thought crossed her mind she felt a hint of events casting their shadows before. If she really behaved irritatingly enough, it was not beyond John to open the jeep door and say 'Out! Keep going till you strike Base. It's the place marked X on the map.'

It was two hard working days later that it really happened—the long walk!

They had crossed a narrow tongue of sandy desert and were finding the rare specimens for which John had come. Pathetic tiny straggly bushes, Kim thought them. Not so John Andrews. From his manner he might have been digging up nuggets of gold.

On the third day, almost out of nowhere, came a sand storm.

To Kim this was terrible, yet in a strange eerie way—wonderful. At first she was not even frightened.

The eastern sky grew black, almost as if this might be a rain storm coming—except that rain could not come from the north-east, across thousands of miles of the Great Sandy Desert which lay to the north-east of their own particular neighbour desert—the Gibson.

Their jeep had been all the afternoon parked under the shade of a lump of bedraggled bushes, while John hunted around for this strange, rare and straggly plant which he so treasured. Now and again he called to Kim.

'Sketch that as it grows,' he would command. He would thrust in a stake by the plant and tie a white tag to the top of it. This was so the plant could be found again later. Each time this order came, Kim, with her drawing-board, and materials carried in her shoulder bag, would sit down cross-legged on the ground under the pitiless sun, and with a fine pencil draw the plant exactly as it grew. The drawing would be to scale if it was a large plant. If small, then she drew it as nature had made it. Later John would dig the plant for his specimen case.

Sometimes John, wandering away in the distance, would be long gone before he came back with news of another find. In these intervals Kim took out her indian ink, her hair-fine drawing-brush, and translated the pencil drawings to ink on good quality drawing-paper.

Then, as the strange haze crept over the eastern arc, she became so absorbed in this last rite of committing the growing plant to paper, she did not hear John come back,

He stood over her looking down first at her work, then at the top of her brown dust-laden hat. He had to admit it was the finest brush work he had ever seen. Some lines were indeed as fine as the hair of a new born child—so shining clear and delicate were the strokes.

He looked down at this strange girl who had the manner of a too-young person one minute, the sharp perception of a gipsy the next: sometimes the quiet contemplative air of a very adult person.

And the way she wore that hat! Anywhere on her head that was comfortable! He would have liked to smile about that foible, but other matters were too pressing.

Right now, as she was drawing, she was someone way out of the world—absorbed in the life of a plant which she translated to paper with such sureness. Somehow her drawings *lived*. She gave them tenderness and a right to existence as if they were human beings.

Then he looked again at Kim herself. She was in a world of her own. She sat cross-legged, her board across her knees, the ink held by a miniature tripod beside her. The tip of her tongue peeped restlessly from the corner of her mouth. Her hat was at that ridiculous angle!

This, John told himself, was why she had that unworldly expression when sometimes she looked directly at him. Her eyes didn't quite, quite focus. He had to see her at the business of drawing to understand it.

'Over my dead body!' he said aloud.

Kim finished one long downward stroke She looked up from under the brim of her hat.

'You mean my drawing? You think it's not good enough?' she asked, instantly ready to give battle. She knew her penmanship was good and even John Andrews, botanist, could not take that piece of self-knowledge from her.

'I was thinking of oculists, not drawings,' he said unsmiling.

Kim wrinkled her brow.

'Oculists? They're eye doctors. Specialists or something ——'

He squatted down beside her and picked up the folder of pencil drawings she had done earlier. He leafed through them casually.

'Sure. That's what they are. Eye doctors. I wouldn't let

one loose on you Kim—except, as I said, over my dead body.'

She stared at him wondering if he had taken leave of his senses.

'You mean an eye doctor might interfere with my ability to draw a straight line, or a curved one?'

'Yes, that and for other reasons——'

'Other reasons?'

He turned his head and looked straight into her eyes. Odd, but it was almost impossible to perceive now, but those very innocent clear grey eyes didn't really focus. Not to the millionth of a millimetre anyway. Yet that very fact gave them their unique expression—almost of inward wonder.

'Never, under any circumstances whatever go to an eye doctor, Kim,' he repeated—flatly giving an order.

She dipped her pen in the ink again.

'I won't if you say so. At least—not while I'm working under your command. Of course, that only lasts twelve weeks in all, doesn't it?'

'Blackmail?' he asked.

Kim looked too innocent to be true. It was those eyes again!

'Well, who knows? In about a hundred years' time you just might need an expert penman at those Botanical Gardens of yours at the Mount.'

'I thought so,' he said coldly. 'All women are blackmailers. Now you have one more reason why I don't like women on my expeditions. They're inclined to twist a man's arm—to get further advantages. Don't you realise the Director at the Mount has University graduates after those jobs?'

'I'm just a typist who can draw,' Kim concluded for him sadly. 'If you had Myree—if she could type as well as draw——'

'Myree can draw very well,' John said bluntly. 'Her main contribution would be a scientific one which, of course, is the most valuable contribution they need at the Mount.'

'She's also very bee-oo-tiful,' Kim added, her head on one side, looking past his shoulder at the great black swathe dominating the skyline in the east. 'She really *is* beautiful, you know,' she added: always truthful.

'We all know that. However, when it comes to a matter of ability, it is beside the point——'

Not so very much—Kim thought. *Not with that note in your voice, Mr Botanist.*

It was time she changed the subject. It wasn't really in very good taste.

'John——' she nodded her head towards the east. 'What is happening to the sky? It can't possibly be rain—not from over there.'

He glanced over his shoulder. Then suddenly straightened up.

'Blast!' he said. 'A raking dust storm!'

'But dust is red, not black,' Kim said puzzled.

'It's what the light does to it. It will change——'

He stared at the sky for several minutes in silence. The black had become purple. Even as they watched it was changing to acquamarine, shot with red lights. To Kim it was becoming an incredible and wonderful sight. Red, like fire, now.

'It's moving fast,' John said suddenly springing into action. 'Can you manage your equipment? I'll get the specimen cases I left back in the bush. Pack all the camping gear you can manage into the back of the jeep. And hurry. Run! You can hear the wind coming!'

Far far away there was a throbbing, then a moaning sound.

Kim heard. She packed her gear at top speed and headed back over the scrub to the jeep.

'Not so easy!' she decided. 'That camping gear is heavy. The camp oven—the sleeping bags. Worse, the cartons of tinned provisions—— Of course, those beastly specimens *would* come first!'

She withdrew that thought. The specimens were John's heart's blood!

All the same, she ran about doing things very hard and fast. She even forgot to look at the skyline again till she had most of the stuff in the jeep. After she had thrown her own equipment on to the front seat she looked up to see what was happening in the eastern arc of the sky. She stood stock still, and gasped.

The great vast cloud was black at the base only. The area above the dark swathe was unlike anything anyone ever dreamed of. A red fire shaped like a wave was lifting itself up into the sky. All around was darkening as if night was drawing on, instead of the midday lunch hour. The mountainous wave-cloud in the east came on, gathering greater fury of colour as it came. There were a hundred different reds in it. Crimson, flame, gravel-brown, tangerine—and all their possible combinations. The swoosh, then rush and roar was of a million voracious death-dealing dingoes. The fiends of hell seemed let loose!

With whip lashes the first of the wind and the dust swirled round Kim.

'John! John! Where are you?' she called wildly. Against the wind she lifted, then shoved the last few items of gear into the jeep. She managed, against the wind, to climb on to the back tray and draw down the canvas covers. She had the wit to pull out the large roll of canvas camp-cover first. They would need more than the frame of the jeep behind which to shelter. The dust and wind were already sweeping under it. Inside the jeep they would surely suffocate.

John, she was sure, was lost for ever in that dreadful pall of dust. He would never find his way back. He would be covered with sand. He would smother. He would lie out there in the bush and die—all by himself.

A mountainous lump gathered in Kim's throat as she mourned in advance.

Oh John! John!

All the time, as thoughts stumbled through her head, and tears for John's certain death were forming mud baths in her eyes, she went on strapping down the canvas cover of the jeep.

She managed to work her way round the side of the jeep once more, lever open the door, and cover her work bag and John's specimen cases which had been left there earlier.

'They are the most important of all. Something for posterity. One day, months from now, they'll dig us out. But the drawings will be found—John's cases too——'

Then she thought of John going for those other specimens far off in the scrub, instead of seeing to their own safety.

She went on working madly at cords and canvas—in the teeth of the wind. It was a very wild howling dust storm now!

'What about those doctors who first drank foxglove tea to see if it really did have *digitalis*. People saved from heart failure just because of that! The man who first ate a mould or fungus, or something, to prove it was *penicillin——*'

Dear, brave, scientific John! She wished she could have lived long enough to put a cross, or more likely a cairn, on the spot where he died. All the same, no one was ever dead till they really died—John was too virile. He could never die.

CHAPTER EIGHT

She had unrolled the camp canvas by now and was desperately trying to hoist it—hard against the wind and sand—to tie it to the jeep tailboard. She heard a stumbling noise that was more relieving to her heart at this moment than reflections on the heroism of scientists. It was John coming—not struggling towards the jeep—but being *blown along* with the sand.

He carried his burden of specimen boxes under his arm.

Safe!

'What in the name of yellow-striped snakes are you trying to do?' he gasped in a dust-choked voice. 'That's too heavy for you!'

He probably couldn't hear much of her reply. 'You'd better put the specimen cases in the cabin. Please don't uncover my drawings——'

'*Your drawings?*' John caught the last words. 'Priceless jewels? I have here a specimen of the genus Duboisia: *myoporoides*, no less. Unknown to grow in this area. More important—*hopwoodi*. Unique!'

His words were lost again in a fit of coughing.

'Then put *your* precious jewels in the cabin too——' Kim shouted against the wind. 'I'm awfully busy trying to tie up this canvas——'

This was the first time he had mentioned the names of his great 'finds'. It had taken sand, sand and sand again to make John forget to distrust her!

The finds—*Duboisia, myoporoides* and *hopwoodi*—were too rare in this state for John Andrews to think of doing anything but exactly what Kim had said. He struggled against the sand-laden wind round the jeep and cached away the specimen boxes. By the time he came back to the rear of the jeep Kim had given up. She sat on the ground holding the canvas before her face trying not to suffocate.

'Here, take this——' John's voice was rough against the thundering noise all around. He swayed about like a drunken man as he ripped his shirt over his head and passed it to Kim. 'Hold it six inches from your face. That'll leave an air-space. You do have to breathe—— Think of the veils the Arabs wear——'

Kim, exhausted, did as she was told. John, as strong as the devil bedriven by the wind, hoisted the canvas aloft and attached it by ropes to the jeep's hood on its lee side. The section usually used as a tent flap, he pinned down to the side of the vehicle. Next he stretched the main sheet outwards and leewards a yard or two, then pegged it down.

Suddenly they were in an air-space. They were not free from dust but were at least in an atmosphere that was breathable.

He sat down, knees hunched up and put his head in his hands. He leaned his elbows on his knees and fell silent. Kim could see the heaving of his chest as he fought for breath.

She said nothing for a long time. When she could see his chest movement was easing she touched his arm.

'Guess what? Storm or no storm, life and death desperation or not, I brought the Thermos and the picnic bag out of the jeep *first*.'

He eased his head out of his hands and looked at her.

She started to laugh.

'You do look funny, John,' she said. 'Like you have a mud-mask on, or something. Only it's all dry. Your eyes are black holes——'

'So are yours,' he said bluntly. 'Where's that damn' Thermos?' Then he smiled painfully, slowly, and in a very tired way.

'I've heard of bush angels, but I never met one before,' he finished.

She scooped the sand away from the picnic basket, opened it and brought out the Thermos. The vanguard of the sand storm had blown across them and was racing away to the west, but its body and tail were still a dusty billowing veil over everything. Kim unscrewed the double Thermos tops, poured tea into the bigger one and handed it to John. She filled the smaller one for herself. They raised their cups to one another.

'Your good, undusty health!' John said gravely.

'Thank you,' Kim replied with equal gravity. 'Long may

you and—what did you call it? *Hopwoodi* something? Anyhow long may it last too.'

'Learn to spell it correctly before you draw it, Kim,' he commented. 'It ends with an "i". Who but a typist would have been so mundane as to think of saving our lives with a Thermos of tea?'

'Myree would have thought of a bottle of soothing oil for our faces too.'

My, even in this grave hour she was being a *meanie* again! The words had popped out—well, unexpectedly——

'Yes——' John said taking a swig of the tea which now had a fine cream of dust on top of it. 'Myree would undoubtedly have thought of everything. But *everything*!'

He said it so seriously that Kim decided he wasn't punishing her. He was thinking in his sandy isolation of Myree—safe with all her brains and beauty—back at Base with a whole host of men, all of whom would be making a play for her attention.

'All except Stephen Cole,' Kim reflected. Funny how she was so sure of him. He hadn't once looked at Myree with interest, but only at *her*—brainless Kim——

'It's a wonderful thing,' she said, out of context and after a long silence. 'It's a wonderful thing to have *someone* who likes you. Who thinks you're attractive.'

John drained the dregs of his tea, asked for some more, then helped himself to a handful of biscuits from the box.

'Meaning what exactly?'

'Well, we've nothing else to talk about so I might as well talk about *me*. I feel grateful to Stephen Cole. He likes me. It sort-of softens me—specially at this moment when burial by sand might be imminent.'

'I'm glad of that,' John commented briefly. 'About your gratitude, I mean. Not about Stephen Cole. Now suppose we consider that imminence of which you spoke. It might bear mentioning now, that other matters are quite trivial compared with it.'

'The storm's nearly gone, hasn't it? At least the worst of the noise has. The dust will die down sooner or later——'

'Later than sooner, by the look of the sky out there. We're marooned in a series of sand dunes that didn't exist two hours ago—in case that fact interests you, Kim. Worse——'

'What could be worse? The sand's red, I know. When we

were children we used to like playing in the sand dunes along the beaches.'

John was silent. Kim had a feeling she'd been making gaffes all over again the way she did at home.

Suddenly her spirits dropped. She ought to have been serious about this predicament. She ought to have talked *gravely* about it.

'You won't navigate us out of here, Kim,' John said more quietly. 'There'll be no sign of our jeep tracks. Probably no sign of the far track back to the old station.'

Kim could see well enough that they wouldn't be able to get the jeep out of this mess. As the heaviest of the dust subsided in the wake of the big blow she could see sand was built up feet high completely covering most of the low scrub trees. There were dunes that were absolute barriers against the passage of a four-wheeled vehicle.

She must think of earnest things. For instance what would Myree—and the men back at Base—say about them being marooned together like this?

Worse, what would John *fear* they might think?

She mustn't say anything funny, or silly about it. She could see, under his coating of dust and sand, that John was being very serious indeed.

'I guess I might as well go to sleep as sit and worry,' was all she said aloud, sorry that her voice croaked instead of sounding dulcet.

John's only answer was to rest his head in his hands again, and his elbows on his knees.

'Then go to sleep,' he said in a disinterested way. 'I intend to do the same myself. There'll be heavy work ahead of us to-night, or to-morrow—whenever this raking dust dies down.'

Kim did indeed sleep—from sheer exhaustion. Her muscular efforts in packing the stores in the jeep against the wind had really beaten her. She slept first in a sitting position with her head in her arms, then finally keeling slowly over till she was rolled round like a kitten, bang against the canvas behind her.

When she awoke it was night. The dust storm, with all its hangers-on of air drifts and willi-willis, was gone. It might never have happened except that the landscape had changed its form, and the moon high in a hazy blue-black sky was rosy pink, with a glorious halo, instead of being merely pale gold. John was up and about.

With the help of a king-sized torch—also rescued earlier by Kim along with the picnic basket—he found the hurricane lamps, the miniature butane gas stove, and one of the larger kits of tinned food.

Kim did the cooking while John cleared the gear out of the back of the jeep and made up a camp bed for her there. Eating wasn't as much fun as it might have been, for they were both hungry but their throats were sore. The raspy vocal chords precluded conversation too. This Kim thought was a good idea. In a state of compulsory silence she could not possibly say the wrong thing again.

When they had painfully eaten tinned salmon, a few fry-pan scones and a small tin of apricots, John set to work by the light of the lamps to unhitch the life-saving canvas from the rear of the jeep and set it up as a proper camp.

Here he rigged up his own sleeping bag, hung up one of the lamps, and set to work examining those precious specimens which he had dug out of the ground, roots and all, while Kim had run for the jeep. He had forbidden her to wash up the dishes or the fry-pan.

'We have a certain amount of water,' he said perfunctorily in his very husky voice. 'There's no reason to be prodigal with it. Till daylight we can't even begin to guess how we'll get out of here. Let alone how long it will take us to do just that.'

Kim did what the aborigines did. She cleaned everything with sand. The fact that the plates and the mugs would not have a polished appearance, and remained stubbornly sticky, was a matter she decided not to waste her conscience on.

Later they slept again. John under the canvas and Kim in the back of the jeep. They were unaware of the utter silence of the night, or the bright pink coloured stars and halo-ed moon. The old old land was so still. It was timelessly indifferent—for thousands of haunted miles around.

In the morning they surveyed their surroundings. This might have been the Sahara except that here and there a rock, or the leafless top of one or two of the taller trees, peered above the sand dunes. As far as they could see the only noteworthy thing in all the world was that the miles of dunes all around were red instead of yellow.

'Not a bit like the beach,' Kim said trying to be bright. 'That reminds me. How do we wash?'

'We don't.'

At this Kim really was aghast. They had a small tank of water—but water was more than diamonds and rubies if they didn't get out of here soon.

'Well . . . just our faces and hands . . .'

'Not even those. Do with them, and the rest of yourself, what you did with the plates and mugs last night. Use sand. You'll be redder but you'll be clean.'

'Like using sandsoap?'

'Exactly.'

'Except it's out of fashion since detergents came in——'

I must stop this, Kim thought soberly. *I'm trying to be way-out again. It doesn't work with John any more.*

With one of the long tent poles John rigged up a mast above the jeep and from this hung a towel.

'That will have to be my land mark,' he said. 'I'll go off in all four directions. One at a time, naturally. When I reach the point short of no return, I'll come back. I'll see what is to be seen of any track.'

It was two hours before John had done with his voyage of non-discovery.

'Nothing!' he said. 'We'll have to strike a course by the compass—which, thank heaven, has no dust in it.' This was one cause for relief, for their only other way of finding direction was by their watches and both were dust-clogged and had stopped.

John took out the map and pondered long over it. Finally he carefully drew a route on it.

'Right,' he said. 'Now I have to test the depth of the sand in that direction. When I come back we'll see if we can move the jeep.'

Even with a four-wheel drive they'd never get the jeep through the sand. Kim knew this. He was trying to keep up *her* morale by doing something.

'When I've tested the sand drifts,' John went on. 'We'll search out the spots where a bit of shrub or greenery is showing. Next we shovel sand away from those trees and shrubs. Even spindly bushes. Finally we fall to tree cutting! Have you got the message, Kim?'

'You mean we'll build a fire as a sort of beacon? Peck and Bill would be the nearest human beings likely to see us, but they'd be miles and miles and miles . . .'

A shadow crossed John's face.

'They were going north—as from the old station. Very nearly in the opposite direction from us,' he said quietly. 'We cut saplings and as many tree branches, or even stems, we can find. We corduroy them. That is, make holding rafts under the jeep's wheels.'

'But we'd only move a few yards at a time that way——'

Kim broke off.

Myree would not have said that. Myree would have known that that was the only way to move a vehicle across sand-dune country.

John was too busy uncovering the axes, a shovel and small spade; all clipped by stanchions on the bonnet of the jeep, to reply.

'You,' he said, turning round once, 'might make some tea. And don't waste the water by warming the teapot first.'

To this last Kim took deep exception. Tea was made in a billy can. *Not* a teapot. He was being sarcastic at her expense. She refrained from saying anything more at all. She did some thinking instead.

Cut down trees! Build a raft! Move the jeep forward a few yards! Remove the raft in the hideous heat that was already descending on them with the high noon sun. Then place the raft, corduroy fashion, in front of the jeep again! Then move the car on another few yards!

'If we work all day and half the night,' she thought, 'we might move the jeep a few hundred yards in twenty-four hours! We must be fifty miles from help!'

People did die in the desert. One often read about it.

As two days and two nights followed one upon another, they soon fell into a routine of each to his own job.

The thing that Kim minded most was John's insistence on the right to ration the water for tea-making. As if she wouldn't be careful herself! Kim, at this stage, had no idea that the heat beating on the galvanised iron of the water tank had been causing evaporation. Neither had she known why

John had carefully covered the radiator of the car with thick layers of the bush blankets. There were many questions she didn't ask, because John was not in an answering mood. He was lost in a world of his own silence as he worked.

Dear God, how he worked!

On the fourth day he told her.

When they finished their breakfast he insisted that Kim had an extra mug of tea.

'You'll need it to-day. You've a long hot job in front of you.'

'Something new?' she asked brightly; anything to change the monotony of their back-breaking work.

'Yes,' he said shortly. 'Take your drawing materials out of that carry-bag of yours. Cover them well against the normal dust blow, and leave them in the jeep. Next fill your bag with the tinned stuff I'll put out for you.'

'There isn't so very much left.'

'Enough for our separate needs,' he said dryly. His face was expressionless.

She wasn't sure what he meant, but she did as he ordered. It was a long time since she had had any inclination to question or even talk. Conversation had ceased to exist—as such. They were saving their natural body juices for their labours.

John put several small tins of fruit and two tins of milk and a packet of biscuits in the bag, then hung it on her shoulder and asked her how it was for weight.

'Not too bad,' she said. 'But why——?'

Instead of answering, he took the canvas water-bag and filled it from the tank. Kim noticed the last of the water pouring into the bag came only at a slow flow.

'It's almost empty!' she said staring at the tank. Then her eyes came back to his face. The immediate facts of life hit her. Hard!

'Not quite empty. Now listen, Kim. And listen carefully.'

He searched her eyes, but he read only puzzlement, then a strange *cheerful* fearlessness. She understood now.

'Last night, after you went to sleep I went out. We've only brought the jeep to an area of deeper sand troughs. I later went over the map. I've made this new one. You know how to use the compass. You must carry the bag of tinned stuff on one shoulder, the water-bag on the other, and *your hat on your head*. Remember, whatever happens—first, last, and all the time—you keep your hat on your head. Do you understand?'

Kim stared at him. The grey eyes, dark-fringed, were unwavering.

'*You* are our chance of rescue, Kim, *if you keep your hat on your head.*' As he said these last words a sudden almost tender shadow crossed his face. Then he went on, 'Sunstroke is your worst enemy. Sooner or later you will come to a stand of banksia trees. We didn't leave them so many miles behind.'

'John. I'm staying with you!'

His face was as craggy as the worst rock outcrop they'd seen since Base.

'You will do as you're told, Kim. When you come to the banksia trees—if you're short of water—you dig down to the root tips. You suck them. They contain water. That is how the aborigines survive this stretch of country——'

'You've put the last of the water from the tank in my water-bag!'

'There is water in the jeep's radiator. It's almost full. That's why I covered it with rugs. To save evaporation.'

'You knew this might happen?'

'Of course. I'm not brainless.'

She shook her head.

'I'm staying with you, John!'

She stood, a small brown dust-covered girl, with unexpected stoical determination in her face: her brown hat at an absurd angle. A shadow passed over John Andrews' eyes again as he looked at that hat-ridiculous. So much of Kim's character was in its dentable versatility. Then he pulled down the mask. He was quite cold and impersonal again.

'Listen, Kim,' he said flatly. 'You'd like to survive? In a small kind-hearted way you would perhaps like *me* to survive? That is very touching of you considering—well—never mind that! Now are you listening—*for the last time?*'

Her eyes said 'yes'.

'I repeat. *You* are our chance of survival. *You*, not me. You are a good navigator. You can read a map. Stick to your compass. Stick to your map—and *keep that damned hat on your head*. You'll reach the stand of banksias before your water runs out. You'll be on the track to the old station. Already there has to be an alarm out. We were due to make contact two days ago.'

'Yes, of course!'

'Once you're on the track to the old station *you* will be found. At the worst you'll be picked up at the old station. At the best—many miles before that.'

'But Peck and Bill were leaving! We didn't tell George Crossman, back at Base, we were going to the old station. We made a deviation from the route——'

'They'll be looking for us *somewhere*. They'll know we were there——'

'How? If there isn't anyone there to tell them?'

John looked at Kim—right in the eyes—for quite half a minute. Then a slow, half weary, half amused smile flickered over his face.

'You left a message on the wall. You told the world in red ochre—*Kim Wentworth Was Here*. Remember?'

She nodded. 'Underneath I wrote—*So Was John*. It was only a joke.'

'A very life-saving joke. It left a message. Now, are you going?'

She nodded.

'Don't die of thirst, or sand storm, or snakebite while I'm gone, will you?' A sandy frog came in her throat. She couldn't possibly show him real concern. He'd slap her straight back in her place.

'I didn't know you thought so much of me.' He was almost amused.

'I didn't, but I do now. That's only because I'm leaving you alone in the desert. Why can't we *both* go?'

His voice was suddenly sharp.

'Because there's enough water in that bag for one to reach the banksias first, even the station track. *There is not enough for two*. We both go, we both—well, never mind that. Besides, I have my *Duboisia* specimens to bring in. That is my first consideration. The weight would be an additional burden——'

'Oh *no*!'

She who loved plants, suddenly raged against them. He could possibly die of rusty radiator water, or another sand storm—but he had to think about his *Duboisia*! Thirst or no thirst, he would stay with his beastly specimens!

John took her by the shoulder and roughly turned her round facing north-west. He adjusted the compass and put that in her hand. Then he tucked the map, with a pencil tied to it, in the bib pocket of her working overalls. He adjusted the straps of the bag carrying the tinned fruit on one shoulder, and the strap of the water-bag on the other for balance. He gave her a push forward. He might have been sending a reluctant child off to school for the first time.

'Now go!' he commanded. 'And remember. Though the heavens fall—*keep that hat on your head*. Even when you sleep at night. Sunstroke is your only real enemy. *And keep walking!*'

She wanted to turn round to wave goodbye. She didn't because she knew he'd hate it. But there were tears stinging her eyes. And in her heart too. She wasn't very brave any more.

'See you later!' she said without turning her head.

'See you later!' he replied. She thought he nearly finished with 'God Bless!'

Her imagination, of course!

Yet she had not misheard!

The words sang in her ears as her feet sank deep in the sand and she steadily ploughed her way forward. *He had said 'God Bless!'* She fixed her eyes first on the compass in her right hand to take a bearing on a distant rock, then on the sand she had yet to force her feet through. He *had* said it! Well, he didn't think her a fool school girl any more——

Her chin went up. She pushed her hat over one eye. The Wentworths were worth where they went!

She hoped her back view, as she trudged over the sand dunes, would pass muster. Myree's backside view would be much more entrancing.

Forward Kimberley Jessica! Into the pale yellow gauze of the north-west sky! Take a bearing on that distant rock peeking out of the sand hills now and again—just to be sure.

She was a good navigator. *He trusted her to get there!*

She loved him for that.

Did she say—*loved?*

CHAPTER NINE

Kim forgot how many days she had been walking. Maybe it was three. Maybe four. At night she slept when she had to; and only where she could half lie, half sit propped-up so she could keep her hat on her head.

She had by-passed the stand of banksia trees, but she still had a third of her water in the canvas bag. She'd gone on very short rations indeed. Yesterday, fearful of forgetfulness, she had begun saying over and over again—'*I must not put my compass down, even at night. I must keep my hat on my head.*'

When she realised she was repeating these words every few minutes she became worried for fear this was a sign of desert-happiness. Or was it desert-haziness? Maybe just other names for 'sun-struck'. She must ask someone sometime. Whichever, it was a sickness that began with throwing away one's clothes, then all possessions. Finally one's hat. After that——

She must think about interesting things. And people. Like the other members of the Expedition, for instance. She would think about George Crossman coming over the sand dunes to rescue her. Next she would think about Myree, and about beautiful things packaged together with Myree. That would be to show she was not desert-happy. Just magnanimous.

She went back to her litany. *I must keep the compass in my hand. I must keep my hat on my head. I must remember not to have another drink till sundown. I must begin thinking of George and Myree and Stephen*——

Stephen's eyes reminded her of the worst part of the sand storm. Red and brown, all mixed up. One day, back at Base, she'd gone to George Crossman's caravan and found Stephen leafing through George's notes while the other man was away with a field party. Stephen had laughed off his presence by saying he was looking for a reference to an important text—*Key to West Australian Wild-flowers*. Kim had offered to lend Stephen her own.

Now, walking mile upon mile over red-brown sand dunes she realised she hadn't believed Stephen that day. Not really.

What had he wanted in George's notes?

It was time to say her litany again. She put her hand on top of her head to make sure she had not yet thrown away her hat.

Her feet told her she was suddenly walking on clearer ground. It was hard and firm. She wasn't lifting her knees waist-high to take each step. She looked down and noticed for the first time that through the sandy overlay small plants and shrubs were dustily showing their heads. She was out of the sand dunes. She looked up again.

Mirage lay across the middle distance shrouding the horizon with its back-haze. Through the dazzle of gold and deep yellow and red she could see the dark distorted figure of some moving creature coming towards her. Dingo, emu, kangaroo, or *man*?

This black thing was foreshortened. It gangled with strange horizontal lines like the TV set when it went wonky.

Next the figure seemed vertical, yet shapeless and mystifying. Then it came out of the mirage into the near-distance.

It was a man. It was Stephen Cole.

Kim felt crying time was due at last, except she never cried on principle. What's more she only wanted to cry because it was *not* George Crossman. She had decided—somewhere on the long walk—that she loved George Crossman. Well, she had to love someone, hadn't she? He was the best and the nicest and the dearest——

She put her hand on her head again. Her hat was safely there. She didn't have to *try* any more. She could give up, as from here.

She smiled, just that much cheerily, not noticing she had dropped the water-bag, and the supply-bag, and the compass. *But not her hat.*

Stephen came on over the sand-strewn distance. Then he broke into a run. Kim stood still.

After all she was dreadfully tired!

Stephen waved both his hands over his head as he came loping fast across the wounding ground to where Kim stood —shock-still—like the bare-leafed, windwhipped sapling tree nearby.

He came to a halt in front of her. And stared. He took in

a deep breath and shook his head, as if for one moment he was wordless. Then he straightened his shoulders.

'So!' he said mustering a grin from a near-stunned face. 'The lost is found! I have you all to myself again, Petso.'

Kim could not smile any more because it hurt her sunburn too much.

He slipped his arm round her and let her lean against him.

After a while Stephen stood her off from him.

'Listen, sweetie. Are you registering?' He searched her unclear eyes with his red-brown ones. 'Where have you left John? Remember him? Boss-cocky of the Expedition? Where's the jeep?'

Kim shook her head, too tired at the moment to remember.

'He stayed behind——' Her throat was cracked and dried and it hurt her to talk. 'He's with the jeep, and——'

'And with his specimens? Is that it? They were too important a find for him to leave? Good heavens! Just how important were they, love? Can you remember?'

Kim shook her head. This was because it buzzed and whizzed. The skin was burned off her nose and forehead. Her hands and arms too.

Then she remembered she had to tell Stephen that John Andrews was roughly three to four walking days away in the sand dunes. And she didn't know anything about specimens. Only about rusty radiator water which was all John had to drink. It was more important anyway.

She was desert-happy all right because it took her a long time to explain the exact direction. She'd noted the land marks.

Stephen took her by the shoulders and stared deep in her eyes again.

'Listen, sweetheart,' he said. 'I need to rescue John, the records and the specimens. Okay? Can you do one thing more? My Land-Rover's hit the bomb over to the right. It's useless. George is with his own Land-Rover six hundred yards over the rise to the west. Can you make it?'

She nodded. 'I can make it—if you go for John. *Now.*'

'I'm going for John, Kim. I'm fit and can go way-out faster through the sand dunes than any girl. And you've given me the land marks. I've my ski sandshoes along with me. George has a pair with the rescue kit too. Tell George I've gone on ahead because it's urgent. I've my own water-bag. Are you receiving, Kim?'

She nodded.

'Right. Tell George to bring the Desert-Rescue kit for *Man and Vehicle*. He'll know what that is. The sandshoes will halve his travelling time. With the rescue kit and its nylon matting we'll bring the jeep out. I'll get there before George, so tell him I'll check on the gear. Specimens too.'

Kim nodded again.

She supposed saying 'yes' to everything—even the bit about John's specimens—was all right now.

She couldn't think of anything else to say anyway.

She was desert-happy all right.

'Get going, my Petso,' Stephen said gently. 'Six hundred yards over the rise. Can do?'

She nodded.

He was going for John. That was all that really mattered.

Six hundred yards! To Kim it was the hardest stretch of all.

She walked stiffly up the rise, then down over the other side to where she could see the Land-Rover in the distance. George was kneeling beside one of the wheels tightening the nuts on the hub. She was almost up to him when he turned his head and looked over his shoulder.

Then stood up—as if seeing a mirage himself. Kim stopped and gazed at him vaguely. She was really here? She wasn't sure, but she thought she had made it.

His face seemed to crease up. He looked as if he might be the crying one. The spanner dropped from his hand with a clang. Then he held out his arms. *Wide*.

Without a word Kim trudged on, straight into them. He wrapped his arms round her and held her tight.

'Dear little sweetheart Kim——' he was saying, a note of incredulity in his voice. He kissed the top of her head.

'That's awfully nice——' Kim thought. 'George *kissing* me——'

He led her to the shade side of the Rover and sat her down on the ground. He then dragged the vacuum cooler from the back of the car and, opened it up, mixed her a drink of tinned milk and egg powder. He put into this a tot of rum from the First Aid box. Then he sat down on the ground beside her, holding her hand round the mug so she would not drop it: his other arm around her.

When she had finished the drink she sighed. For five silent minutes George cradled her against his shoulder watching the new life creep back into her poor sun-ruined face. When she opened her eyes he was amazed to see them alight with a sort-of determined will.

'You must go for John——' she said.

He nodded. 'Of course.'

'It's important—you see—he has *special specimens*——'

George's eyebrows went up. 'He has to be found for his own sake, Kim.'

'I know. But his specimens must be saved too. He stayed because of them. And for a record for Myree too. You see, Stephen's gone for them. The records I mean——'

George frowned. He sat quite still thinking hard. Then he looked at Kim again, long and thoughtfully.

'We're right on the station track, here, Kim. Could you make it in my Rover?'

'Yes.'

'Stephen's vehicle is out of action. We'll have to make sure we get John's jeep back, and going——'

She nodded again.

'If you can't make it back go to the homestead, Kim, just park by the side of the track. We'll come for you sooner than later. There's everything in the Rover. Water, food . . .'

She was nodding again, like a little old wise woman who was minute by minute coming back from some distant fantasy place.

He pulled her to her feet and sat her in the car while he removed the gear he needed to take with him to salvage John and the jeep. When he had finished he came round to the drive seat and looked at Kim again.

'You are right on the station track,' he repeated. 'Sixty miles by the speedometer. Can do?'

'Can do!' she replied solemnly. She couldn't smile because the sunburn hurt too much. She started up the engine instead.

She put her head out of the window, the hat-ridiculous funnier than ever. George took her face tenderly between his two hands and kissed her full on her sun-cracked lips. Then he stood back.

'Atta girl!' he said. 'You'll make it!'

'I'm on my way.' She let out the clutch pedal and pushed the gear stick into first. Then on her way she was. Her dust-cloud was like a flag of disdain for all things frightening in the outback.

In the blazing static stillness of sundown, some hours later, Kim drove up to the broken-down station. She braked to a stop, then sat looking at the homestead.

She rested her elbow on the steering wheel and her chin in the cup of her hand and gazed at the desolate skeleton of what had once been a home. Clear-sighted sense had been coming back to her in waves ever since she had left George.

She stared at the straggling letters scrawled in ochre on the wall.

Kim Wentworth Was Here!

and underneath——

So Was John.

She cocked her head on one side and thought about that message.

'Famous words, but not last ones!' she thought.

At the same hour, six days later, John Andrews drove up in his jeep, alone. Stephen and George had made it out to the dunes in two days and one night. The sandshoes, ski sticks and male strength had given them vastly superior speed to Kim. Then there had been a day or two to fix the jeep, and another day to get it across the dunes.

It was sundown when John dropped out of the drive seat to the gravelly earth. Kim was sitting on the last of the door-steps of the old ruin. She looked at him with a considering air. It was important, she felt, not to make this moment too dramatic. After all, he was the Boss, and she the Hired Hand. He wouldn't want a 'scene'. She would make it casual.

She looked at him as he came towards her, looming in his tall rangy way above where she sat. He looked down at her, not smiling, but not anything else either. Sort-of *considering,* she thought.

Kim picked up a packet of cigarettes and a box of matches from the step and held them up to him.

'I heard you coming,' she remarked—very very casually. 'I recognised the sound as belonging to the jeep. It had to be you because I knew you wouldn't leave *Duboi* . . . What was the rest of that name?'

'*Duboisia*,' he said taking the packet from her and shaking out a cigarette. He lit one, flicked out the match and looked down at her again. 'You guessed the first thing I'd like would be a cigarette?'

'Yes. You said you were running short when the sand storm blew up.'

'It was kind of you to remember.'

John leaned one hand on the door frame and stared past the fallen outhouses to the sunset. A tree with its die-back finger was a black etching silhouetted against a sky so vivid it wounded the eyes.

'You know——' Kim went on conversationally, after a minute's silence. 'We really could have saved a lot of time ——'

John did not move his position but his eyes came round to hers again.

'How?'

'Well! . . . Apart from sturt pea, mulla mullas and spinifex there's a clump of *Duboisia* down the slope behind that old broken-down woolshed. I found it the day before yesterday on one of my walks. It's probably not the special *hopwoodi* one. Then again, it could be——'

John straightened up as if an electric charge had gone through him. He stared at her.

'For crying out loud!' he almost exploded. 'You didn't touch it? You didn't fool round with it? You didn't——?'

'I didn't do anything with it,' Kim said coldly, chin up in the air. 'I was too busy doing the housework. I swept and cleaned—that was quite something, considering the dust that had blown in here. And I have your dinner nearly ready.'

John stared at her.

'My *dinner*?' he asked slowly.

'Well, yours and George's and Stephen's. Why haven't they come? I don't even have a triangle to remind them it's the hour for eating. Of course the sunset ought to tell them ——'

John's expression was like the one he'd worn at the Mount when she'd first seen him. It could have meant he would like to upend her and smack her—*hard*. All because she was constantly full of surprises.

A cigarette waiting? *And dinner too!*

His hand went back on the door jamb.

'They've gone on north-east from here,' John said. 'They'd left the second Land-Rover a mile or two in the sand north of where you were picked up. We fixed it temporarily. Then we found an old wool track. The map showed it led to Bim's Stopover. That's a place boasting a radio service, a store, garage, pub, and airstrip.'

Kim nodded. 'They want to let the world know we're all well?'

'That, and to get some replacements for Stephen's Rover and my jeep. The Rover had pranged the sump box. I've lost a tooth from the crown wheel of the jeep.' He paused. Then added—'We're stuck here for a day or two, Kim. The jeep wouldn't last another twenty miles.'

Kim stood up now.

'That's nice,' she said as she turned towards the doorway. 'You can study the *Duboisia* behind the woolshed, and I can draw it, record it and tag it. All's well that ends well, because we'll not be wasting more time, will we?'

'Where are you going, Kim?' John asked abruptly.

'To stir the stew. It's made of an assortment of tinned stuff, but not as bad as Peck's pineapple-and-jam concoction.'

He watched her as she passed him, stepping her way precariously through the broken doorway. He threw his cigarette stub on the ground, put his foot on it, then strode after her.

'Kim!' She turned and looked at him for a long second. He held out his hand. Slowly she put her own hand in his.

'Kim?' There was something dangerous—yet possibly tender too—in his eyes. They were a very dark blue at this moment. Dark as thunder on the mountains. Or pain.

'Don't say anything, John. You don't have to.'

Their eyes met and their hands held.

'Damn all heretics!' he said suddenly. 'It's like—it's like taking advantage of a very young, but great-hearted girl.'

He might have kissed her then, Kim thought. A fellow

adventurer, as it were. But the 'very young' description spoiled it.

'The water in the trough by the bore is warm, John,' she said, her eyes unwavering. 'It's wonderful that it comes up out of the ground, isn't it? A sort of built-in hot-water system.'

He dropped her hand and turned away.

'If I haven't longed for a bath!' was all he said, but he slammed his hat back on his head with a certain fury as he went out.

It was not a day or two, but a full ten days, before George Crossman and Stephen came back with one repaired Land-Rover, and some of the more urgent spares for John's jeep.

Those ten days had been all-heaven for Kim, though she declined to mention this fact to John. She had to appear and behave—as he did—absolutely professionally. This was specially necessary as some more specimens of the less important of the two *Duboisia* species were found in their natural state in other areas not far distant from the homestead. But alas, no sign of the prized *hopwoodi*.

As John hunted and found certain specimens, so did Kim draw and make records for him. Day by day they recovered from their privations. Neither mentioned them again. They had more important things to do—like be real dedicated botanists.

When John went off by himself, knapsack over his shoulder—which he did most of the daylight hours—Kim spent any spare time she had painting in true colours a copy of the sketch drawings she had done for her own private record, from the coast all the way to Manutarra. She brought up to date her notebook, with its drawings of her own interesting but *botanically* unimportant finds hereabouts. Candle-spiked hakea, the wild lilac hibiscus, yellow-flowered red-nutted illyarrie, the crimson native pomegranate, popflower and the lovely mauve spiked feather-flower.

It was the colours, so brilliant, that fascinated Kim.

Then, on the fifth day, Peck and Bill came back. It was a morning when John had been working close to the homestead.

'What-ho! What-ho!' Peck shouted with glee when he saw them sitting on the doorstep drinking their morning tea.

'You two had the weddin' bells an' all? Heard way up the track you'd been off in the sand-plain country. This the honeymoon, eh?'

He slapped his old dusty hat at his knee with pleasure at the thought.

'No pub bills when you dig in here at the ol' shack, eh mate?'

John showed no reaction to Peck calling him 'mate', nor to the suggestion of quibbling at bills. He was inclined to ignore Peck's talk of wedding bells and honeymoons, but he was annoyed that Kim was exposed to this brand of outback humour.

When he had an opportunity later, after the old prospectors had been given tea and a welcome, he mustered Peck into a corner and briefly gave him a short lesson on good taste in a few tough but well-chosen words.

'Sorry mate!' Peck said, not understanding anything about taste or manners, anyway. 'How was I to know it was like *that*, eh? Not married at all! Well, you live an' learn, don't you? You don't look the sort of chap——' He had a gleam of so-called enlightenment in his faded red-rimmed old prospector's eyes. John's jaw took on a sudden aggressive look and Peck, reading the signs aright, took cover. He reckoned he had things to do like unpacking his swag. It was beyond him to understand the nature and the composition of a scientific expedition.

John, watching Peck's bruised and corny fingers, dickering with the straps of the swag, realised the desert-dyed prospector was on the way to being old as well as a little bushwhacky. He relented and offered the old man the only kind of grin of goodwill that he could muster at the moment. He gave the problem of definition and explanation to the stars to manage. It was beyond him.

The complications of having women on the trip lay with *other* people!

The pantry which Peck and Bill had taken over for the night was adjacent to the timber-walled spare room which Kim had tried to make habitable. In a housewifely mood—perhaps to impress Peck and Bill—she decided later that day to sweep out the latest layer of dust. The old tree branch came back into action again.

John had gone on to the plain in a not very civil mood, she thought. She found it hard to believe he minded the two prospectors coming back.

She swooshed with the leafy end of the old branch to the accompaniment of Peck conducting a monologue with Bill.

When she paused to wipe the beads of perspiration from her brow she heard her own name.

'Nice girl that Kim is too——' Peck was saying. 'Whatcha know, mate? They aint even thinkin' of weddin' bells. I kinda thought that feller John was a nice bloke. He fair near knocked me down when he got me in that there corner—jes' fer mentionin' the subject. Makes you kinda wonder how some people live, don't it?'

Bill's reply was a grunt, a satisfactory answer to Peck if not to Kim's startled ears.

'Thet means he aint the marryin' kind. Or maybe he's got himself a girl back some place else. Like he asked me would I get a message sent to some girl called Marie, or something, if we go back through Bim's Stopover. Said he'd write it down and they could send it by radio from the pub. Maybe he has 'em, but don't wed 'em. Sleeps an' moves on, eh?'

Kim didn't wait for Bill's answer, if any. She gave up sweeping out old shacks as a vocation from that moment. She went back to the living-room and the stew pot: although this last was once more Peck's concern. He had brought with him a fine haunch of kangaroo steak.

Stirring Peck's stew, she thought again of Myree.

John was sending Myree radio messages!

'"He has 'em but doesn't wed 'em!" That means girls in numbers! Would that be better than being in love with just *one* girl? Myree or any other?'

Yet it ought to be Myree because Myree was beautiful. As far as Dr Andrews was concerned, she was very clearly a double-doer tryer too!

CHAPTER TEN

Peck and Bill stayed the bare twenty-four hours at the old homestead.

The next day they departed. They were off to a hush-hush place—'north a bitaways just out of Bim's Stopover', they said. They'd heard, back a week or two ago, a whisper of a *find*. Some bloke had come in to the Stopover with a pouch of gold dust.

If they, Peck and Bill, spotted George Crossman and the Land-Rovers as they went along, they'd pass on the time of day. A heft of kangaroo steak too maybe.

All this was said—on their departure—with Peck's chuckling goodwill, and an occasional nod of the head from the silent Bill.

Kim and John waved them off from the edge of the weed-wild paddock that had once been the home of thousands of sheep.

'Bill, old mate, old mate!' Peck said after the last head-turn and as they trudged on round the curve of the track, their swags strapped to sticks slung over their shoulders. 'Didn't they look a right tied-up pair standin' by that wait-a-bit tree waving us orf like that? Well, you never can tell, can yer? It'll make a good story to tell the blokes up at the Stopover. They like a good story up there. The ways of them city folks! It kinda gets yer wonderin' don't it? Nice fella. Nice girl too —only a bit young fer thet kinda caper——'

If Bill was inclined to tell anything at all he did not put it into words. Peck did not expect it. Silence, he had always reckoned, suited Bill right down to the ground.

Back at the old homestead, the next few days passed as they had before the two prospectors had come.

Then on the tenth day George Crossman and Stephen came.

A short while before their arrival John had come in from a plant-hunt back of the rise beyond the clay paddock. Kim was standing in front of the homestead shading her eyes as she looked to the north.

'Land-Rover is coming,' John said, stacking his satchel and specimen box side by side. 'I recognise the sound!'

Kim was excited. She also felt a sudden twinge of regret. It might have been lonely, and except for the wild-flowers everywhere scenting the air, desolate. Yet this camp in the old broken-down homestead had been fun in its own right. They'd been busy—John in his wild herbarium of a million square acres: she with her pencil, her pen, and paint box.

John pulled his jungle hat farther down on his brow, and looked out from under the shade of the brim. He glanced at Kim. She had a curious stubborn look on her face.

'By the rheumy sound of that back-wheel drive it's not only a Land-Rover. It's the one George was driving!' he said.

'With or without the spare part for the jeep?' Kim asked.

'Not to worry. If we can't salvage the jeep you'll be able to return with George.'

'That will be fine and dandy,' Kim replied still not looking at him. 'I go, and you stay.'

He was surprised.

'Did you burn the last of the stew, or something, Kim?' he asked, an edge of amusement in his voice. 'Your natural flair for hospitality at stake? Haven't we enough supper for George? *And Stephen?*'

Kim ignored the verbal underlining of that *And Stephen*!

'We have. But it wouldn't really matter if we hadn't, would it? I mean, with all those brains they have between them they'd have remembered to bring something to add to our stores. Well, wouldn't they?'

John's expression became fixed. 'I think you're afraid they might have been absent-minded about stores. Too much Ralph Sinclair in your past, I'm afraid!'

Kim took half a minute off—to think.

'Do you know Ralph really well?' she asked, pretending mere conversation. She was still looking at the growing dust-ball, and being careful to keep her voice natural.

John, his hands in the belt of his shorts, rocked backwards on his heels. Then slowly forward again.

'I know Ralph's a first-class research man. Also that he has a whacker of a reputation for being absent-minded. He was present-minded enough when you departed from his company, Kim. He tried to get C.O.C.R. to change its plans. He wanted to keep you.'

Kim looked at John, almost disbelieving.

'Did he? Did he *really*?' Her eyes were suddenly shining. 'Oh, dear darling Ralph! I was a meanie to him. I let him down. I was sorry afterwards. It was too late. But——'

'Yes? But what?'

'Thank you for letting me know, John. It makes all the difference——'

'A difference to *other friendships*?' he asked directly, challenging her, though not looking at her.

Kim was really startled this time. John's eyes weren't so blue she noticed. Not now that he stood looking into the bright afternoon light. They seemed to be examining distant horizons again.

'You mean Stephen?' She brushed this off uneasily. 'Well, you see, I have to be friendly with Stephen for Ralph's sake. A sort-of bargain I made. Oh, I can't exactly——'

'Bargain?' John switched his glance quick as lightning. He was looking right at her now. Kim was puzzled.

A distant sound, growing louder, had become a thrumming.

'Look!' she said. Anything to change the subject. 'Here they come. Round the bend.'

She could never explain to John that half-witted threat Stephen had made about Ralph's doctorate!

The Land-Rover became a reality. Minutes later it was roaring down the track before it slammed to a stop. George spilled out of one side and Stephen the other. As Stephen was nearest Kim he shouted a joyous greeting. Then, when he came up, he flung his arms round her. Out of the corner of her eye Kim could see John and George Crossman shaking hands.

Stephen took her by the shoulders and held her back from him.

'Darling girl. What are you mumbling and bumbling about? Some loving words of cheer for me after ten long days' absence? Don't forget you have to show me every little jot of work you've done—just to prove you haven't been wasting the funds of the mighty C.O.C.R. in my absence.'

Kim blinked as she looked into the brown eyes eagerly

scrutinising hers as if to read some hidden message. He had underlined the '*every little jot of work*'. Why had John's mention of Ralph's name made her meeting with Stephen suddenly give her a jolt of fear?

And yet she had been grateful to him before. Because it was *someone* to *appear* to love her a little? Give her feminine ego a lift-up! It had been crumbs from the rich man's table to recompense for the glamorous bitchery of Celia and Diane. *And Myree too!*

She turned away from Stephen to greet George—whom she really did love in a good, quite selfless way.

George Crossman had finished telling John he had a new, but barely run-in, gear box in his Rover. Also some spares—but not all that were needed—for the jeep. Stephen's Land-Rover had had to be left behind. A new axle was a major job——

'They flew some parts up for us from Perth in forty-eight hours to Bim's Stopover. By the way—here's a love note for you John. A radio "hullo" from Myree back at Base.' He handed John an envelope, then turned to Kim and held out both hands. Somewhat mutely she took them. He held her back and looked at her. There was a split second of silence while Kim looked at George with her eyes, while her mind watched John open that note. He read it carefully, and equally carefully folded it and stowed it away in his shirt pocket—the left side. The one over his heart.

'My, oh my, Kim!' George was saying. 'You look more like a desert rat than a girl these days. Brown all over. Sunburned! And look at those small, very horny hands! What in the name of wild dingoes have you been doing with them?'

Kim was not amused.

'The sun out here burns everyone brown,' she explained spelling it out in syllables. 'As for my hands! They're not small, and not *very* horny. I've been peeling wild yams for dinner.'

'Yams?' He was incredulous. 'Out in this wasteland?'

'Certainly,' she said loftily. 'In some far distant time the inmates of this homestead planted parsley and yams behind the wash-house—now derelict. They all went to ground, then emerged wild but edible. I wouldn't expect a botanist—involved with long scientific names—to understand that.'

Stephen gave a shout of laughter.

'She sounds like a lecturer I once had. Old Wilkinson-Brown. He was ponderous as a hippo.'

Kim's backbone stiffened. Dr Wilkinson-Brown? He had been a lecturer at Crawley two years back. In the same department as Ralph Sinclair. Had he also lectured in other realms in the Eastern States later?

'There's something inside on the stove, George,' John Andrews was saying. 'If it's the yams and wild parsley that make it edible I can recommend letting all garden vegetables run to seed——'

The two men turned away. John led George Crossman to the place where he'd stored his specimen cases.

'I've something here to knock you sideways, George,' he was saying. 'You'll have to look at this collection right away. If I'd only had the microscope—which you took off with you—I could have cut some slides!'

'We'll leave the two young ones to the kitchen,' George agreed with a shrug. 'Do you know, John, I had a feeling they might be mating-up back at Base. Stephen had that certain look in his eye. I was a bit anxious——'

John Andrews was silent.

'Sorry,' George amended quickly. 'I know you don't like shinannigans on field work. Nothing too foolish going on anyway——'

'I wasn't thinking of Kim,' John said briefly—too briefly. 'I was thinking of Stephen. I'll have a talk with you about that later. I want to show you my *Duboisia myoporoides*. Better, and unique—two specimens of *hopwoodi*. I found any amount of the first. Kim found the bigger clumps here on this old station. Not the *hopwoodi* of course. I found *that* right out beyond.'

'She found *Duboisia* like she found wild parsley and yams?' George was incredulous.

John, who had bent over his specimen case, straightened up. He stared at the other man curiously.

'You just waking up, John?' George persisted mildly. 'That girl knows more about wild-flowers and native plants than a lot of trained scientists—though I admit she's allergic to their botanical names, and possibly their valuable chemical extracts.'

John turned back to his specimen case.

'If I'd had the microscope,' he repeated. 'I'd have some conclusions at this stage.' He unstrapped two of the cases.

'You were always a stickler for regulations, John,' George said. 'It was my job to take the microscope. Part of the chemist's equipment. You're plain botanist!' He laughed to take the sting out of his joke.

'I'll lift other plants hereabouts at the last moment,' John went on. 'Yes, I know the regulations. I sometimes blast them. Meantime Kim has made the live drawings.'

He fished in his pockets for a cigarette. As he lit up he turned and watched Stephen and Kim entering the old homestead. Stephen had his arm along Kim's shoulder.

John's eyes met George Crossman's.

'If you want to do a little salvaging, George,' he said evenly. 'Forget the microscopes and prise Kim loose from Stephen Cole. That's an order for *security reasons only*. I think you're the man to do it. She feels well disposed towards you.'

George glanced at the other man quickly.

'What news from Base?' John asked relaxing, not waiting for an answer.

'Nothing but good news. We received messages at Bim's via Nookbennie, on the two-way. They're on the right wavelength there for Base. Everyone's at work and most of them have found something of prize interest. Myree Bolton's outstripping them for her own topic. She has a first class research brain, John. She's fast and cool. Also confident.'

John, like George, looked out to the west. The sun was declining and the sky was changing from white to pale blue. Then came amethyst, and the beginning of the sunset glory.

'I know,' he said briefly. 'It's been in my mind to give Myree an appointment at the Mount. I picked her quality when she first did that stint of work with us last year. She has a sound analytical approach.'

He turned back to George, a question in his eyes. 'Would she come?'

'You ask. She'll come!' George said bluntly, giving John the message—if that was what he wanted. The double-loaded message. Myree would come to John, for John—as much as she would come to the Institute. Everyone in the Expedition knew that.

'Good. Now let's get on with these specimens. Ready for the bonanza, George? I have it here in my perforated bag. *Hopwoodi.*'

'I thought you could be joking.'

'I'm not. Look at it. A unique find! The aborigines chew it as a medicinal drug.'

'I can hardly believe it,' George said doubtfully. 'It was thought to be extinct. My heavens, John, we may have here another of nature's wonder medicines. Another *quinine*? Or *penicillin*?'

'You're the organic chemist, George. You have the microscopes and equipment. It is as startling a find as *digitalis* from a common English hedgerow.'

George stared at the miserable straggling tree plants. How unprepossessing! Yet what magic they might possibly yield!

Suddenly his thoughts went off on another track. He looked at the other man quickly. 'You've kept those specimens under lock and key? *The whole time?* Out in the desert?'

John flashed his rare smile.

'They were kept under my dehydrated, all but dead, body. Even when snatching moments of sleep.'

'Good fella!' George was obviously relieved.

They had a wonderful feast that night. Stores from Bim's Stopover almost made Christmas of it.

'No more spoiling those artistic fingers peeling yams, Kim,' George said with a grin. 'Those drawings you've done, and the sections too, are superb. You wouldn't marry me, by any chance, so I can have a scribe like that by my side all my days?'

John lifted his eyes—but not his head—to see Kim's response. She laughed, almost gaily. 'My first proposal of marriage!' She clapped her hands with delight. 'I could—yes I *could*. I do have witnesses, you know. Oh! It would be lovely!'

Stephen had been leafing through some sections in Kim's own personal note-book. He had picked it up from amongst her materials. For the first time since his arrival he was silent and seemed not to hear the others' conversation.

Not even George's proposal, Kim thought, a little disappointed. It was only a joke, but a lovely one!

A minute later she had forgotten Stephen's inattention to

listen to George Crossman's praise of her 'gift'. He was really letting himself go! Someone in all the wide world appreciated her abilities!

Dear George!

In the morning they packed, ready for departure.

John had to take the jeep back to the Stopover because the engine part George had brought had been a temporary one, lent by the local garage. The permanent part was being flown up to the Stopover three days later. Stephen's Land-Rover would have to be left there, at the garage, indefinitely.

The first rule of the Expedition came into operation again. The members must travel in pairs.

Out in front of the old house they were deep in conference.

'I'll take Kim, the specimens and the records, in the Rover,' Stephen offered, volunteering a shade too quickly. 'We could get back to Base in no time——'

'Sorry. No!' John interrupted bluntly. 'George and I are the senior members of the Expedition. Therefore responsible. You and Kim are juniors, Stephen. We divide our forces.'

'I guess I'll be the one to take Kim, eh?' George said grinning with pleasure as he looked at her. 'You're mighty popular, Kim. We're arguing over you.'

John is not—Kim thought irrelevantly.

'*Excuse me!*' she said aloud, having a sudden and daring thought. 'If John agrees I would like to go to the Stopover, You see——'

They all stared at her—*waiting*.

'I don't see at all,' John said quite briefly. His eyes were narrowed against the burning light of the sun and he looked as if he might call her 'that school girl' all over again.

'Well—— You see——' Kim went on with a careful mixture of gladness and sadness in her voice. 'Nobody asked me what I used for sweat rags on that very long walk through the sand dunes. Nor what happened to the two shirts I threw by the wayside because my hands were full of a compass and a water-bag and things like that. You see—in that heat—even an extra shirt was heavy. Not to mention—— Well, I'll spare you details.' She shook her head. 'And nobody asked me where I found clean cloths to do the dish-washing in this fine old pioneering homestead——' She paused to watch the looks of perplexity that came into the men's faces. This perplexity was tinctured with a foreboding of what she might say next. She could go into details about underclothes!

Kim, each knew, was capable of saying *anything*.

She lifted the leg-hem of her work shorts.

'Nothing underneath!' she said regretfully. 'Absolutely nothing at all. You do understand, John? I *need* to do some shopping.'

She tilted her hat forward over her brow, tucked the thumbs of her hands in the braces of her khaki work suit, and looked at John Andrews. Her eyes wore that faintly unfocused expression that made them so unconsciously beguiling.

The thought of Kim with nothing under those khaki working clothes caused Stephen to give a yelp of laughter. He cut this short when he saw the expression in John Andrews' face. At the same time he felt the back-kick of George's heel.

'You do see what I mean?' Kim was asking earnestly. 'It's sad. It's too bad! I have to say it again—— *I need to do a little shopping.*'

John swung round on his heel.

'Stephen,' he said in his 'ordering' voice. 'Put whatever might be left of Kim's gear in my jeep, including her work bag. In between looking over the Harrods of Bim's Stopover she might feel inclined to draw some *sturt pea*, or even *spiked feather flower!*'

He wasn't being funny, so neither George Crossman nor Stephen laughed. He was angry because Kim had won a point with an indisputable piece of feminine strategy. The girl had no underclothes—so to Bim's Stopover she must go!

Stephen, who had not planned for this, felt defeated, but after a minute's thought he cheered up. He'd particularly wanted Kim with him. *Those records*. However, with luck, he might arrange another line of contact. At Bim's Stopover he'd manage to get in touch with his boss in the Eastern States by the radio. Something was bound to come of *that*!

George Crossman took the view that Kim had made a gallant showing for herself. She hadn't asked John, himself, Stephen, or those cranky old prospectors they'd talked of, for their spare clothes. She'd used herself up on that long, heroic walk; then used her talent for drawing, and her underclothes for cleaning—all in the line of active service. The least John could do was to take her to the Stopover to buy herself a few returns.

George was one hundred per cent on Kim's side. Later, when John had cooled down, he would agree too.

With the jeep recently tuned-up at the Stopover, and John angrily bent on getting there, the pace was packed on and it took only two days, at top speed, to make the trip. In the whole of that time, night and day, John had not slept, even when Kim had taken her stint of driving. They had not talked very much either. Kim thought this could be like travelling with a thunderbolt, temporarily resting. Then she smiled at her own successful ruse, and accepted John's reaction.

Found in the desert with a girl who wore no underclothes! She was a little sorry for him, after all. During some moments in the long drive she guessed he felt like thrashing this particular girl!

Nearing Bim's Stopover, wuzzy with no sleep for forty-eight hours, John Andrews himself wondered *why* he felt so angry.

Why the hell hadn't he noticed she was using her own things to provide a bit of cleanliness, and a few comforts at the old homestead? As for those shirts thrown away on the long walk! How did a man like himself say 'Thank you' adequately to someone like this girl? She always seemed to steal the 'punch line' in the end herself!

Kim herself suspected that John *knew* she had manœuvred him into taking her to the Stopover. She didn't blame him for being angry. Not really.

They began in silence and that was the way they ended up—bowling down the track, in a cloud of red dust, into the Stopover.

The town consisted of one store, one garage, one pub, and a red-brown claypan for an airstrip. The only trees in sight were in a clump behind the pub. Then nothing but spinifex grass for hundreds of miles around!

'Over there,' said John as they slammed past a timber and galvanised-iron building with wide verandah under which a number of men sat drowsing in the shade, 'there is your Harrods. I'll take you to the pub first. I dare say they have plenty of water. There'll be enough for a bath anyway. This is artesian-basin country. It all comes up from underground. Like in the trough at the old homestead.'

Kim's skin was thick with dust and caked with perspiration all over. She felt that pub had better have plenty of water! But, willy nilly, first she would go to the store. She hadn't forgotten that crack about her yam-peeling hands from George. She was going to do what she knew Myree would have done. Have a beauty-cure, even if she gave it to herself. That would rock Dr John Andrews out of his black temper and his wicked silence!

She sighed, for she knew no beauty-cure could ever make her look like Myree. It couldn't make her an inch or two taller, for instance!

John parked the jeep behind the pub and went inside to book two rooms. Kim rounded the outer walls of the baked and peeling building, then went back along the dusty street to the store.

She fished in the bib of her work suit for her wallet; pulled out one of the five-dollar notes her brother Jeff had given her, and said——

'Two large pots of face cream please. One cleansing cream and one tonic cream.'

'Dearie! You sure do look as if you need them!' the stout woman behind the counter said. 'Your poor face! Oh dear—and those poor arms too! Anything else while you're about it?'

'Yes, lots,' Kim said brightly. 'For the moment a bra, and a shirt. Inexpensive please. Oh and a pair of shortie pyjamas. I'll come back for other things later when my skin—the part underneath these togs—is fit to try things on.'

Back in the pub, a two-story affair with a wide veranda and dusty wooden-lace trimmings round the balcony, Kim was shown by the manager's daughter to her room.

'I expect you'd like a bath first?'

'You expect very right,' said Kim with a wry grimace. 'Where is it please?'

'Down the passage, turn right and you'll see it.'

'Thank you very much.'

'Call me down the staircase if you want anything more. I'm always willing.'

'Oh thank you very much,' Kim said again.

'I'll send you up a cup of tea in half an hour. How's that?'

'Thank you very much,' Kim said all over again. She guessed she sounded like a record player. She could hardly explain her dire need to bath and be clean, *clean*! And *not* have horny, dust-ingrained hands. Or a sunburnt face!

CHAPTER ELEVEN

An hour later, John Andrews, bathed and shaved, went downstairs to exchange the usual necessary totems of goodwill with the hotel manager. In any one-pub town in the outback the hotel manager was the most important inhabitant. John knew one always paid one's respects as if to the Lord Mayor of a City to that particular father-figure *first*.

'Quite a big place you have here,' he said easily, after they'd exchanged the usual pleasantries and were sampling their first friendly drink; one on the house, as per custom. 'Many station people outback here?'

'More'n you'd think. We're right in the district where the station-owners can get the Wet when the cyclones cut a swathe over the north-west. Sometimes a blow-across from the sou'wester later. It's pick country for grazing north of the breakaway. But terrible in the drought——'

'Rain in summer and a chance of it in winter! That's why it's such good wild-flower country I suppose.'

'Ah. You're the bontanist feller who's been parked back on Skelton's old station? Pity about that place.' The manager shook his head regretfully. 'The salt came through, you know. Seepage. Spoilt the pasture. Too near the sand-plain for safety——'

The man glanced up from his drink and looked at John from under hooded eyelids. He was a big slim-jim of a man, with a friendly face, but wise and knowing eyes that were deep-set.

'You had a girl back there with you for a couple of weeks? She's booked in Number Five. My daughter took her up!' he said.

There was something hidden in the tone of his voice. Not unfriendly, but full of portent. John sensed it.

'My co-worker. A technical assistant,' he said briefly, taking out a cigarette. 'We occasionally have to take members of both sexes in a scientific expedition, you know. Women's rights in a world of equality—and all that!'

The manager accepted one of John's cigarettes, also the lighted match to the tip of it.

'She's a botanist too?'

John's eyes went silver cold as he watched the other.

'Not precisely,' he said. 'As I said, she's what we call a technical assistant. A necessary adjunct.'

'Don't mistake me, Dr Andrews,' the other remarked in an easier voice. 'I don't mean anything oblique. But you'd better know those fellers in there——' he nodded his head towards the wooden partition that divided the main bar from the manager's private saloon where they now talked. 'They like something to yarn about now'n again. Livens things up for them. They don't care a hang what any other man does, and mostly they mind their own business.' He paused. 'But——'

'Yes? But what?' John's voice was studied. Studded with ice-chips too.

'Well . . . *You* have to go back to civilisation sooner or later. Well, you'd better know what went on. *And goes on*. It's not my business, and I don't care a darn. I'm being friendly about this. If you want to know I'll tell you.'

'I want to know. Go ahead.'

'There was a road-train—all wool—passed through here on its way to the main link-road out west day before yesterday. Twelve bale-laden trucks hooked on to a diesel header. You seen those wool road-trains? This one had aboard two drivers, four lookouts, a maintenance man—and a couple of prospectors known round these areas as Peck and Bill.' He paused, then went on. 'These last two were conning a free ride. They'd already hitched one from a station-owner to the road-head. You receiving your end, Dr Andrews?'

Dr Andrews' eyes were wary—and dead cold at the same time.

'Go on,' John said, very clear.

'Everyone was in town on the way to a woolshed dance out at Binni-Carra Station. That bar in there was crammed full. Everybody from anywhere was passing through. That happens when there's a woolshed dance on. It only comes once a year.

Peck and Bill squeezed their way in and old Peck had to live up to his reputation as a yarn-spinner. He yarned all right. One tale after another. One about a girl and a chap picking a sand dune and a broken-down homestead for a honeymoon. *Some honeymoon*, was the general concensus of opinion in that bar. Do I go on?'

'You do.'

'Skelton's place?'

'Okay,' John said levelly. 'So what? In scientific circles, even mission circles, our sort of community-living has to be accepted.'

The manager nodded his head thoughtfully.

'So there's field work? So girls have to go too?' He shrugged. 'It's all okay by me. Like I said—I don't care a darn. But people up here are conservative. Landed people always are. It's a patriarchal land anywhere north of the Twenty-sixth parallel. You try and convince 'em it's okay for girls to be stuck out alone with a man on a science jaunt—*in amongst the sand dunes*!'

'Why should I?' John Andrews was too civil.

The atmosphere between the two men was getting stickier, yet each was trying to communicate.

There was a long silence while the manager filled John's glass again, and then his own. They'd both stubbed out dying cigarettes, then lit up again.

'Well, that ought to settle that little matter,' John added briefly. 'What'll we talk about now? The weather?'

The pub manager wiped his chin with one hand and stared at John.

'Guess I'd better let you have the lot,' he said.

'There's more?'

'There's more.'

'Okay. Go on.'

'First—up hereabouts—and farther north, there's an unwritten law against talking about women in the bar. Not done. You understand that?'

John nodded.

'When it does happen it doesn't mean anything particularly pleasant for the young lady concerned,' the manager said. 'Second. One car load going through to the woolshed dance took exception to Peck's yarn—on the principle I've just mentioned. There was a bit of a fight. Oh, no heads broken!

The reason this feller took exception was he'd worked for another feller down south, and kinda liked him. A forester. You know, one of those types grows trees for the retimbering of the forests down south? This forester feller's name is Jeff Wentworth and he was given to taking his kid sister down in the forest with him. This feller in the bar had seen her more'n once. I go on?'

'You do.'

'Written in red ochre on the wall out at Skelton's old homestead is a bit of a legend, it seems. How'm I going?'

John's stony silence was a form of comment.

'According to Peck and his mate, the legend written on that wall reads—*Kim Wentworth Was Here*. And some more too. The name's the same. Have I said enough?'

John's hand was cold steady as he tipped the ash from his cigarette into the tray.

'So this feller?' he asked evenly, half Antartica in his voice. 'This worker-friend of Jeff Wentworth's had a fight in a public bar in an outback town over Jeff Wentworth's sister? Is that what you're telling me?'

'I'm sorry, Dr Andrews. I'm downright sorry. I thought about it hard and long, after you came in an hour or so back with Miss Wentworth. You see—her name went down on the register along with yours. I couldn't help but know who you two were. So will the rest of this span of the outback. And the story too. I reckoned—after I thought hard and long—*I ought to tell you*. Some day—maybe ten years hence—someone's going to tell that forester Wentworth about that bar fight. I reckoned-up you ought to *know*. The girl looks too nice to have her name chucked about the outback by Peck or anyone else. Yarns grow, you know. More gets tacked on ——'

'Thank you. I take your information as part of the service,' John said. 'Will you have another drink? Two's enough for me.'

'For me too, this time of the day. But I'd like you to know I take it as an honour to have one of you scientific chaps come in here and pass the time of day with me.'

'It's a pleasure!' John said turning away from the counter. He added—'Thank you for telling me. You were quite right. It is something I should know. As leader of this particular Expedition I'm responsible for Miss Wentworth.'

'I thought so. I'm glad you're not taking offence. By the way, the cook's preparing a fine brush turkey for dinner to-night. We keep a good table here. Hope you enjoy your stay.'

'Thank you.' John's dignity was impeccable. 'It'll be a matter of a few days, I think. I'm waiting for a spare part for the jeep. It's being flown up from the south.'

He walked out of the door, across the main hall, down the side passage to the courtyard at the rear of the hotel. He walked across the gravel space to the mulga clump—the only grove of trees in the whole town—then stood staring across the bushland into nothing.

The manager wiped his hand over his chin, and shook his head as he watched John's back go through the door. His wife came in from the side veranda and looked at her husband.

'You tell him?' she asked.

'Yep. I had to. Only fair thing to do. Nothing to it but what old Peck made of it, that's for sure. Peck's idea of a good yarn. If only it hadn't dust-balled into a bar fight!'

His wife nodded in agreement.

'There isn't anyone in the outback who didn't hear that radio message from some girl called *Myree* at the Expedition's Base.' She reminded him. 'You remember you gave it to that other science chap to take back to Skelton's old place? Then there's this other message came over the air this morning. Did you give Dr Andrews the new message, Joe?'

'Jumping kangaroos! I forgot. It has that raking word "love" in it again! They'll know about *that* in the bar too. That talking *air*! Send Ted out with it will you? I'd say that Dr Andrews' love affairs has got him in one big fix. Any time someone'll start another fight.'

'I like the girl upstairs. Kathy does too.'

'Well—notwithstanding—you'll have to give him that radio message. The law says so.'

'I don't believe anything against that girl upstairs, Joe. Well not yet, anyway——'

'You tell that to her brother the forester come the day he arrives, if ever.'

Upstairs in Number Five Kim was bathed and clean at long

long last. She had done the remnants of her personal washing. She put on the new bra and shirt she'd bought at the store. She sat on the stool in front of her mirror and was busy scooping out dollops of cold cream. Then spreading this snowwise on her face.

Over the shoulder of the curved mirror she had a view of the yard. She saw John Andrews walk across the squaré and come to a stop under the mulgas. Her hand, spreading cold cream half an inch thick on her face, came to a stop too. She rested one elbow on the dressing-table, and her cream-messy-chin on the back of her hand. She sat quite still as she watched John.

The tall rangy figure was not very relaxed! His back was *too* straight. He'd dug his hands in the pockets of his trousers as he stood there and stared away into nothing.

'He must be *thinking*,' Kim told herself, 'About something very important! Not very unworrying either——'

She watched him. First he rocked back on his heels, then forward. He took out a cigarette and lit it. Next he threw the cigarette on the ground and put his heel on it. He walked round the yard, his head bent in thought. Finally he came back to the mulgas and stood gazing out at the wilderness again.

'Something on his mind!' Kim nodded her head in sympathy. '*Duboisia hopwoodi* I expect.'

She felt a little sad for him. He was awfully alone out there.

She dug her fingertips in the cold cream again, and slapped on another layer.

'If I leave it an hour?' she reflected, meaning the cold cream. 'Will it do anything for this poor awful face of mine in that time?'

She leaned forward and stared into the mirror quizzically.

Then she began to add layers of cream to her arms, to the backs of her hands, and in between her fingers.

When she looked up through the window John was no longer there.

'He's lost himself,' she thought. 'Poor Dr John Andrews! So High and Mighty! He has to walk round a yard all by himself!'

What had he been thinking about? Of something more than *Duboisia*—even the *hopwoodi* kind? There'd been a thing very stiff and angry about his back. Then tired. Then *stooped*.

Some minutes later Kim heard firm footsteps come up the linoleum-covered staircase, turn the corner of the corridor, and come four doors along. Then stop.

The knock on her door sounded very aggressive indeed. Next came John's voice.

'Kim? Have you something on? May I come in?'

She swivelled round on her stool.

'Well, I do have something on,' she said doubtfully. 'But you won't be able to see through it. I've cream all over my face.'

He turned the handle, and came in. He closed the door behind him and stood, leaning back against the door frame, his hands on the knob behind him.

He gazed, more than stared, at the girl on the opposite side of the room. The window behind her made a halo of light round her newly washed hair.

Her bare feet were smaller than he remembered noticing. Her shorts and shirt were sparkling fresh. It was the rest of her that all but held him transfixed. Her arms, hands, throat and face were covered a half-inch deep by a foam of white snow—all except for a slit that was her mouth, and two round holes through which a pair of grey eyes stared at him, wide and so very ingenuous.

'I'm sorry for this intrusion,' he said trying to sound formal. 'I wanted to ask you an important question.'

'Oh well . . .' Kim began. 'That is . . .'

She wiped a dripping dollop of cold cream from her eyebrow with one finger, and looked at him over the tip of her cream-laden nose. 'Is it something I've forgotten? You don't mind me in face cream, do you? It's my sunburn you know. It——'

She could see the outline of the oblong radio message in his shirt pocket. It was the unmistakeable red of the envelope they put such messages in. Funny, but the thought of Myree sending him messages *here* while he was busy with being saved from the aftermath of a sand storm, made the satan in her want to give battle. Right now that particular devil was having a wonderful time romping around inside her chest.

Myree hadn't spent four days and four nights, or had the skin burned off her nose and her forearms, walking through sand dunes.

'Do you think you could listen carefully to me for a few minutes, Kim?'

The expression on his face said he meant something serious. Kim banished the devil in her chest forthwith.

'Well . . . If you don't mind my appearance,' she said blinking cold cream from her eyes. 'Ought I be dressed for the occasion, or something?'

Darn! She was making a way-out gaffe again! And he really was deadly serious.

He caught her eyes, snow-ringed with cream yet with that unique, faintly unfocused expression of studied wonder in them.

He held her eyes with his own as he walked, quite slowly across the room. He was so tall, standing above her, she had to crick back her head to see his face. A splash of cold cream fell from her cheek and landed with a silent plonk on her shirt front.

'Will you marry me, Kim?'

She didn't move. And neither did he.

Utter silence.

He looked down and she looked up. His eyes weren't so icy any more. They were almost gentle—or did she imagine it?

Or was she, *or he*, just a little mad? Desert-happy?

'I beg your pardon?' she asked politely, not believing her ears.

'Will you marry me, Kim?' he repeated.

She lifted her hands, and with her fingers, one on each side of her face, wiped the cold cream away from her eyelids upwards to where her soft hair capped her forehead.

'Darn!' she said. 'Now I'll have to wash my hair again.'

The expression on his face changed.

There came the oddest of odd looks into it. Kim tried to think of the right word, but gave up.

Would she marry him?

'I'll think about it,' she said nodding her head, as if to an offer of an afternoon walk. 'Do you think you could ask me again to-morrow?' She had an unreal feeling of acting a stage part: the dialogue already written for her—— He was sun-struck of course.

He bent down, put his hands on her shoulders and shook her to make her understand.

'*Kim. Will you marry me?* Don't think about it. Just marry me, and we'll sort it out afterwards.'

She thought she saw some light.

'You mean you like my drawings? They're good, aren't they? It would be useful to have me along with you all the time—day and night—so I could keep on drawing! And make you famous as a botanist? Like helping my darling Ralph Sinclair get his doctorate?'

'Something like that.' He dropped his hands from her shoulders, turned away and walked round the room looking at the floor.

'Something like that—if that's the way you want to put it,' he said. '*But I need you.* It's imperative I have you with me all the time——' His voice lightened a little. 'We could make a success of it you know, Kim. You really are a splendid cook. You were quite housewifely out there at the old home-stead. Of course——' He broke off.

'It's a pity you mentioned those last two accomplishments,' Kim said gravely, watching him. 'I mean about the cooking and being housewifely, because I had a solution to your troubles. Only I don't know if those two things fit. That is—I'm not sure. Well, not exactly——'

He stopped circumnavigating the room and came to a halt.

'What *are* you talking about, Kim?'

'Myree Bolton. She can draw—almost as well as I can. But not quite. She doesn't *have* to have a pen-hand as fine as Ralph Sinclair needed. But she's a real botanist. This time next year she'll have First Class Honours. Right now——'

Kim thought of that folded radio message in the shirt pocket over John's heart.

He took out a cigarette and began tapping it on his thumb-nail.

'I know all Myree's attainments. They couldn't be bettered,' he said quite brusquely. 'I had thought of offering her a job at the Institute by the Mount next year. She'd be valuable for the particular work there and to . . .' He broke off.

Funny how she, Kim, was always giving Myree away to her own possible future employers! First Ralph, and now John. Wouldn't Myree be mad if she knew. *Kim donating her as a gift to eligible men!*

Meantime she hazarded a guess at what John was up to.

Me in the back room out of sight—doing the cooking when taking time off from drawing, typing and tagging—probably somewhere between the soup and the frozen vegetables! Meantime Myree in the front room! Twin beds, or a double one?

Kim's small chin firmed, and her eyes darkened.

Oh no you don't, Dr Andrews! No you don't!

Anyhow what was this all about?

'Dear John,' she said with calculated gentleness. 'Thank you for the compliment. Wait till you've tried my Irish stew or my chow mein. I'm good at *burning* things like that.'

She swung back to the mirror. In its reflection she looked at him, the latest cigarette unlit in his hand, his wonderful handsome head framed by the door behind him.

Her heart misgave her.

'I'll think about it,' she added, almost too quickly. 'I'll give you my answer in the morning. Would you wait that long?'

He put the cigarette back in its packet, and stood staring past the shoulder of the mirror out into the courtyard. His eyes were full of shadows, and *tired*. Kim's heart dropped a beat.

If he doesn't go away in less than one minute, she thought sadly, *I'll get up and throw myself at his selfish scientific head. Cold cream and all!*

John's eyes came back to her.

'Fair enough, Kim,' he said quietly. 'It's quite a big step to take. Leave it till the morning.'

He turned on his heel, opened the door, went out and shut it behind him. His footsteps fading down the passage weren't so heavy as when he had come. The very sound of them on the old linoleum caught in Kim's heart strings.

One or other of us is mad, she decided, and wished she really could cry—something she refused to do on principle.

'Clearly I could do with a change of name and a change of tune too. What motto would go with 'Andrews', I wonder? No more "Wentworths are worth where they went!"'

She slapped on another lot of cold cream to hide her face from herself. There wasn't much left in the jar.

Kim thought about that strange proposal of marriage all the evening; and later between jagged razor-backs of sleep.

John wore a kind-of-kindness in his manner at dinner: much like a man wearing knight-of-old armour. He waited for Kim before he went into the dining-room. He pulled out her chair with a certain firmness about the gesture, as if it was his usual duty, and more than just good manners. He passed her things like the cruet and the glass dish containing the bread—long before she wanted them.

He asked her questions about her home, her family and about her brother Jeff. Why was she so fond of Jeff in particular? He smiled, and looked at her quizzically when she told him about the sofa with the padding falling out, and about her wild-flower plot. Also about the tank to catch the rain-water from the roof in winter.

In fact, she hardly recognised him as *that man*!

'Diane and Celia think the tank spoils the salubrious beauty of the back garden,' she told him. 'Funny, but they never notice the weeds, or the broken gutter on the garage.'

She watched John guardedly as she went on.

'About my family—the female side of it——' she explained. 'They're foresters. Oh no, my sisters don't climb or fell or grow trees like Jeff and my father. They sit in the office at headquarters and write up records and keep charts. That sort of thing. Still, they were *trained*. Like you were—at the University. They don't understand about wild-flowers though. Undergrowth is a mere hazard in the forests to them.'

'You really love those wild-flowers, don't you?' John said. 'That's why you want to paint them, as well as draw them for the records?'

'Yes,' she replied thoughtfully. 'It sticks a nasty long pin in me to see the flowers on paper just as *sections*. I like to give them colour too. I like drawing things tiny—the tinier the better——'

John, crumbling bread with one hand and twisting the stem of his wine glass in the fingers of the other, went on looking at her. He took in the wide-spaced frank grey eyes; the half shy, half daring smile. She was like a prankster who might, for the fun of it, bring a scorpion out of a cigarette box any moment.

A wisp of regret, light as the brush of a feather, touched him as he looked at the deep sunburn on her face and throat and arms: the brown scratches on the back of her hands, and the last remnants of physical tiredness at the back of those same grey eyes.

She'd been through as severe an ordeal as any he'd been through himself. Yet she had not said one word about it. The smile and the ready wit had come as easily as on those first few days at Base. His only concern about her then had been her attraction to Stephen Cole. He'd had a certain curiosity about her leaving Ralph Sinclair, of course. He'd made up his mind early—when he thought of her association with Stephen—that if anything special or unique were found he'd have to make it plain these finds were confidential.

'Have you thought over the question I put to you earlier?' he asked, almost abruptly. He was suddenly serious, all over again.

Kim pursed her mouth, put her head on the side, and contemplated the peeling paint on the ceiling of this very old outback dining-room.

'Ye-es——' she said slowly. Her eyes came back to his. She smiled, just that much impishly. 'You'd better look out,' she warned. 'I might accept. Then where would you be?'

CHAPTER TWELVE

After dinner Kim went for a walk by herself around the gravel yard of the hotel. She took a studied interest in the clump of mulga under which John had stood so thoughtfully this morning. Perhaps they had some particular mesmeric quality about them. She looked the trees over: also the view beyond them across a wasteland of weed and spinifex.

She shook her head perplexed.

'Something must have given him odd ideas while he was out here.'

If not the trees, then what? There weren't even bats in the evening air and she didn't really think there were bats in John

Andrews' belfry either. At dinner he had seemed quite sane —only kinder. It had made her heart quicken just a little madly.

I've a jolly good mind to accept! She shot these parting words at the darkling sky. The last pink tinge on the western horizon was a fade-out of the dying day.

But what a day it had been!

She went upstairs and decided she'd go to bed on the grounds that she might have a try for 'beauty sleep'. She didn't want to be way-out, or to make gaffes any more. She didn't want to have jokes inside herself as a protection against being hurt. She wanted to look *beautiful* in the morning.

She could never be really beautiful. Not like Myree——

She didn't want Myree in the front room being a clever botanist while she, Kim, cooked and swept and washed—also kept her skill with a fine drawing pen—ready for use come John's demands.

It wasn't good enough. And looking at it another way, it was absurdly funny! *Yet she wanted to say 'Yes' to John Andrews!*

She couldn't bring herself to admit, let alone say—*'I love him.'*

She went on thinking it all out—even in her sleep. Some of the things she thought in those half-dreams had woken her right up. They were ideas like sleeping with John: his head on the next pillow to hers.

John Andrews was not present at breakfast.

Changed his mind? Forgotten? Had second thoughts?

Kim ate her way steadily through cereal, steak and two eggs, then too much toast and finally two cups of tea. Still he didn't come. She felt fed very full. It was all, of course, an excuse to stay at the table in the hope that he'd come.

When she had finished she delayed even longer. She watched the few through-travellers to Perth finishing their breakfast before they revved up their cars, or station-wagons, and wended their way farther along hundreds and hundreds of miles of track—first sand and clay, then gravel and finally the bitumen, till at long last they would come to civilisation —close by the shining River Swan—far, far away.

But still John did not come.

Eventually Kim could stay in the dining-room no longer.

She stood up, pushed back her chair, tilted her chin as she imagined proud people did, and walked the length of the dining-room to the door.

There—all the time—out in the main hall, leaning on the office counter talking to the manager, was John.

Kim allowed her chin to lower and her smile to wither. She didn't care for him any more. He didn't have to do this to her.

However, it was bad manners to show feelings in public, specially as John turned round and said—*in a very pleasant voice*——

'Good morning, Kim.'

Had he been off-beam yesterday? A sort-of delayed bush-whackiness?

She knew the manager was watching her very curiously. Had she some butter on her chin or marmalade on one eye-brow? *Or something!* She felt almost desperate, but had to hide it.

'Good morning, John,' she said in a steady voice. 'Did you breakfast early, or not at all?'

'Early,' he said politely. 'The radio calls come through between seven and eight, and I was expecting at least one message. Hoping for two.'

'Did you get them?' Her eyes flew to his shirt pocket: the one over his heart. He seemed, standing there, so tall, so sun-browned in a neat way, and so good to look at. Her bravado cracked and her heart dropped. There was a folded paper in that pocket. More messages from Myree?

Something inside Kim toughened.

Myree wasn't going to have everything. Wonderful looks, wonderful figure, well-to-do parents who *cared*! Nice furniture, a luxury home, a University education, brains—and a crackerjack job as a botanist when her Honours Degree was confirmed!

No, not at all! Not everything! Not absolutely everything without even a crumb left over!

She stood quite still and looked at John, meeting his eyes, smiling ever so determined a smile.

He watched her face with its grey eyes a little clouded, the mobile mouth with its controlled quiver. Also the little wisp of hair that fell across her forehead.

'Shall we go for a walk, Kim?' he asked quietly.

'Yes, rather. I'd like that very much. Morning's the time for walking, isn't it? It gets too hot later.'

The manager went on looking at her curiously. Too curiously! Then his gaze shifted to John. He tapped his front teeth with the nail of one forefinger. But he said nothing.

John straightened up. He put his hand under Kim's arm.

'Let's go then,' he said.

He turned at the door, lifted his hand to the manager, who nodded back.

Once they were outside John asked her where she would like to go. His hand, very firm and not to be withdrawn, was still under her arm.

'Round to the courtyard,' she said promptly. 'There's a clump of mulga trees there. Even at this hour of the morning a little shade would be nice.'

'The courtyard? Are there some mulgas there? My impression of the place was that it was as empty as the plain.'

Kim stole a glance at him. He looked slightly puzzled, that was all. Not in the least like a man who was about to tamper with destiny. Or even one who remembered decision-making by the mulgas yesterday.

He hadn't even noticed he stood under trees—if such lean wispy things could be called trees, anyway.

They arrived at the shady spot. There was an old wire fence nearby with the top wire slack from long use by people who preferred to go over a fence than walk round the front exit.

John dropped Kim's arm. He sat on this top wire, and treated it as a swing. Kim sat herself down on a stump. They looked across three yards of brown gravel at one another.

'Why the mulgas?' John asked, looking at her quizzically.

'Well, you see, these trees must have a certain type of magic. A *something*, if you understand what I mean?'

'I don't.'

'Well, they do things to people. Cast spells. At least, I guess they do——'

John shook his head so slightly Kim wasn't sure he really did it at all. He reached in his pocket—the right hand one—for his cigarettes. Kim wished he hadn't done that. It reminded her of what was probably folded neatly away in his left hand pocket. This made her waver in her decision. Then she remembered that Myree couldn't have everything. Not the world, and the cream in her coffee too!

John was lighting up, his head bent over his cupped hand so that Kim could see the thick black mat of his shining much-washed hair. No more red dust in it now. That hair did things to her—like stir her heart.

'You might have forgotten you asked me a question yesterday,' she said summoning Wentworth courage.

'But I haven't forgotten——'

Then she rushed her yard—rails, fence, muster paddock, and all. 'The answer is *yes*,' she said.

After that she could have died. She didn't know why she stayed sitting perfectly still, *and still breathed.*

John flicked out the match, threw it on the ground and put his boot on it. He looked up, quite slowly, and met her eyes. He saw a queer mixture of sadness and gravity, and *courage* in Kim's face. The set of her chin, the stillness and stubbornness of her soft and generous mouth put a finger of remorse on his heart.

'Thank you, Kim,' he said gravely.

For the first time since she was roughly seven years old she was at a loss for words and for the quick answer; the challenging retort.

Her eyes misted over. Her hands were in her lap so she gripped them together. This was a help.

'I'm sorry I said that,' she said carefully. 'Perhaps you had forgotten you asked me. Or didn't mean it——'

His cigarette was burning itself away to ash. He had to shutter his eyes a little from the spiralling smoke.

'I had not forgotten. And I did mean it.'

Kim smiled with relief. Her hands lay still again in her lap.

'Oh, that's good!' she said cheerfully. 'I thought I was making one more of my way-out gaffes again!'

'Getting married is not a gaffe. It's a serious business.' He dropped the half-smoked cigarette on the ground, and put his foot on it. He stood up and held out one hand.

Kim stood up too and gave him her hand.

'I suppose it's a little early for kissing?' he asked gravely.

'Well—we could try a simple one.' She put two fingers of her free hand on her forehead. 'Just there, for instance—as a sort-of start.'

He leaned forward, cupped the back of her head with his right hand, and planted a kiss on her forehead.

'How's that?'

'Very nice, thank you. What do we do now, John?'

'We go down to that crazy store in this one-horse, one-pub, one-garage town, and get a temporary engagement ring. It will probably be brass, or nickel. It will have to do for the time being. I want the small world of Bim's Stopover to know that we are *engaged to be married*. A ring always helps. An outward sign, you might say.'

How quaint he was, Kim thought, puzzled, but somehow touched. He might want her only for usefulness but he was doing all the right things. Maybe, some time in the long distant future——

Well, not to daydream now! In her own good time she'd oust that Myree! Or would she?

'It's a very nice store,' she said defensively, trying to hide a sudden shyness. 'You'll be surprised. It's peeling paint outside, and has iron sheeting for a roof. It's not much better inside, but it does stock *everything*——'

John held her hand all the way down the dusty red road to the store. He didn't seem to mind that the two or three people about, mostly lounging outside the hotel or the store, watched them. This, Kim thought, was very odd for a man who was coldly dignified, aloof and sometimes angry—as a general way of deporting himself.

When they passed the window of the hotel's office, the manager looked up, and gave a wave of his hand.

'Do you have a special personal friendship with the manager?' Kim asked puzzled.

'Everyone has that relationship with the Keeper-of-the-Pub in the outback. A matter of diplomacy when in distant parts. Next place to doss down is two hundred miles away. As a matter of self-preservation you make the pub's manager your best friend.'

'I see,' Kim nodded thoughtfully. Actually, she didn't see at all.

They found a gold ring—not brass or nickel—in Stopover's

all-purpose store. True, it was only fifteen carat gold and the stone in it was a local gemstone. This flecked stone shone like an opal, and Kim loved it.

'We'll buy you a proper one when we get back to Perth,' John said. Kim shook her head.

'No, thank you. Well, not for an engagement ring. I love *this* one. It's mine——'

She broke off. Now was the wrong time to be sentimental. It was much too early!

'When do you think we'll get to Perth?' she asked. 'Will you mind faded curtains, wear-holes in the carpet and the stuffing coming out of the sofa at our wedding?'

'I wouldn't mind them in the least. However, we're going to have our wedding right here in the Stopover. We'll ask the whole town. That would account for about twenty people. So to make it a merry one we'll ask the station people from around. Stockmen, rouseabouts, yarders, ringers, and the whole shearing team—if there happens to be a shearing team in the district.'

They were on their way back to the hotel. John wasn't holding her hand any more.

Kim stopped and stood quite still, looking at him, puzzled.

'Well, what's wrong with that?' he asked, a very succinct note in his voice.

'Everything. I'm under twenty-one. I can't get married without my parents' permission. We'd have to go home to get it, wouldn't we? I know in advance they'll be—well, they *might* be difficult. You see, I'm the youngest and Celia and Diane aren't married yet. Jeff, of course——'

'Jeff?'

'He won't mind. He'll love it—my getting married *first* ——'

'I'm glad to hear that.' John seemed to have an odd cold note in his voice. Now that they were 'engaged' he appeared in danger of changing back to his old aloof self. He was being firm about what he wanted.

'We'll fly Jeff up on the freight plane that brings the spare part for my jeep. I'll send an urgent radio message.' He added—'He can tuck in with the cold storage goods in the plane's tail.'

Kim smiled scornfully at that.

'You don't know Jeff,' she warned. 'He has a will of his own——'

'I expect I'll know him very well shortly. If he can't give you permission we'll get a local magistrate to do just that. There's always one around somewhere. Generally one or two of the station owners are J.P.s. Barker the pub manager will know.'

'A *special* licence?' Kim was dubious. Also painfully aware she wanted John to be *right* about all the rush. It didn't leave time for a change of mind. Or for Myree to appear on the scene.

'The marriage laws have been modernised, my child,' John said as if explaining simple arithmetic. 'The officiating clergyman, or magistrate, has to give notice—on the certificate, *after the event*—that he had known the couple for nine days. Yesterday was one day and to-day is another. That leaves seven. With a little pressure or persuasion, I guess we can get Barker to push the calendar dates about to the tune of another three or four days.'

'Isn't that unscrupulous?' Kim was thrilled to see this man—Dr John Andrews, taking the law into his own hands without batting an eyelid. It made her marriage more sure than ever. In spite of the ring on her left hand, she still hadn't believed it would come off.

'Am I unscrupulous, or merely determined?' he asked surprised.

'A little of both, maybe——' she said. 'But I don't understand. I mean, why . . . Well, why so soon——?'

'You didn't go to the School of Hard Knocks, that's why. You're not really worldly, Kim. Not for the outback. Out here the law is a thing for man's convenience. Often it has to be the instrument of his survival. It's adjustable—north of the Twenty-sixth parallel.'

She couldn't think of anything quick enough or wise enough to say to *that*!

They walked to the hotel, John's hands in his pockets now: Kim's hanging, a little lost, by her side.

Half her mind took in the fact that Mr Barker was leaning on the sill of his open window, watching them. Across the track two stockmen, in dusty pants, high-heeled stock boots, and wide dusty stetson hats—obviously in town on station business—glanced at them. They said something to one another, then grinned—a little too knowingly: and John saw them.

They reached the shade of the pub's veranda-shelter.

'Do you think we might practise that art of kissing once more?' John asked suddenly. His expression was studied, very matter of fact. Then it changed. His eyes softened and there was a kindness—almost like regret—in them.

'It's a little public,' Kim said doubtfully. She was quite bewildered by this new change in John. Also uncertain——

'The more public the better.' John's voice was extra firm. 'I quite liked it the first time. How about you, Kim?'

He wanted to kiss her in public, yet he wasn't anything now but sort-of *impersonal* about it.

'Yes. I think I did,' she said judicially, but wary.

'Then, here goes.'

He put one hand under her chin and tilted it up. His other hand slipped round her shoulders. This time—right out for people to see—he really kissed her, full on the lips. It was a kiss that made Kim blush. It was so full of promise. And yet —*was it*? She hadn't known that kissing would be quite like this. There'd been the young man down the street at the garage. And Ralph Sinclair had kissed her in an absent-minded way at the end-of-the-year parties. Stephen Cole had kissed her in a messy way on the lips. She had been very much put off by that!

But this kiss!

'There goes my heart!' Kim thought soberly. 'I can't pretend any more, even to myself.'

If only it was night: and he could kiss her like that again! And again, and again!

Maybe she could . . . Well what? Help him really to love her—*as a person* and not as a pen-hand and housekeeper? Could she?

Jeff came on the freight plane together with the jeep's wanted part. Kim was so overjoyed to see her brother she all but forgot her queries and doubts for quite an hour, while she recounted all that had happened since she left home.

Jeff's brown face was creased with his usual easy-going why-worry grin as he listened to his young sister.

'Well Bratto!' he said when he too finished his own news. 'I stirred the old shanks and went finding out all I could about this Dr John Andrews as soon as I received his radio message. I sent him one back bang-on; just to let him know I was coming. *But with a divided mind*. You understand?'

She nodded.

'Phew!' Jeff was saying. 'A handle to his name and all! You can guess what Celia and Diane had to say——'

'I can guess, but don't tell me. It might make me runaway mad all over again.'

He grinned.

'Well, you guess wrong. And it won't be the first time, Bratto. They started ringing up all their pals, saying—"*My sister Kimberley is, of course, engaged to Dr John Andrews. You do know who he is? Tops in his field. Leading botanist in the state. Yes, of course. Everyone has heard of him!*"

Kim stared at her brother.

'Not really!' she asked, incredulous.

Jeff rumpled her hair where she sat in a wobbly cane chair beside him on the pub veranda.

'Absolutely! Basking in reflected glory! Nothing like a bit of snobbery for that pair of pure beauties. It's the handle to the name, that's done it. Same with Mum and Dad too! They sent their love: but didn't have any spare cash. They'll write, and all that. We'll have a wedding present for you when you get home!'

They both laughed. Then Kim sobered. It was funny, but she didn't want to get her own back on Celia and Diane any more. She didn't even want to laugh at them. She really did love her parents——

'What did you discover about John?' she asked, suddenly serious. 'Everything good!'

'I couldn't find anything wrong, that's for sure! I tried you know. Darn' hard. Just to be certain. Everybody gives him top marks all along the line. I'm still waiting to discover the reason for wanting to marry, so very pronto-wise, a bratto like you.'

'It couldn't be that I'm attractive?' Kim asked cautiously, expecting a roar of laughter from her sceptical brother.

For the first time Jeff looked at his sister with serious intent.

'I can't sort-of think of you as grown up——'

'That's been the trouble,' Kim was stubborn once again. 'I've always been the kid sister. The infant. The babe in arms.

All because I was born ever so much later than the rest of you. Not really wanted either, you know!'

'Rats to that!' Jeff stroked his chin reflectively. Then he shook his head. He straightened his shoulders. 'Well,' he declared. 'On with the game anyway! That is until——' This time he looked at Kim with severity. 'That is—until I find out something I don't like about him. I'll still keep trying, just in case. Meantime, I guess I'd better do the brotherly act and have a talk with him. Where the heck is he anyway? What's he like? Short, squat, cross-eyed? Why's he keeping out of my way?'

'He's tall and he's handsome—very. He's not keeping out of your way. He's giving me a chance to see you alone. Actually he went down to the garage to work on his jeep with the mechanic. Your plane brought a needed part for him. The crown wheel in the differential had lost a tooth. Dust and oil had seized up something crucial.'

'So he was out at the plane when I arrived?'

'No. He stayed away on purpose. He wanted you and me to meet each other alone.'

Jeff nodded his head. He was again puzzled but nevertheless he approved of this piece of tact on the part of his future brother-in-law.

'Dr Andrews? Phew!' he said again, wondering how his young sister had pulled this one off. He still found it hard to believe she was really grown up. He looked at her furtively.

She was pretty all right. She had on a new striped cotton dress. That store down the road couldn't be as bad as its shabby dust-covered outside indicated.

Jeff's heart smote him somewhat. Why hadn't he seen Kim with a man's eyes before? She had a way-out gamine charm, and those eyes were really beautiful in a big way. A bit short-sighted or something. It added to their charm.

Of course some feller'ud fall for her!

'He's coming up the road now,' Kim said. Jeff detected a small note of anxiety in her voice.

Now why that? he wondered thoughtfully.

He took in the tall rangy figure of the man coming along the road. Black hair, a square brow. Good strong features. A man's man all right. Tough maybe—in a wiry way. Anyway he looked it in those brown outback clothes.

Jeff stood up.

'Guess I'll have to talk with him.'

Kim was unexpectedly and drastically self-conscious. 'You go and meet him, Jeff. I think I'd better—— Well, it might be easier if I'm not here.'

Jeff watched the tall figure moving nearer. The man came on in a leisurely way, yet there was confidence and a natural ease in his walk. He was a man no one could easily buck. Jeff decided that in advance.

'I can't talk to him out here in the middle of a raking dust track,' he said nonplussed.

'Just shake hands with him,' Kim said quickly. 'Then drift him round to the courtyard. There's a clump of mulgas by the fence. That's the place for talking. The best people settle affairs of business in the shade of those mulgas. It's very much done, you know!'

Jeff glanced down at his sister.'

'Ducking it?' he asked wryly. 'You just want to run out and leave me with the right to sock on the jaw: or be socked on the jaw?'

Kim nodded.

'That's right,' she agreed. 'But the shade under the trees helps. It sort-of mesmerises, or something——'

Jeff grinned.

'Okay. Bratto!' he said. 'You skid inside. I'll take care of the Queen's honour, the realm, and Dr Andrews. You go slap up your beauty with yet another make-up. I'll take him to pieces if I think it necessary.'

'He just might do that to you by mistake,' she said soberly. 'Watch his left hook, Jeff.'

She reached up and kissed him. 'He's very, very strong!' she added.

'Hell!' said Jeff rubbing the point on his jaw bone where the kiss landed. 'As if I were a kissing man, and all that! This feller coming up the road might take the first jab at *me*.'

'He's also quick on his feet!' Kim advised demurely. She didn't exactly flee inside, though the feeling to do so was very strong. She did the opposite. She was so sedate that Jeff, watching her, shook his head once more.

'Don't understand girls,' was all he remarked as he stepped off the veranda and walked out on to the dusty road.

In the hallway, Kim was still being so carefully sedate, she nearly walked into a stranger. In the darkness-after-light of the inside hall, she failed to see the well-dressed man who had arrived on the same plane as Jeff.

'I beg your pardon,' this same man now said courteously. The trilby hat he had worn as he alighted from the plane, was now in his hand.

'It was my fault,' Kim apologised. 'I'm afraid I wasn't looking where I was going.'

He smiled down at her from a benign seniority of between forty and fifty years of age. Yet there was something *too* kindly and too curious in his eyes.

'It takes fifteen seconds for the pupils of the eyes to adjust from bright sunlight outside to the sepulchral gloom of an outback pub's hallway,' he said, explaining for her. 'Quite impossible for you immediately to see anyone. Even me.'

Kim put her head fractionally on one side. She wasn't sure she quite liked him. *Too* polished. Or was it the way he said what he said? Yet his voice was pleasant and he was being kind.

'You would be Miss Kimberley Wentworth?' he enquired, still smiling. Kim's heart dropped a beat, though she had no idea why. It was as if he was a messenger of a not-very-gay fate. Someone who might know the true facts about special licences; and brides-to-be under age! And *nobody* outback called her *Kimberley*.

He saw the sudden gleam of anxiety in her eyes. In the long silence that followed he considered the girl's disquiet. It could be—it was possible—this very disquiet would be an advantage. He might revise his planning.

'How do you know my name?' Kim asked.

The man indicated the register on the counter nearby.

'Like all mere mortals I had to sign before I could enter and take possession of a room. A place to lay my head, as it were,' he said with that too-kind smile. 'You had to be the Miss Kimberley Wentworth registered here. There do not seem to be any other young ladies round about. You have an interesting name, Miss Kimberley.'

'I was called after a pioneering forebear. It's quite a common name in this state.'

'Of course, of course!' He spoke so pleasantly, yet somehow his soft voice did not tally with the hard vigilant expression in his eyes.

'The tycoon look,' Kim thought. 'As seen on television of course!'

'I didn't know I was signed in with my full name—Kimberley——' she began, out of her unease.

He raised his eyebrows slightly.

'Oh? Someone else signed for you? Not very proper my dear young miss!' He smiled in a pearly-toothed way to indicate a joke. But the eyes still looked hard at her.

'Yes. That is to say——'

Being a bratto had its virtues after all, she decided. She went back several mental leaps to the being she was before John had asked that irrational but fateful question.

'I have a limp in my right hand,' she added cheerfully. 'From over-work you know. Like a housemaid's knee, only in the upper limbs. Or should I say "fore" limbs? I always get someone else to do my writing for me.' She smiled, her head still slightly on one side, as she looked at him out of the wide windows of her clear, dark-fringed eyes. She had a feeling he nearly said—*But not your pen-drawings of plant sections, my dear*. Which was ridiculous. He couldn't know anything about *that*, of course.

Kim found it easier to stay her old self just long enough to get away from this man.

' 'Scuse me, won't you?' she said, almost too brightly. 'I have things to do to my face and hands. I'm expecting a visit from two important people. Right now they're out under the trees in the courtyard discussing the season's wool prices. *And the cost of maintaining just one lamb!*'

She edged round him, then ran up the linoleum-covered stairs.

'*Me being the lamb!*' she added to herself. She had an uncanny feeling about this man in the tailored suit who wore shiny shoes *in the outback*. And who had been curious enough to find out her name from the register!

Kim sat down in front of the mirror in her room. Over the left hand shoulder of the mirror's frame she watched through the window the trees standing in the absolute silhouette stillness of a blazing hot midday.

Nothing stirred in that courtyard. Even the flies had gone to sleep. The whiskers of dried grass round the fences were spike-still. The mulga leaves, slim and pointed, were lifeless.

Kim watched as round the corner of the main building came the two men. John, head bent, was talking very quietly, but with a sort-of compelling air. Jeff, hands in pockets, walked beside him. He looked down at the gravel ground as he did so: and kicked a pebble schoolboy-wise.

They came to the shade of the trees and there they stood, both looking out over the wasteland of spinifex to some unmeasurable distant place where the sky met the last rim of shimmering mirage land. They rocked back a little on their heels as they exchanged words.

The two men in her life!

Kim slapped cold cream on her face. Then some more. Finally she wiped most of this off and patted on a covering cream. She had never thought about wanting to be beautiful before. Not much anyway. But now it was different——

She dropped her hands to the table in front of her. What were they saying to one another—out there under the trees?

She knew when she had first fallen in love with John Andrews. She'd been trying to cheat herself for ages, that was all.

He hadn't had a handle to his name then. Or appeared to be anyone likely to claim fame. He'd been—*that man*: standing there in the dazzling sunshine of the Mount, with the lovely shining river stretching away in bays and shoals and wide expanses below the cliffs. He had looked at her, and the look had struck a glancing blow at her heart.

As she had left that day, she had turned her head once. He was smiling at something that pleased him about a plant. It was a glorious flashing smile that almost took the shine out of the river. Bang had gone her heart all right!

Ever since, she had played at a game of chance—blindfolded. And lived on hope and a camouflaged daydream.

Cheated *herself*?

The two men under the trees had turned round. *They were smiling!*

Kim, watching them through the window, drew the deepest breath ever.

It's going to be all right.

After much thought, she put on the cotton dress she had

worn earlier for fear Jeff would recognise any change and tease her about it in front of John. She must remind Jeff that when John was around, teasing was out of bounds. Besides, she was a working girl now on a good wage. She could actually afford a new dress or two. Even a diminutive trousseau.

How strange and impersonal John's signature had looked on the pay cheque and the official cover note that went with it! There had been the date, her ranking—Technical Assistant—duration of work, period, and finally the magic *J. S. Andrews: Officer in charge.*

Her thoughts raced on as her hands raced too. She looked in the mirror.

If only I could look like Myree would look——

Somewhere she'd read that 'envy' was one of the seven deadly sins. Okay, she'd eliminate 'envy' from her character make-up as from now. Besides, Myree wasn't getting everything this time!

Oh dear! What a meanie mind I have, after all!

She would think about her pay cheque instead. One hundred beautiful dollars. Oh lovely money!

Mr Barker, the pub's manager, was back behind his counter. He looked up and offered a sly grin as Kim came downstairs.

'Well, how's the engaged couple to-day?' he asked. 'I heard your brother came in on the plane all right. I see he's registered. Kathy fix him with a good room?'

Kim nodded.

'Yes, thank you.' She hadn't seen Jeff's room, but this mention of 'registering' was an opening gambit. She leaned against the counter and fingered the petals of a pink everlasting.

'There was another man who signed in too,' she said, as if not really all *that* interested. 'He looks so different from an outbacker. Did you see him?'

'I saw him ten minutes ago.' The manager put his finger under the last name written in the register. 'Name of Harold M. Smith. Now that surname is one I often see written in the register. Funny how many Smiths tread the dust of the good old outback.'

'Is it so strange?' Kim queried with her head on one side. 'Actually there are Smiths right at the top of the social ladder, aren't there?'

'I guess that's why so many people use the name,' Mr Barker remarked dryly. 'Snobbery!'

Kim laughed. 'This man who arrived to-day spoke to me. He was *very* nice. I came in out of the glare and all but bumped into him. I wondered how someone like that could come on a *freight* plane. I mean——'

'It's the only plane for another two days. Anyone can get on a freight plane if there's room. He could be one of the Charter Company's men. Main-Office type. Anyhow, what about that brother of yours? How did he manage a berth?'

'Oh easy!' Kim smiled her most urchin smile. 'He came as extra staff-hand to handle the freight. He has to go down to the airstrip this afternoon and do just that. Move the freight landed here! Jeff knows all the lurks about travelling cheap ——'

'Same with this other chap, I guess. Except this Mr Harold M. Smith didn't come dressed as a cargo hand.'

'He's a sort-of executive type, don't you think?' Kim suggested.

'Like I said. A "Main-Office" character!' He looked at the young girl with a bit of a grin, then added—'If you really want the news of the day—and most people in the Stopover do—this Mr Harold Smith did not state his business. Kathy was at the desk when he came in. He did no more than make enquiries about a certain Mr Stephen Cole—one of Dr Andrews' men, if I remember rightly. A scientist or something. Mr Smith saw the name in the register—dated back a while—and mentioned casual-like that he knew Mr Cole. And where could he meet up with him now.'

'He asked *Kathy*?' Even Kim's face was dead-pan. Very unusual for Kim.

'Yes, he asked Kathy. She passed it on to me because when that Stephen Cole was here he just about burned up the "blower" sending messages through the radio base north of here to *Sydney*—where this feller comes from.'

He looked up and caught Kim's grey eyes fixed on his face.

'Well, nothing to that!' he finished off abruptly. 'You'd know this Stephen Cole, I guess. Why does he want to send a spate of messages from *here* anyway? He could send 'em all backwards to the coast from your Base, couldn't he?'

'Not really,' Kim said casually. 'He might have thought the Land-Rover wouldn't be absolutely certain of getting back to

Base. And he had to leave a vehicle here at the garage. They're fixing it now. Base couldn't reach us out at the old homestead. Too far from a transmitting station. We don't have the new 25 watt transceiver either——'

'Well, Mr Cole didn't look like the over-anxious kind to me. A bit self-confident. Brash, I'd say!'

'He's not either of those things,' Kim said quickly, team loyalty up in arms. At the back of her mind, however, she felt a prickle of anxiety.

The man behind the desk watched the doubt and the unease cloud Kim's face.

'An old sweetheart, eh?' he asked. 'This Stephen Cole?'

Kim shook her head.

'Just a friend.'

'Guess all you people in the Expedition have "special" friends?'

Kim made no comment because she was still deep in thought. The manager decided not to tell her that yet another radio message via the base at Binni-Carra had come in for Dr John Andrews from the Expedition's headquarters. This was the only wave-length that could communicate from the west. He remembered the message——

When are you able to return. Important I inform you of arrangements to meet you. Please reply at earliest date, Best love Myree.

This girl, Myree, had sent too many messages signed with that word 'love'. Now here was Miss Kim looking pink and thoughtful about Mr Stephen Cole!

The manager, with a vested interest in seeing this wedding come off, decided to forget, temporarily only, where he put the written copy of this latest radio call. A proper monkey he'd look with the people around about if someone threw a jinx on this wedding. What with big orders of fresh fruits and salads coming on the freight plane—extra staff taken on—the safest thing he could do was forget *all* radio messages *in* or *out*. That mob back at the Scientific Base could find out about the wedding in God's good time. He, Joe Barker, not being God, was not going to do the telling.

Through the open door men's footsteps could be heard coming round the veranda.

Kim stopped leaning on the counter. She straightened up

as if touched by magic. The unpleasant cobwebby man named Mr Harold M. Smith ceased to exist.

She had to meet the two 'Js'! With an air too! How would Celia or Diane—*even Myree*—do it?

Her heart started to beat far too fast. She looked at Mr Barker, but in vain. Worldly wise, he had decided this was the moment when paper work in front of him was more important than the affairs of his paying guests.

Kim watched the door instead.

She saw the grin on Jeff's face, and that a shadow flitted across John's eyes, as they came in. Then John smiled too! Her relief was almost overwhelming because mixed up with it was a longing that he might one day really love her.

'Hullo, Kim!' John's voice was a matter of fact. Yet was there something else, indefinable, too?

'I have your brother's blessing,' he went on. 'Shall we all three go in and celebrate with a drink?'

Kim was fresh out of words so she just nodded. Then caught Jeff's eyes. He grinned, a little wickedly. John looked over Kim's head towards the desk where the manager was leaning on it stroking his chin with one finger and now looking up at the trio with an expressionless face.

'Will you come and join us?' John asked him. 'This could be your wedding, you know.'

What did he mean by *that*? Kim wondered vaguely.

Mr Barker grinned, but shook his head.

'Not mine. Yours,' he said. 'You look like a family party. You go ahead and I'll keep any unwelcome strangers out of the parlour. By the way,' he said looking at Jeff now. 'Talking of weddings, I'm standing you one right here in this pub that'll be the best ever for this year's takings. It's my party. Are you on?'

Jeff stared at the manager as if he was seeing a man from Mars.

'Look here——' he began. 'I'm the bride's brother——'

'I'm her sponsor,' Mr Barker said in his slow flat way, yet in a voice that conveyed the outback authority only the town's Boss Cocky wielded. Not a hint in it of the crates of fruit and salad already *en route*. 'Give me seventy-two hours and I'll run a wedding that'll give this district more of a kick than it's had in months. Don't count the cost because I'll rake it back in the bar. I always do. Bedroom service too. And more. That's the way we manage things up hereabouts.'

Jeff laughed, though somewhat abashed. This was a flat statement of fact, but a wonderful one. He himself could barely muster enough to run a small wedding. *But the whole district?*

Mr Barker bent his head as if once more to pay attention to his desk work. 'Well, that's settled!' he said as if finalising a very insignificant account. 'We gotta bring 'em into town now'n again! Goodwill and lamb's wool for business, you know!'

'Mr Barker, you're a darling,' Kim said diffidently. 'You could even be a super-darling——'

'You say that to the six-footer on your right, young miss. He's your first claim. Elsewise you might be letting loose fighting words.'

John looked at Kim.

'That's right,' he agreed quietly. Once again he was wearing his smile—not quite so remotely now. It did awful things to Kim's heart. 'Let's go and have that drink,' he said. 'Mr Barker, Jeff and I will talk the matter over later.'

They turned to go through the swing doors into the parlour as Kathy came into the main hall from the back. She looked thoughtfully at the diminishing figure of Kim between two outlandishly tall specimens of man power.

'You tell me something, Dad,' she demanded, leaning on the counter. 'Whenever there's a nice stray girl who books in at this pub, and some straight kind of a feller at the same time—me, Mum and the cook find ourselves with a wedding on our hands.'

'You been overhearing?'

'More or less.'

'Well, it's like this——' Her father reflected on the parlour door with studied interest. 'There's only the race-meeting out at Binni-Carra Station in the next three months to keep us lively in this place. They wouldn't keep any staff down at the store or the garage, or even out at the air field, if we didn't have some social life. And we'd be broke. It needs a wedding, or some such, to liven up the place. Give it a good name as a Stopover for social life. Brings people in——'

He glanced round at his daughter.

'It's good for business, my girl,' he advised. 'The station people come in here instead of going two hundred miles up the track to Blain's Find. Now, if we could stage another big "do" before the Wet hits us, we'd be in pocket for the rest of the year. It's what the district people can spend here instead of up at Blain's that matters.'

His daughter looked at him thoughtfully. It was true that most of the weddings they'd had at Bim's Stopover had been a success. People kept coming back to celebrate anniversaries. The station-owners around tended to drop in at the Stopover for months afterwards. *And spend money*——

As for herself? There was Don down at the garage, of course. Dad was always asking him up here—— Was there a subtle meaning in that remark about another big 'do' before the Wet?

Kathy turned and went back through the dining-room to the kitchen.

'Mental telepathy,' she told her mother. 'I've just found out Dad's been trying to put ideas in my head.'

'That's your father all over. What's he up to now?'

'Kim and Dr Andrews. They'll get married all right. Her brother's all smiles. All the same, strikes me there's something sort-of *missing*——'

Her mother lifted an apple pie from the oven and set it on the table.

'Any just cause or impediment?' she suggested. 'That what's worrying you?'

'Could be. They don't seem so very in love to my liking. Funny sort of way they are with one another—— Sort-of distant——'

'They don't have to show feelings like some I know. Don Carter down at the garage for instance. What's more, right now your father's got other things on his mind about this particular wedding.'

'Like what?' Kathy asked handing her mother a fresh oven cloth.

'Well, between you and me, your father has those wedding certificates ready drawn up for Mr Soames from Binni-Carra to take the ceremony. Him acting as local magistrate for the occasion. Your father keeps those legal documents in the safe for the J.Ps. that might need them—there not being any government office round these parts. It happens all over when you get this far outback. The pub's a real social necessity——'

'Oh yes, I know all that! When Mr Soames isn't growing more wool than anyone else round about he's baptising or marrying or burying.'

'Here dear—move those pies along will you. There's more to come. What was I saying?'

'Something about Dad making out the wedding certificates for Mr Soames.'

'Yes. That's right. That's the point. I don't reckon your father really knows the law like he thinks he does. And Mr Soames is that forgetful. I'm just hoping that getting Kim's brother to give permission is good enough. Kim says she's only nineteen.'

'But Mr Soames can give permission, can't he? He did for Nan Richards from Windy Station.'

'Yes, but he *knew* Nan. He doesn't know Kim. He hasn't even met her yet. He's supposed to know them both for *nine days*!'

'So what? Dad's met her. That's good enough isn't it? Mr Soames'll take Dad's word for it.'

'Well maybe. Let's hope anyway. So long as some bush-whacky loon doesn't blow in and speak up when that question about "just impediment" gets asked.'

'Oh, for goodness' sake, Mum! Dr Andrews wouldn't do anything that wasn't in the book. He's too important. A scientist, and all that! Besides what bush-whackers are likely to come?'

'Well, there's that Peck and his mate Bill. They'd have heard there's a wedding on—wherever they may be. They love a yarn, and when they've got one they tell it from one end of the state to the other.'

'Well, tell Dad to lock Peck in the dog-house if he does blow in,' Kathy said succinctly. 'I don't want anything to go wrong. I like Kim. She's nice. She's a bit nervous about something, and when I come to think of it——'

'Don't think too hard dear. You'll addle your brains.'

'Come to think of it,' Kathy persisted. 'There's those radio messages about "love from Myree". There'd be a lot of girls jumping out of their skins if someone like Dr Andrews came along kidnapping them. He's that attractive.'

'You keep your mind on Don Carter. He's nearer your mark, my girl!'

CHAPTER THIRTEEN

It took three more days to organise that wedding. Some people, determined to come, had to travel from far. First they had to finish mustering-in the sheep, for the shearers who were due in the district from next week on. The air—per radio and radio telephone—was lively with voices. People far and wide, who had never heard of Kim Wentworth or Dr John Andrews, were determined to come to *any* wedding at Bim's Stopover. But first the mustering had to be finished! The wedding had to wait willy nilly.

Kim wasn't the only one counting days on her fingers. Kathy and her mother, with some relief made it the bare nine days since Dr John Andrews and Kim had come in from Skelton's old homestead. The only problem now was that *Mr Soames still had not met the bride and groom*. Not a soul far and wide was certain whether that mattered or not. Neither Mr Soames, J.P.—from the distant reaches of the muster-yard at Binni-Carra—nor Mr Barker, manager of the pub and Boss Cocky at Bim's Stopover, were saying. Dr John Andrews appeared to have a mind sky-high above such negligible things as crossing 'ts'.

Everyone that could be mustered was busy cooking, decorating, giving Kim advice about what to do with the white linen dress she had bought down at the store with her pay cheque. And whether she should or should not wear a hat.

John Andrews and Jeff Wentworth went for long walks along the dusty streak of track or across the drying grasses of the plain talking endlessly—not of Kim and weddings—but of forests, plants, and the uses to mankind of trees. Also of the obscure remedial drugs that certain plants gave to suffering humanity.

'*Myoporoides* was a find enough,' John Andrews mused aloud. 'But *hopwoodi*! Of course it's George Crossman who'll hit the headlines with its chemical values. *What a find!* It'll make history!'

'It's thought to have been extinct these twenty years——'

John spared time from high thoughts to give his future

brother-in-law a cold look. 'No one's looked for it out here towards the *western* desert fringe before. That's all!'

'Okay, okay!' Jeff agreed cheerfully. 'So long as you don't make mistakes in *human* relations: never mind plant species. You scientist chaps——'

'Meaning?' John asked him, his eyes losing their blue and turning a dark grey.

'Nothing! Nothing!' Jeff said quickly. 'All the same, it's strange how some people do make those mistakes. Take Kim, for instance. She's not what she seems. If you know what I mean.'

'Kim can err in her judgment of *people*?' John asked the question bluntly.

'Kim was brought up by the *whole family*,' Jeff parried. 'She came into the world a long time after the rest of us. She didn't have much chance of experience—— Too many wind-brakes!'

John Andrews was silent.

'Suppose we change the subject,' he said presently. 'Let's get back to your own topic. I've personally listed two hundred and eighteen varieties of eucalypts—that excellent gum tree. I could possibly add another thirty to that with investigation. Those flourishing in unexplored pockets of the Sandy Desert, for instance.'

'Then don't forget to let me in on them,' Jeff retorted. 'I could muster an expedition from the Forestry Department. C.O.C.R. would back us, as with you people. Certainly—if we could get the kind of tycoon *you* landed. One who'd give us a handsome contribution to the costs——'

'As long as he doesn't come along in the guise of a spy for an industrial chemist,' John said so quietly Jeff was startled.

'You get that kind mizzling in too?'

'We don't get them. *We have them*. The thing to know is when they're around. Then you keep a guard on your discoveries.'

'*Hopwoodi*, for instance?'

'*Hopwoodi* by all means. It's a narcotic known to have been used by the aborigines very effectively. Priceless, if reared, for some chemists! The sick and the ailing——'

'Then you'll keep very quiet about it?'

'I will. George Crossman and you are the only two who know exactly what I've found.'

'Thanks for trusting me,' Jeff said, pleased at this compliment.

'We're fellow scientists aren't we? You'd have any amount of top secret stuff down in the karri forest, wouldn't you?'

'Right you are. Very hush-hush. By the way, I suppose Kim has had to do the recording? Maybe the drawings? A bit of a responsibility!'

'Yes, Kim knows what she's doing. She's a member of the team——'

Jeff took this statement as a general compliment to his sister. A good way to begin a marriage.

They walked on without speaking for a long time.

Then John broke the silence unexpectedly.

'I'm interested in that man Smith who's staying in the Stopover. A character out of type. Giving no account of himself——'

'Maybe out after gold prospectors?' Jeff hazarded. 'Since this state burst out of its seams with its big mineral discoveries those types are busy snooping all over the place. You positively trip over them. Generally they have a fat cheque book to buy out the prospectors, or to pay for information.'

'In which case Peck and Bill had better keep away from the wedding,' John mused. 'Bill can't talk, but Peck can't stop. They might find the stakes pulled out of their own gold claims overnight.'

Kathy, having experience behind her, allocated herself to the role of bridesmaid.

Kim was grateful. Actually Kathy didn't give her any choice. A submissive girl, she pointed out, was femininely attractive to men.

'I guess it will take forty-eight hours to turn you into a picture-girl instead of a burned-off piece of brush in from the spinifex,' Kathy said looking Kim over judicially. 'My, when you first came in from that sand plain, dressed in brown dust and a tangy shirt, you sure looked a real waif.'

'What, me?'

'Yes, you! We really do have to do something about that face!' Kathy shook her head as she gazed at her victim. 'You've improved it. I'll grant you that. But for a wedding we have to make it extra-super.'

She looked at Kim in a considering way. 'Oatmeal's the thing,' she said at last. 'Oatmeal packs from now till D-Day! You're not the only bride that's come in out of the wilds to the Stopover to get herself married-up tight. I've found oatmeal helps a lot. Gives the doubting Thomas something to look at—instead of think about.'

In no time Kim found her face, neck and arms, firmly encased in a thick paste.

This was to be the pattern for two hours each day until the wedding ring was firmly on that third left hand finger. Kathy graciously allowed the eyes to remain uncovered so Kim could while away the imprisonment by finishing the important duplicate of John's notes and drawings.

The things she did for Myree!

Also she wanted to put a few final touches to the early record she had made of her own solo trip from Perth in the south, to Manutarra, the jump-off roadhouse for the Expedition.

'Well, just as well to get on with some work,' Kathy agreed. 'You can't go spoiling the honeymoon with ink and paints, you know. Have to stay a "picture-girl" till that's over, at least.'

The very thought of 'honeymooning' alarmed Kim, but she wasn't going to worry herself thinking about it *now*. Actually, she couldn't bear to. Better to work and keep her thoughts on more familiar things like the flowers on either side of the road up the Bindoon Hill, and the miles and miles of golden wattle east of the Greenough Flats.

If only—if only——

No, she couldn't finish that thought either.

On the afternoon before the wedding—while Kathy was safely out of sight helping with the decorations—there came a tap on Kim's door.

She was lying stretched prone on the floor, the pink tip of her tongue peeping from one corner of her mouth. Her mapping pen was in her hand, the ink bottle handy, and a large sheet of drawing-paper spread out on the floor before her.

'Come in!' she answered absently. She finished a line and began another. Of course it would *never be John*!

The door opened, but there was only silence. Kim carefully shook a blob of ink from her pen, then turned her head.

It was the man from some-city-nowhere. Or was it Sydney? Mr Shiny Shoes.

He stood in the doorway, sleek and suited, looking at the front-side-down figure of a young girl who was swathed in a sheet, her hair tied back in a towel and her face covered—except for the mouth and eyes—in a paste of porridge.

He smiled at her as if amused. But in a very friendly way. *Much too squeazy a smile*, Kim thought.

'I'm sorry I can't get up,' she said. 'It's the sheet you know. It's all I have on. And it's only pinned in one place——'

'Please don't. I wouldn't disturb you for one moment—except that——'

'Except what?' she asked politely.

'I wanted to tell you how delighted I am about this very unique outback wedding. I wondered if I dare—— That is, if I may make a suggestion, and which you might receive kindly.'

'Yes?' Kim's eyes didn't widen, but that was because her eyelids were all but fixed by the oatmeal mixture.

'You don't mind if I speak to you in the guise of a favourite uncle?'

Strange, but Kim noticed he had behaved exactly like that. And he wasn't that. She hadn't any uncles at all. He moved over to her bed and began casually looking at an open record book with its page of finest hair-line drawings.

'Goodness me,' he said, by way of winning favour. 'Such exquisite drawings! What wonderful eyesight you must have. Minute work!'

Kim was used to a bohemian way of life at home, so she saw nothing remarkable about a middle-aged man coming into her room. Anyhow the door was wide open—and he was being friendly in his own peculiar squeazy way.

'Oh I have very good eyesight,' she agreed. 'That's a very important record book to me. I had to be super-careful.'

'And this very thick book is full of such drawings? All annotated?'

'Full—up to date. Why did you want to be my favourite uncle?'

He was turning pages of the record book with one hand. With the other he seemed absent-mindedly to be taking from his inside pocket *a cheque book*.

'I would like to give you a wedding present,' he said glancing down at Kim. She decided he must have quite a gallon of oil on the hinges of his face.

'That's very kind of you,' she said gravely. 'But I'm not having any presents. Not for this wedding anyway. Of course, you could send something to the spastic children. Or to the Wild Life Society. You could write to Prince Philip about the last. Someone gave him a cheque for £200,000 for that. In sterling of course. It would be $400,000 in Australian money. wouldn't it?'

That was a statement outrageous enough to startle him surely!

His smile was a little fixed now.

'Roughly.' he agreed. 'Of course Bank Exchange would account for a little more——'

'You don't mind talking in terms of thousands of dollars?' she enquired She wormed her way up to a sitting position, carefully adjusting her wrapping sheet as she did so. Perhaps he was rich enough not to be dented by *anything*.

'Not at all. I'm a very wealthy man,' he said meaningfully.

Kim bit the end of her mapping pen and stared at him.

'Then which is it to be?' she asked, wondering if he was mad, or bad, or both. And how far she could go with her remarks.

'That depends on you,' he said smoothly. 'I'd like it to be the Wild Life Society with a nice percentage to you for giving me such sound advice. I happen to be interested in wild life. Plant life very particularly. I don't suppose you could bring yourself to let me have a look through your record book in some idle moments? To-night for instance? I daresay I would feel all the more eager about that gift if my interest was really stirred by *some new or exotic find*.'

Kim put her pen down, drew up her knees and wrapped her arms around them. She cocked her head on one side and regarded her visitor.

'You're very generous,' she said. 'I guess I'd better take you up on that offer before you change your mind. You could send my percentage to the Herbarium at the Mount in Perth.'

Mr Harold M. Smith looked over the drawing-book at the young girl on the floor. He couldn't read her expression because of the over-all coverage of the face-pack she was wearing. Nevertheless his sound business ear was tuned-in to what he diagnosed as a genuinely naïve, very young girl, speaking quite *seriously*. The din of thousands of dollars would have a crashing sound in the ears of such an unworldly person, he decided. He'd spent two days taking good stock of her.

'Done!' he exclaimed.

She had *accepted* in words, *clearly*. Irrespective of where the offer was supposed to go! Whether he paid out any money or not, she had agreed in principle. He had her hooked, for agreement even in words, was a contract.

He stood up, putting away his cheque book as he did so.

'Well now, I must leave you to your beauty care. That is what all the mess is about, isn't it?' His face was creased with more smiles.

Kim nodded her head.

'Not that anyone could realy make me beautiful,' she said regretfully.

'I'm sure your good fairy attended to that long ago. A little sunburned, perhaps. But easily remedied.'

He was still smiling.

'Now is this the record book I take along with me?' He still held the book he had leafed through in his hand. 'I'll return it to-night. Or to-morrow at the latest. Of course I'll take the greatest care of it. I see it has a beautifully drawn map of the environs you have traversed *lately*.'

Kim thought a minute. She thought best when she had the handle of a pen or a brush in her mouth, so she picked up the pen again, and chewed on the end of the wooden stem. 'Quite lately,' she agreed. 'In fact *my* latest. Those are most *precious* records.'

The man filled in more time by standing silent, in case she said more. He leafed through the book again. He could see the latter part of it was done with fresh ink, and paint. He guessed she was adding up dollars in that small, towel-shrouded head of hers. These ingenues were just so easily impressed! It was almost a shame——

'You won't forget to send the cheques?' Kim asked at long length. He looked up a shade too quickly and only managed to mask his eyes with an effort. 'There are *two* cheques, aren't there?' she went on simply. 'One to the Herbarium: and the other for the Wild Life Society.'

Was the girl shrewder than her fey-like simplicity implied?

No. Even the porridge-mess on her face could not hide the clear candour in her very large eyes. The amount of the money talked—had mesmerised her.

'Two cheques it shall be,' he said moving to the door with a soft tread, taking the book with him. 'Meantime I'm giving instructions for the very best wines to be served at that wedding reception to-morrow! No. Don't thank me, my child. It is my privilege to a fellow lover of wild plant life.'

'I shall think of you with deep feelings as I sip it,' Kim said quite earnestly. 'When I lift my glass you'll know I'm drinking to you, won't you?'

'I shall know you are thinking of me,' he said. 'Why not? I'm the favourite uncle, aren't I? Back to your beauty care, my dear. You must look beautiful for to-morrow.'

He went out, closing the door silently behind him. He had her *offer to accept money*. That was all that mattered. She was rather a nice little thing, *really*!

Kim sat buddha-like swathed in her sheet, and thought very hard.

Mad, or bad—was her final judgment of Mr Shiny Shoes.

Oh well, she had yet another group of sketches to do on the sheet of drawing-paper lying stretched on the floor. Better do it now before her face-mask cracked because of too much talk with a cheque-happy tycoon.

She didn't for a moment believe the madman would send cheques of any kind: to anyone, anywhere.

So long as he returned that record book! That was her only care. After all—it was *hers*. And very precious.

Not to think about it now. To-morrow was her wedding day!

The wedding preparations had gone on during all that day. Meantime dozens of dusty cars and station waggons were driving up, off-loading equally dusty passengers to fill the pub.

Kim had not seen John since dinner the night before. Jeff, Mr Soames, J.P., and some of the station-owners who had already driven in, were busy giving what they were pleased to call a 'Bucks' party'. The women folk who had come with the men, had already wished Kim lots of luck, then settled down to tea and a free-for-all gossip. It was their wedding too and all they hoped for was a really beautiful bride to make the whole thing worthwhile.

Kathy made no bones about where Kim should be—walled up in her room, wearing a face-mask and plying a needle.

'I've pressed the dress and you've yet to sew those everlastings on your hat,' she said.

'Thank you,' Kim said. All this kindness called for docility. She was in Kathy's organising hands, and there she had to stay. Actually she wanted to see John. She didn't know why, only that she wanted to *see him* very badly. If he came to say good night to her this latest face-pack would end all prospect of nuptials! She said so, feeling that Kathy might be understanding about this.

'I'll lock the door so he can't come in, just to make certain,' Kathy was very determined. 'Besides it'll be past midnight before they're finished in that parlour, and the bridegroom is not supposed to see the bride on the wedding day . . . even if it is only in the early hours.'

Kim with no other course open, submitted. She only hoped that inch-wide gap below the door was big enough to allow Mr Harold M. Smith—the tycoon with the oily smile—to return her record book as promised. Her diminutive amount of packing had already been done.

She had an awful fear that John might change his mind and take off for the fringe of the Gibson Desert in the night. After all, *hopwoodi* was more important to him than perhaps any bride, let alone Kimberley—Kim for short—Jessica Wentworth. Supposing he changed his mind? Funny how, later alone in her bed, she began to have doubts of herself too! Maybe she was cheating *him*, as well as Fate!

People from miles around were still pouring into the downstairs hallway. They had come from far and wide. All yesterday, then through the night, and now this morning, they came—the men in their brim-shading slouch hats, their voices drawling as they talked, and their wives in pretty cotton dresses, their sun-dried skins hidden under careful layers of make-up. The children were in shorts, mini-skirts, or slacks. They had tumbled out of cars, or station waggons, as the vehicles pulled up in the dusty road by the pub. Their laughter, and calls to one another, all seemed to say the same thing—'There's a wedding at the Stopover! We've come!'

The noise in the bar had been thunderous for hours. Upstairs in the ladies' sitting-room the chatter and tinkle of tea cups had been incessant.

'You see what I mean?' the manager said to John. His finger was stroking his chin as he leaned on the counter top. 'Half this mob won't go back for three days. It's the only break they get. We have to have a party now and again at the Stopover. We're bulging at the seams already. There's more to come too!'

John could see this state of affairs for himself. And said so.

'It's like this——' Mr Barker drawled on, his finger still stroking his chin. 'If your wedding could give that Kathy of mine ideas—why you'd be kind-of doing us a good turn, Dr Andrews. Me a good turn for business, and this lot all over the pub would get another bit of a break from sheep, fences and windmills.'

John barely smiled. 'Do you whistle up weddings as a matter of business, or of habit?' he asked.

The manager straightened up from the counter. He planted both hands down on its top and looked John Andrews squarely in the eyes.

'It could be that I like seeing people enjoy themselves,' he remarked with some emphasis.

John took out a cigarette, tapped it on the counter, then lit it. He took quite a time, and for the whole of that time Mr Barker kept his eyes unwavering on his wedding guest.

'I'm beginning to think you are capable of anything, Mr Barker,' John said very quietly.

The manager had leaned his elbows back on the counter. Once again he fell to stroking his chin with his finger.

'Let me see,' he said making an effort at brain raking. 'What did Peck say? Seems like I don't have a memory that good.' He looked up sharply. 'Tell you what, Dr Andrews. I'd sooner have Peck yarning in my bar than any other. He's a regular attraction. If he bogs down at Blain's Find, way up the track, he kinda has a habit of drawing my customers away from me. Not much trade in these parts you know. The Stopover and Blain's Find compete with one another quite a bit. This wedding now——'

John blew a spiral of smoke ceilingwards. He looked straight at Mr Barker for a good thirty seconds, then turned away. He went into the bar and bought himself, and the two men on either side of him, a drink.

'I needed that,' was his only remark.

CHAPTER FOURTEEN

All went well for Kim on her wedding morning. The record book had been returned—under the door. John had not gone to any desert, let alone the Gibson. Kathy reported that he was downstairs, first having had breakfast with Jeff, then yarning with her father.

The last of the face-packs came off. The tip of Kim's nose had grown a new skin over the days. The freckles were subdued. Her skin, though tanned, was as clear as her dark-fringed eyes.

She had washed her hair while under the shower, and Kathy then set it with the help of dozens of bobby pins. The captive was next commanded to sit near the window and not dare move till the 'coiffure' was dry.

The white linen dress lay creaseless on the bed beside a biscuit-coloured straw hat, which was now delicately trimmed with the everlastings. Kim gazed at this particular decoration lovingly She even went so far as to wonder why she had not become a milliner instead of a typist.

Lunch, sometime later, was brought to her on a tray by a fussing Mrs Barker. Finally—as the clock's hands seemed now to have whizzed round—Kathy came back in her guise of bridesmaid. Out came the bobby pins, and swish went the brush till Kim thought she was certain of a sore head.

Next the linen dress was put on, and patted down. Kathy tried three different ways of settling the straw hat on the bride's head before she was satisfied. Kim, letting her minister, had her own intentions as to the angle at which she would wear her hat. She would do something about *that* later.

Lastly, right on the hour, Jeff came rat-tatting on the door.

'Are you dressed and ready, Kim? Heaven save us, so you are!'

He walked round and round his sister.

'You know what!' he said puzzled. 'You sure look beautiful. How'd you manage it?'

'Oatmeal porridge,' was all Kim said.

How she went down that staircase and into the decorated dining-room she never afterwards knew. It was all a daze. One minute she had been in her room, and the next she was looking into the bronzed, lined face of Mr Soames J.P. from Binni-Carra Station. John, tall and anonymous, was standing beside her. He was wearing a fine new set of khaki drills—as such a thing as a suit was not known in Bim's Stopover—except in the case of Mr Shiny Shoes Smith.

Kim's thoughts went on being hazy and dazy too.

I'm being married! Did John notice the wild-flowers on my hat? What is Mr Soames saying? Who ever would have thought of a dinner bell for a wedding march! John! Oh John! Where are you?

Words were spoken: responses made. Time marched on.

At the side of the dining-room, almost hidden by the crowd, Mrs Barker was becoming more agitated.

She had seen Peck and Bill come in. They stood a few inches inside the door, their ancient felt hats dusty as ever—though they had the grace to carry them in their hands, and not on their heads.

Peck was grinning. Was it a *knowing grin*?

'It's all right, Mum,' Kathy whispered standing near her mother now. 'For all we know it might be the law for a brother to give his sister permission and all that. And Dad and you've known Kim and John nine days, even if Mr Soames hasn't——'

'It's only what *Peck* might say at the wrong moment,' Mrs Barker answered in a desperate undertone. 'He always likes a good yarn. He won't be able to keep quiet when Mr Soames asks that question! He could speak up, even as a joke.'

'You mean that one about "anybody knowing just cause or impediment?" Nobody knows what "impediment" means anyway,' Kathy whispered back. 'At least not in the Stopover——'

Two minutes later the moment came! Mr Soames looked up, and took in the whole congregation with one magisterial glance.

'*If anyone knows any just cause or impediment*——' He forgot to drawl, and became sonorous. He delivered as from the Bench—'*why these two should not be joined together in legal matrimony*——' he paused, then added—'*let him speak now, or forever remain silent.*'

Mrs Barker looked dizzily around in the stillness that followed. Nothing could be heard inside or out—not even a willi-willi prancing across the dusty gravel yard. Mr Mystery-Smith had gone, after paying in advance for a large amount of champagne for the wedding. A Land-Rover had called for him, and whisked him away in the early hours of the morning.

All that Peck did was shift his weight from one leg to the other so he could lean against the door jamb more easily.

'*Then I pronounce you man and wife!*' Mr Soames declared.

Mrs Barker decided not to faint—a diversion she had planned in advance. Instead she beamed with relief.

Kim stood suspended in time and space. She wondered why she felt *stunned*.

Man and wife? What had she done? Who was this tall, silent man of will beside her? *Why had he asked her?*

'Now kiss the bride,' Mr Soames was saying.

There was a hand touching Kim's arm. It belonged to the stranger. John Andrews. He turned her towards him. It was the first time she had *looked at him to-day*.

His face was quite serious, and his eyes were dark. *Concerned?* Was that possible, after this fraud? Then she saw—far back in the very recesses of his wonderful eyes—a tiny light.

Dear God! *This man was her husband!* It had all happened like a flash. Maybe it was the way madness came on.

There was a silence in the dining-room as everyone waited, some standing on tiptoe.

John took Kim's pixie chin in his free hand, bent his head and kissed her.

It was so gentle and chivalrous a kiss! It seemed as if the sky had opened one chink. She nearly, very nearly, saw into Heaven!

She would never be the *little sister again*. She would be the wife of a botanist who one day might be famous. Dr John Andrews!

She turned instinctively to where Jeff was standing.

'Give everyone a smile, Kim,' he whispered. 'Don't look so scared, Bratto! They're all waiting for that smile. That's right. Now another. Good, it's a real beauty. Now your colour's back! Jumping kangaroos! I thought you were going to faint!'

The pub manager on the far side was now wringing John's hand. Mrs Barker was bustling up with much relief in her face. The details of the reception—yet to be—were temporarily forgotten. The men—some of the girls too—swarmed round John. Kim was cut off from him by a wall of flowery dresses.

Jeff, the care-taking brother, took her arm in his. 'Keep smiling, *Bratto*,' he commanded.

'I'm still *me*, Jeff? I'm not that much different?'

'You're not different at all, except for that ring on your finger. Not to worry, Kim! You never really did worry. Now did you? You had your own way mapped out of the trees right from the start. Well, you've made it. Now you've got yourself a first-class husband. You're free of that mad hatter's tea-party back home. You've cut and run——'

'Is that why you came up? To help me escape?'

'Partly. Once I got here I took a shine to this feller John Andrews.'

The wedding guests were swarming round her.

Jeff beamed. 'Like I said,' he finished in a whisper. 'Not to worry! Most people feel shaky the first five minutes of finding themselves married——'

The guests were crowding Jeff away from the bride.

The men were still taking it in turns to wring John's hand, while the girls, and children, fluttered around Kim. Everyone loves a pretty bride, specially this one in the lovely shady hat, who had such wonderful dark-fringed grey eyes.

'You look lovely!'

'My, aren't you lucky! How'd you get someone so good looking like Dr Andrews? A real science man isn't he? Can he fly in space?'

'Who did your make-up, Kim dear? Kathy! Well, come to think of it she always does. We always have our weddings here. Kathy's always the make-up girl!'

Kim answered questions, smiled willingly, and exchanged kisses with absolute strangers who suddenly had become loved and loving friends.

Then, as minute by minute passed, her fright retreated. Something else was taking its place. A sort-of muted, mounting excitement. Her heart could just possibly be beating to the sound of happiness.

She was married to John. She would make her marriage work. She could do it. She was not Kim Wentworth, the bratto, any more. She was Mrs John Andrews.

The incredible had happened.

Her heart lifted and lifted, up into a wonderful world of hope and anticipation as she kissed and was kissed by all around her.

She saw Peck's brown wrinkled face peeking impishly through the door in the far corner. It could have been the face of Pan, it was so wicked. But heart-warming too. She wished he wasn't too bush-shy to come and kiss her. When she got the chance—— *Well, look out Peck! You're in for some kissing too!*

The moon lifted its shining apricot globe over the eastern stretch of plain as Kim and John went out to the jeep. They were in their work clothes again—all freshly laundered and ironed by the pub's laundress.

Now was the time to drive away—together and alone. Silver shone everywhere—on the pointed leaves of the magic mulgas, on the iron roof of the pub, round the curves of the massive water-tank. But mostly in people's eyes.

'Guess you'll have to wait to start that honeymoon till you gets to Skelton's,' someone fresh from champagne celebrations called out. 'Mind the snakes in the spinifex, Dr John! It's their rousing time. No bedding-down in the bush!'

John, having packed everything in the back, and then checked that Kim was comfortable, hefted himself in the driver's seat, and revved up the engine. Kathy was the last to put her head in the window.

'Lots of love, Kim,' she said. 'Look what you've done to me and Don. We've *nearly* decided to get married. Well, maybe—— Dad's gone in to open more champagne—in case!'

'Oh Kathy, I'm so glad!'

'We'll sure make out better than you two!' Kathy said with a grin. 'Mr Soames'll have known us both for the legal nine days. More'n with you two. We'll be married *good and proper*! Very legal! No mistakes about *us*! Not to worry Kim. No one'll let on about you two——'

Kim was very tired by this time. Too tired. Half her mind was taking in the medley of good wishes from the other side of the car. Yet some semi-dormant self inside her pricked a listening ear. *What had Kathy said?* What did she mean about Mr Soames knowing people a legal nine days before he married them? That frightening word '*legal*'.

'Goodbye—goodbye—goodbye!'

'Goodbye Bratto!'

'Goodbye Jeff darling!'

'Bye-o Dr John! Take care of her. Don't lose her in the sand dunes! Put a leg-rope and halter on her.'

All the goodbyes were said, and Kim leaned out of the window, waving till the last moonshine figure was lost amongst the shadows of the old pub.

John swung the jeep on to the track leading away to Skelton's. Kim wished he would stop the car and kiss her. She waited and hoped for it. She was too diffident to make the first gesture. That was *his right*. She was also very tired.

She leaned forward, pulling her feet in a little, and wrapped her arms round her knees.

'Are you tired too, John?'

'A little.' He glanced at the huddled figure beside him, the moonlight putting a silver halo round her head—the hat-ridiculous was back in its rightful place. 'It was a good wedding, wasn't it? Are you happy, Kim?'

'I'm nearly happy.'

'*Nearly?*'

'Why did we get married, John?'

'We're right for one another. Moreover——' He peered into the stream of light shooting rays from the head lamps, the better to see the track. He was driving very fast.

'You were saying something,' Kim prompted.

'We have a long time in front of us in which to get acquainted,' he said.

There was another silence. Kim unwrapped her arms and leaned back. Inch by inch she edged herself sideways towards him.

'John?'

'Yes?'

'What did Kathy mean about Mr Soames knowing *them*—meaning Kathy and Don—more than nine days? Something about making sure of being *legal*: better than us. Better than us about *what*?'

Her head nearly touched John's shoulder. She felt his arm muscles stiffen. Then he was, all of him, taut.

'Kathy was excited, and had a fair quota of champagne. She was talking rot. Nine days' notice is needed for a special licence. Mr Soames had that for us. Jeff saw to it. He went out there to Binni-Carra.'

'Oh. That was the day before the day before yesterday? I wondered where he had gone. I was doing my drawings snowed under by Kathy's oatmeal. Did my skin look all right, John? Not so dreadfully burned?'

'I like your skin burned.' He slowed down to a crawl to manage a bad twist in the track.

Now, Kim thought. *He might stop altogether*——

But he didn't. The jeep was safely out on to the straight again, and going fast.

'You managed to finish all the records, and the drawings, while Kathy had you walled up in that bedroom?'

'Yes. Every one of them. The duplicate for Myree too. They're locked in the Number Four case. I'm glad I finished them. I was lonely, in a way. I wanted . . . well——' she couldn't add—*I wanted to be with you*. He hadn't said anything about missing *her* in those last few days.

'I had much to do. I needed to check and repack the specimen cases. Make my own notes and bring the official diary up to date,' he was saying. 'I thought you were busy at wedding preparations. I'm glad you managed to get your records done.'

Kim gingerly rested her cheek against the sleeve of his jacket. He took one hand from the steering wheel and slipped his arm around her.

She expelled a long breath of relief, and closed her eyes.

Nearer, nearer, nearer, she thought. *Soon, if I'm ever so careful . . . 'subtle' they call it in marriage-guidance circles . . . I might break down that barrier.*

The moon was shedding a cold light everywhere, making the world very beautiful. It was signalling the hard fact that temperatures dropped a long way down out here on the fringe land. Blazing hot at noon, but three-blanket cold at midnight!

'You must have been too busy to be lonely,' John said thoughtfully.

'Oh, I had one visitor. That Mr Harold-tycoon-Smith.'

'Smith! I wondered about him. Why did he make a present of the champagne for the wedding, Kim? I was uneasy about that. Was it a gift to you personally?'

'To us both, of course. Well, he's rich and some rich people like to throw their money around. Make a fine gesture and all that! He wanted to do that for the wedding, so I let him.'

'You let him?'

'Yes. I let him,' she smiled to herself at her own airy but low cunning. 'It was easiest that way.'

Against her cheek, down her side where his body touched hers, she felt those muscles tauten again. The arm round her was no longer nearly caressing her. It stiffened. Then he withdrew it. Both hands went on to the steering wheel again. He bent his head forward as if to see the track better.

'You *let* him, Kim?' he repeated carefully. 'Is it wise to let strangers be so generous?'

Kim sat up straight.

'You think I'm not very sophisticated, don't you John?' she asked in a not so small voice. 'You really think I'm like that school girl you met at the Mount, and who would not go home and be good? If she had done that she wouldn't be here in this jeep now.'

'And married to me,' he added quietly; thoughtfully. 'I'm glad you came back that day, Kim.'

Why didn't he stop the car and say so with his arms round her? *How did she ask to be kissed?* Did she have to make all the moves in this barrier-breaking exercise?

The old Kim in her woke from a temporary slumber. Hers had been the listening ear that had cocked when Kathy had said something about getting married good and proper. Legal, *not like herself and John.*

'Do you know?' this other self said in a voice light and inconsequential. 'I wouldn't be surprised if what Kathy said didn't have a point. We weren't married in a church because there wasn't any parson: or any church. Do you think we're really married? I mean, tight and for ever more? Were we supposed to have gone and seen Mr Soames ourselves?'

'I shouldn't raise sleeping dogs, if I were you, Kim,' John said abruptly. His voice had a chill in it. This turned Kim to ice as suddenly as if she had been plunged from heights into a snow heap, though she realised she had brought it on herself.

Out of her deep-freeze her voice came almost sadly.

'I always seem to say and do things the wrong way. I always have. Even now—I can't even get married *properly*: legally——'

John pulled the jeep over to the edge of the track and braked to a stop. He leaned back in his corner and looked at the moonlight flooding Kim's face. It shone in her eyes giving them a silver glint, making the infinitesimally unfocused way she looked at him utterly beguiling, tweaking at his heart strings where before the only heart he had ever had had been for plants—wild, mysterious and unknown. What *was* it about her? Her absolute candour?

Perhaps it was the unique expression in those very beautiful eyes. Childlike, yet paradoxically deep with hidden thoughts and ideas that were perhaps unique too. *Ideas* were the most precious jewels in the world.

'Perhaps you do things the right way *for you*, Kim,' he said soberly. 'It is we workers, with too much on our minds, who miss the points of contact that make us known to one another. What strange quirk of your very generous heart would make you see anything worthwhile in a man like Mr Harold Smith, for instance?'

'Oh, I didn't see anything in him,' Kim said, immediately more cheerful. At last, at *last*, she and John were going to talk heart-to-heart. 'Actually he wasn't at all a likeable man. Too squeazy. But he liked me. At least, he liked my drawings. He said they were *exquisite work*. Quite an expression, wasn't it? I mean for a man like him to use?'

John straightened up. The air around him—like some preamble to a thunderstorm—was suddenly electric.

'He liked your drawings? You showed them to him?'

'Oh yes! He saw my record book on my bed. He borrowed it for a whole night to look at the drawings.'

'God in Heaven!' It was a prayer, not a blasphemy.

He put his elbow on the steering wheel, and his head in his hand.

Kim sat still, suddenly terribly cold.

'Get out and walk home, Kim,' John said through tight lips. 'Otherwise I might thrash you.'

She stared at his head where it rested in his hand.

There was a long dreadful silence.

If I weren't miles and miles and miles from anywhere I would do just that, she thought.

She would need a compass in her hand, a water-bottle over her shoulder and *her hat on her head*. Endurance too!

She had thought that once she was married to him, she could make it work!

Well, he had never said he loved her. Much worse, now *he didn't trust her*. Then why had he married her?

She knew well enough why *she* had married him. *Love*. Oh what a wounded word was that!

Maybe they weren't properly and legally married, after all. Like Kathy said. He was the one thinking up excuses not to love her—well heart-to-heart anyway!

So what had it all been about?

With all her will Kim tried *not* to be frighteningly miserable.

It was her wedding night!

Moon shining out there—go away: and stay away! I want to cry!

But crying is something I never do!

CHAPTER FIFTEEN

They sat there in silence.

John had lifted his head from his hands long since. He edged back into the corner. He had taken out a cigarette, then later killed the butt dead in the ashtray.

Kim sat sideways-on, her knees hunched up on the seat between herself and John. Her cheek rested against the leather of the back-rest.

It seemed the moon would reach its zenith and wane in the wake of yesterday's sun before they could find a way to communicate again.

To Kim it was an aeon of time since they had spoken. And this was her wedding night! She knew the silence was of her own making, because she could have explained. Yet something inside her would not let her speak. Pride? Stubbornness?

Both!

Degree by degree, the temperature fell, as it always did at night. Her eyelids drooped over her eyes. She was so tired that not even the black band round her heart could keep her from beginning to doze off.

Here, in this car, there was only John's silence. She could not bring herself to explain to him—anything at all. He had built up the barriers, not she. She hadn't the will power, or even the wish, to break them down. She was too hurt.

He did not trust her! Unreliability was a more deadly matter for a member of a scientific expedition than for anyone in any other situation.

John and his *duboisia hopwoodi*!

It occurred to Kim, on the point of drowsing right off, that she was jealous of a wild plant. Strange, because she had always loved them—the wild things and the bush flowers!

Near-sleep almost took the barb out of her pain. Even so, a jhingi must have walked over her grave, for she shivered.

John moved, and lifted his head. The moonlight was so clear he could see the eyelashes lying on Kim's cheek. He had felt that shiver—across the distance that separated them.

'I'll get the rugs,' he said.

Kim did not answer. She had settled for sleep as being her only armour: a panacea for her woe.

He turned the door handle silently, then moving quietly inch by inch, he edged himself out backwards and dropped to the ground. He reached in the cabin for his torch above the dashboard. Still Kim did not move.

He went to the rear of the jeep, and pulled out the rugs, also the basket containing the Thermos and snacks that Mrs Barker had provided. He tied down the back-flap of the jeep and brought the rugs and basket round to the cabin.

Still Kim had not moved.

John stood quite still and watched her. The light washed her face gently with its soft opalescent glow. She looked very pale and very young—all silvered over by the moon.

He could see the rise and fall of her gently rounded bosom as she breathed.

John pushed his fingers through his hair. He could not keep the small muscle at the corner of his jaw from working.

He hefted himself up under the steering wheel, bringing one of the blankets with him.

'Kim——' he said gently. He took one of her hands but she did not move except to take a drawn-in breath that had a tiny break in it.

'She was too inexperienced to know what she was doing——' he told himself. 'That swine Smith! At his age——!'

John manœuvred one of the rugs over the top of the steering wheel, then behind Kim's back. He put his hand under her arm and drew her to a sitting position while he wrapped the blanket around her. His hand and arm could feel the warmth of her young body through its thin cotton shirt. He held her against him while he tucked the blanket round her. He rested his chin on her head so that her face lay curved in his neck.

He sat holding her for one long frightening moment. But she did not move.

Then he folded the sides of the blanket over her breast, tucking it in all round, and let her ease back against the seat.

He slung the second blanket round his own shoulders and leaned back in his own corner. He had left the Thermos and basket on the ground outside. He did not care for its contents any more.

He closed his eyes and fell to thinking.

Then, at long last, he too slept.

At dawn Kim awoke. She was stiff, though not as cold as she had been in the early part of the night. Nor as lonely. She could feel the blanket snuggled round her. John had not really meant her to get out and walk after all. He had covered her, and kept her warm.

Could she have been too stupidly stubborn? Yes, because it wasn't the first time in her life.

She couldn't bear to look at his face where he half sat, half leaned across the corner of the seat, his eyes closed. So intimate a view hurt.

She began to feel awfully hollow. When John woke up, he'd feel hollow too.

Kim wormed her way out of the blanket, then out of the jeep. The cold of the night had given way to the chill of the early morning's east wind. Even as she stood out on the track the wind was dying by degrees, and the warmth from the newly rising sun was brushing her arms and her face.

Then she saw the picnic basket on the ground on the far side of the jeep. The Thermos tea would be hot. Wonderful! The sandwiches and scones would still be fresh as they were wrapped in plastic coverings.

She looked around for a water-hole, then followed the tracks left by generations of kangaroos, snakes and goannas towards a small dip in the land on the right. There, a few white ghost-gums stood leaning forward as if looking at treasure. Here was a water-hole. It was big enough to wash in. The water was pure and safe because she could see that bush animals had been down here only last night. The tracks were moist and fresh.

Kim cupped water in her hand, and drank a little.

'If I'm not dying or dead by the time I get back with the billy-can,' she reflected, 'I'll be certain sure this water is not poison!'

She went back to the jeep and unpacked the cups and saucers and two plates. She put these in a pile by the side of the car. She walked a little way into the spinifex, spat on her fingers and held it up to the wind. This was to make sure of the wind's exact direction. Next she scraped some dried leaves together and lit them. She watched to make sure the smoke blew in the direction of the small kidney shaped claypan she had chosen. She couldn't afford to add a grass fire to her other mistakes.

All was well, so she put more broken sticks to her fire, then dampened them with a fine sprinkling of red dust.

'Now you make coals while I fetch the water——' she advised the fire: her only friend at this particular moment.

By the time she had brought back a billy full of water,

John had woken. He had shaken off his blanket and was removing himself, tousle-headed and stiff, from the jeep.

'Good morning,' Kim said pretending not to be nervous: not smiling, but trying to be bright. Her words had to tread gently on tiptoe from now on. 'Your cook didn't walk away after all! Here she is; bright and early. You did want a cook and a good housewife, didn't you, John? Well, fire's alight, breakfast is set. All we need is the billy to boil.'

'It's too early in the morning to be practical, Kim,' John said, an elaborate *quietness* in his voice.

'Me practical? Nobody ever called me that in my life, John.'

'Perhaps nobody called you by the right names *ever*—in your life. Is that the water-hole over there by the gum trees?'

'That's it, and the water's pure.' She hesitated, then added quickly, hoping still to sound bright. 'The kangaroos, snakes, emus, one goanna, *and* I—all have had some. We're still living——'

'Thank you. You need not have experimented. It's marked *Drinking Water* on the Survey map.'

Kim deflated. She hadn't thought of the Survey map.

John took his towel and soap from the back of the jeep. Then, running his fingers through his hair, went to the water-hole. He didn't look back.

Kim carried the billy to the smouldering fire and set it between two stones to boil.

'Sad!' she thought. 'We are exactly as we were before we ever went to Bim's Stopover. It's just as if nothing had happened. There wasn't any wedding. We're part of an expedition. That's all.

They had their breakfast, cleared up with haste, then packed themselves back into the jeep. The climate between them seemed set for fair weather only. They were back to starting day—as from Base!

Kim commented with care and exactitude on the interesting types of fauna and flora, as they crossed the plain. John told her which to record and in what category. Now and again he glanced down at her bent head, as the tip of her tongue in the corner of her mouth, she controlled the workings of her sharp-pointed pencil in spite of bumps and swerves by the jeep in top gear.

He said nothing of his thoughts. Kim had put up the toughest of all defences—her own professional role.

Towards noon, when they should have been nearing Skelton's homestead, John handed Kim the Survey map and told her to navigate him along the arc track that cut round the south of the mesa country, instead of from the west as before.

'If we found *duboisia* unexpectedly in the homestead area we might as well check its limits,' he said.

Kim took the map from him and studied it carefully. She intended to be the perfect navigator. She had her professional pride along with her too!

She marked the route they were to take. Presently she moved her pencil along the map, back to places where they had been since first leaving Base.

Then her thoughts *did* wander.

They had been together here, and here. And here! Her pencil touched each place, and rested there.

John looked down at her bent head. How her hair, under that ridiculous Kim-ish hat, shone in the hot light of noon! It infuriated him all over again to think of that lecherous Smith at the hotel making overtures to her. What the devil had been his real name? The master-mind for industrial spies, of course! That stuck out a mile. Those fellows seemed to *smell* when and where there was a likely 'find' by an expedition. A grape-vine leak had told its own tale. The botanists were looking for finds of *chemical* or *pharmaceutical* value.

Keeping the jeep at an even speed he watched Kim's pencil making its cross-country journey on the map—moving back over the way they had come.

The long leg to the first night's camp! Then the longer leg to the old homestead! Next came the journey to the desert fringe. The dust storm! The pencil moving, staying, pressing on, told the whole story all over again.

It told of the walk through the sand dunes. Kim's walk, alone, for four days!

She lifted her head and looked through the windscreen. He could see the lashes drop for one moment over her eyes. He saw the sad curve in the line of her mouth: the furrow on her brow.

The jeep came to a stop with a jerk.

She looked at John quickly.

'Kim!'

'Yes?'

He took his hands off the steering wheel and held one out to her.

'Kim?'

She looked at his waiting hand. It was so full of promise: of security and *peace*. She blinked her eyes. She looked up again, straight into his eyes. Then she put her hand in his.

John drove on—one hand only guiding the steering wheel. They said nothing at all.

They drove on over the breakaway west of the mesa. They burned up the red ironstone outcrop, turning north-east now over blistered red land. They rounded the hillocks clothed in spinifex, then rattled down through unexpected gorges that split the country like canyons. Here John had to release Kim's hand for he needed both hands on the wheel as they twisted in between tall shade-giving cadjebuts, and over mats of wild ferns, then up on to the plain again. The jeep swept on between vast blankets of mauve mulla mullas, flannel flowers, and cotton-tails. The ghost gums stood still in scattered loneliness. A blue-tongued lizard idled dangerously across their tracks.

As the sun began its westering they caught the rose glow of the rare miniata, and here and there splashes of sturt pea lying blood-red across the ground. Here was velutina, burgundy-coloured rufa and occasionally the flaming paradise flower.

They were again in the land where trees, bushes, and myriads of wild-flowers grew abundantly.

It was Kim who first broke the silence.

"I know why Peck and Bill never want to leave this land ——'

John's reaction was unexpected.

'Leave Peck and Bill out of your kindly musings, Kim,' he said. 'That pair are better lost than found.'

Kim was startled. Wasn't 'the war' over, after all?

'I thought you liked them?'

'I do. When they keep out of my hair——'

'Why, what do you mean? Peck was very well-behaved at our wedding. Kathy was surprised—— He has quite a reputation!'

John eased his manner.

'Yes, they were quite presentable,' he agreed. 'Possibly Peck and Bill did us a good turn. I don't suppose we'll ever really know.'

'Know what?' Kim was really puzzled now.

'The ways of people who inhabit this misbegotten stretch of no-man's land—— They're all mysteries. They're in a world of their own.'

He swung the jeep up the last rise, round a vast hump of boulders to bring it out on the tableland. Away to the north and east was the haze of the desert fringe.

'We could almost call this home-country,' he said, changing the subject. 'I think we'll make the old ruin by sundown. Before that if our luck holds.'

Kim looked at the map, then at her watch. 'We're doing fine——'

He decided she would never know the antecedents of their wedding. Luck could help him with that subterfuge. It had to do just that!

'At sundown,' Kim was thinking, 'like the flowers in the bushland I will fold up my own prickly petals for keeps. Maybe with *luck*, to-night——'

She dared not let her thoughts go farther than that.

They were both thinking of 'luck'. Courting the lady in their hearts.

Soon they were running along an old sand track.

'Something passed this way last night,' John said. 'A Land-Rover by the depths of those tyre marks.'

'Going or coming?' Kim asked. 'I hope there's no one camping at the homestead.'

'Going. Watch and you'll see where the rear wheels skid deep in the sand. It possibly by-passed the homestead on this track.'

Kim watched, and when John pointed out the tyre marks she recognised the smudged angled swerve tracks for what they were. She was relieved. Whoever had passed this way had gone west, *away from the homestead.* She and John would, please God, be all alone.

A little later Kim noticed a fine pencil of smoke rising way over to the north-east.

'Look, John. Smoke! Could it be an aborigines' camp?'

'That, Kim,' John said steadily—he'd been looking at the smoke for some minutes—'is from the homestead. It's just over the rise. Someone has lit up the old stove.'

'Oh no!'

It was wrung from her. Her heart dropped with a clang that could have been heard right across the outback.

'I'm afraid so. We have company.'

Silence fell. Kim felt there was absolutely nothing to say. Perhaps John was conscious of this too. His own silence seemed full of loaded patience: yet unspoken barbed comments.

Please don't let me get prickly again! Kim begged of her latest companion—Lady Luck.

They drove between leaning rotted fence posts, across what had once been the station's gravel square; past the tottering timbers and rusted iron sheets of falling outhouses—next the water trough that still functioned with its lead from the water-bore. Then round the corner of the crazy dilapidated old building to the 'front'.

There, fifty yards from the homestead, was parked a utility —and a small caravan hitched to the tow-bar behind it. *This was one of their own Expedition's outfits!* It bore the identity-plates.

John slammed the jeep to a stop. He sat, his hands on the wheel, and stared at the vehicles.

Kim's face froze. She said nothing. Neither did she move. The windscreen in front of her seemed fogged.

From inside the homestead there came the clatter of something falling. A cup? A billy-can? Then a man's voice was raised in excitement. He was speaking to some other person. *Two*, if not more, were camping in the homestead!

A minute later they came out of the gap that once had been a doorway.

Myree and Stephen Cole!

The air was moveless and the heat of the late afternoon

enclosed the jeep and its occupants like a steam vapour. Yet Kim was stone cold. Every little part of her *ached* with that cold.

'Oh no!'

The words were wrung from her again.

Not Myree! Beautiful, selfish, predatory, brain-box Myree! What had she, Kim, done in past years that she deserved this?

'Yes, Myree!' John spoke so quietly it almost frightened her.

Could there be relief in his voice? Or had she dreamed it?

Kim looked at him. If possible her heart dropped lower. He didn't *seem* deadened by frost bite or withered by hell fires within. He was masked and walled-up—all over again: except that he was getting ready to smile at Myree. Fighting to keep it professional? The leader catching up with his team?

John turned the door handle. Kim saw that he really was smiling at the other girl. Myree wreathed in poise and charm was coming across the gravel stretch to meet them. She carried herself with the manner of a born hostess greeting late arrivals—except that she looked only at John. She smiled only at him. John returned the smile.

CHAPTER SIXTEEN

Kim unfroze slowly. She would have to play it the old way—as when Celia and Diane set out to take all her about-to-be admirers from her. She'd smile it out. She would have to do that, *or just lie down and die.*

John was already out of the jeep and on the gravel. He was looking at Myree and—*yes*—continuing to smile!

Kim let herself out of the car. She felt dreadfully stiff but would rather have died than show it.

She straightened her back. Resolution, if not pride, suddenly possessed her.

Myree and Stephen were not going to have John. Not even over her dead body. She would think of something artful and awful to do to them. The kind of things Jeff's 'Bratto' used to think up once upon a time. Then it came like a flash—the

Idea Brilliant—for it was born out of an old forgotten piece of knowledge.

It was Stephen who gave it to her. He wore a sort-of forced smile as he came forward to meet them, *and he put his hand up to smooth his hair*. It was a gesture—the hand smoothing the red-brown hair—that did it. *She'd seen it before*: the way he did it from the centre part, then down. Now she remembered where, and how she had known of him. A glass darkly was shattered.

She knew what she would do about it too!

She smiled at Stephen. Then, not even doubtfully, she smiled at Myree. This last was wasted because Myree was devoting all her attention to John.

'I can't believe it,' Myree was saying, looking lovely in spite of the place, the hour, and the puzzling frown on her beautiful forehead. The heavenly peaked eyebrows were hovering just a little higher. Her smile was as brilliant as ever, if a little *determined*. 'I really refuse to believe that you two are married! A mistake, of course! We heard about it at Base. We could make contact on our very simple transceiver with one of the stations north of us. The people there said they were going to a wedding. Yours! Well, I ask you? We did laugh!'

'It's quite true,' John said, so mildly that Kim looked at him quickly.

'We decided it was a mistake,' Myree repeated determinedly. 'A confusion of names about who was at Bim's Stopover . . . about *who* was getting married. John, it's not true! I simply don't believe you!' She laughed a little shakily.

Kim pressed her hands down over her overalls as if to smooth them. Then she pulled her battered hat forward over her brow. She was back to her old self, all right. She *felt* like it. She looked only at Stephen from under the brim, and dug her hands in her side pockets.

'Hullo!' she said brightly. She hoped she sounded baleful too.

Stephen sensed something was not quite usual about Kim. He stood quite still, watching her carefully. His uneasy smile flickered to rest. Then he decided some kind of quick natural exertion was necessary.

'Petso!' he said mocking her, yet still *watching* her like

he'd watch a snake likely to rear and strike. 'Petso darling, you've let me down. You've gone and married someone else. Or have you? Do I beg or steal a kiss? What John says can't really be true, of course.'

Kim shook her head. Her eyes went on watching him, and her smile was just too consciously Mona Lisa-ish. She had put on her so-called 'inimical' look.

'Sorry Stephen. I don't have any kisses to spare on Wednesdays. It is Wednesday, isn't it? Anyway, they're expensive. Kisses, I mean. *Very*——' She paused, looking at him sideways. Then finished—'Or aren't they expensive? Those ones back at the Base, for instance?'

Stephen looked away for a split second. Then he straightened his shoulders.

'Kisses expensive?' he asked, trying to sound incredulous. Could she possibly guess at that trading of information with the industrial chemist? How could she? He'd covered all his tracks. Did she mean 'kisses' as a code word, or a warning? *What was she up to?*

Stephen glanced obliquely at John Andrews, partly to escape the expression in Kim's eyes, partly to play for time.

'Funny,' he said, back to joking. 'I can't imagine John in any kind of kissing situation——'

Kim refused to blush at that image. She had business to do with Stephen. A trade-in to effect. Two could play at that game. She went on looking at him in a knowing way on purpose. She meant to make him uneasy.

'By the way, Kim,' Stephen hurried on. 'They'd all heard, back at Base, about that four day walk of yours. Everyone's still goggling. Couldn't quite believe it, you know——'

Myree, only a yard or two away, looked round quickly. She had heard this last remark of Stephen's.

'Why so, John?' she asked turning back to her quarry. 'Why did you stay out there alone? You, as leader, were the important one——' She gave a little laugh. 'It is rather convenient to be the girl in the party sometimes, isn't it? I mean—first preference to being saved, and all that."

John pushed his hat on the back of his head.

'It was not quite like that——' he said mildly.

'Oh, I know. Don't tell me. Your precious plant finds, of course! You were quite right. It's in the tradition of great scientists to make personal sacrifices. You will be quite a hero, John.'

Kim was thinking that John was regarding Myree with too much interest during this speech. His eyes were searching the other girl's face. Myree noticed it too. And liked it. Kim tried not to let her heart drop any farther. It was probably rock-bottom already, anyway.

She had yet to fight the good fight——

'You thought possible death by thirst or privation was worth special valuable plant finds?' John was asking Myree quizzically.

'Of course you would be like that, John! It's in the tradition—as I said. We were sure you found something special out there. That is why George Crossman let me come here. By your own book of rules I had to have a partner.' She laughed again. This time as if making a jolly joke of it all. 'Hence Stephen. I had to *find* this place. Stephen had been here before—except for George who couldn't be spared.'

'Of course,' John pulled his hat to its right place over his brow. Then he took the thing off altogether, folded it, and pushed it in his belt.

'Stephen knew the route.' He nodded his head thoughtfully. 'The obvious partner,' he concluded.

Stephen squared his shoulders.

'Let's face it, Boss. Being an extra I was the only one not wanted urgently at Base. The poor girl had to have someone to change the wheel when she blew a puncture.'

'Don't make small of yourself, Stephen,' Myree said with an overdose of kindness in her voice. 'You were most useful.'

Stephen made a grimace at Kim. This last phrase was damning with faint praise.

'You see?' he said. 'That's all I am. Someone who is useful. Like the caretaker, or something.'

'Well . . . it's my turn to make use of you now,' Kim said with a docility that did not deceive Stephen. 'Way back we saw the smoke signals of the fire in the stove. Does the billy boil? We haven't had any lunch. Nor afternoon break. Let's make tea? You and I, Stephen——'

'It's on the boil, Petso,' he was very eager to please. He was uncertain of Kim, and mistrusted her gentle docility. Also her willingness to leave Myree to John,

Trouble brewing—was the message flashed to the back of his mind.

John, with one hand in his pocket, and the other wiping dust from his forehead, was already dug into an involved scientific discussion with Myree. Kim guessed it was about the wonder 'find', and the duplicate of records he had ordered specially for her.

Why can't John see what she's doing? Kim's inside voice almost wailed as she asked herself the answerless question.

She walked with Stephen beside her towards the hole-in-the-wall that was the homestead's front door.

'Come on in, Kim-girl,' Stephen invited, too casually.

She felt a flick of sadness for him. He scented danger. And how right he was!

'Cast your hat somewhere, sweetie. There's nothing to put it on, as well you know. By the way——' He went on talking as if words might ultimately avert the thing he possibly feared. He had seen recognition of a special kind in Kim's eyes. She had fooled *Smith*. He'd already discovered that. Not without brains was the little Petso.

'By jingo! And by the way!' he went on. 'We laughed our heads off when we saw that six inch scribble on the wall outside. *Kim Wentworth Was Here!*'

'Yes,' Kim said gravely. 'And underneath I wrote—*So Was John!* You saw it when you were here before, Stephen. Maybe it saved our lives then. Now it puts a sort-of claim on the homestead doesn't it? *Our homestead!*' She was very meaningful about this last bit.

He was fiddling with the billy on the stove. He turned round and looked at her.

'Myree might say, right now, possession is nine points of the law——' he began, pretending cheerfulness. 'We're in possession——'

'But our names were on the homestead *first*, Stephen dear ——' Kim persisted.

That 'dear' warmed his heart just when he needed it most. He lifted the billy off the stove.

'Yes, my pet. What can I do for you?'

Kim was standing quite still in the middle of the old weathered floor. She had not taken her hat off. She had it cocked at a curious angle over her brow. This way she felt it gave her stature! Made her look taller.

'I want you to take Myree away. *To-night*——' She said it quite simply as if she was spelling out a one-syllable word. Her eyes under the brim of that dusty, waifish, worse-for-wear jungle hat were clear and frank; yet determined.

Stephen put the billy on the hearth, fetched four cups from the camp gear in the far corner and began to ladle boiling tea into them.

'Come, come!' he said jokingly. 'Myree has a mind. And knows how to make it up. Darling Kim, she has come out here to find something that John knows about and that will be invaluable to her work. You don't really think she'll budge?'

'No, I don't. But she could be kidnapped.'

Stephen looked up as if he'd really seen a snake. He now waited for the hiss and fang.

'You wouldn't be a little desert-happy, Petso?'

'Don't call me "Petso", Stephen. I'm not that any more.'

'Sit down, Kim. You make me uncomfortable. If you aren't the Petso, what are you?'

'Well,' Kim said, considering. 'You could have said I was a blackmailer. That is, if you'd known me a little better in the olden times, back at the Base.'

Stephen, the tilted billy of tea in one hand, stared at the girl in front of him.

'*Blackmail?*'

'Don't be so surprised, Stephen. You've been dealing in it a long, long time. So you know what I mean.'

He put the billy down, squatted on his heels and went on staring at Kim. She noticed he was a little paler now. All brashness gone.

She moved across to the wall: then let herself slide down so that she sat on the floor, her sunburned legs stretched out before her She dragged off her hat-ridiculous, and plonked it on the floor beside her.

She looked out through the doorway to where John and Myree, now both of them leaning on the bonnet of the jeep, were still deep in talk. *Very possessive talk too*—Kim thought *—even if it was botanical*. She had to play the valiant; and the unscrupulous with Stephen—but inside her heart was crying.

She knew that Myree might be too strong for her. Myree carried too many guns. Even now—out there—looking up into John's face, talking vivaciously, smiling into his eyes, Myree was playing for a knockout win. For *her*, there were no such things as 'marriage-lines'.

Kim closed her own eyes.

'Talking about blackmail——' she remarked.

'Yes,' said Stephen. 'Talking about blackmail?'

'I'll trade secrets with you, Stephen. I know why you went to the other side of Australia to work for that man Smith—or whatever his real name is. "Matthews" I think you once said. That was what the "M" was for in his signature at the Stopover, I guess. You had three years of studies in Botany behind you—then, like the ass you are—you borrowed someone else's assignment and sandwiched it into your own. They stood you down for that, so you couldn't take out your degree that year.' She looked across the short distance between them. Stephen passed her a cup of tea, then sat back against the wall himself, and sipped his own tea. He was silent.

'I'm right, aren't I?' she asked.

'Go on,' he said tonelessly.

'You minded that very much, Stephen,' Kim said gently. 'But it was a two year suspension only. Though you've taken longer yourself. Why? You could go back and finish——'

'And face Professor Watts again? And those lecturers?'

Kim considered this.

'It takes courage——' she agreed at length, her head on one side, cogitating. There was a long silence. Then she finished—'Seems like a better way of life than taking money to act as a "spy" for an industrial chemist!'

He glanced at her quickly.

'You *knew*? *I* mean— *why* I was in the Expedition?'

'You asked too many unnecessary questions, darling Stephen. Specially about plants I was supposed to keep confidential: and which had to do with medical uses. Then there was that scrounging through George's lab. That was all back at Base. Before we ever came out here. I only surmised but——'

Stephen sipped his tea, an excuse to keep his eyes averted.

'And I thought Myree was the one who had brains!' he said after a long silence.

'She has too. That's why I'm afraid of her.'

'With John?'

'With anyone.'

Outside the sun had gone down. A wonderful pink and

mauve haze clothed the land. It made Myree—where she stood talking eagerly to John—almost ethereal in her attractiveness.

'That man Smith——' Kim went on, out of a void of silence. 'He borrowed my record book. But it was only the record and drawings that I had done from memory of my own trip up from the Darling Ranges as far as Manutarra Pretty, but that was all. Quite irrelevant to the Expedition. Nothing really botanical in it. He had to bring the copy he made of it, in the still dark hours of night, to you—out here—to interpret. You had to tell him that's all it was—a girl's own picture-story of her travels. Was he very mad about it, when you told him?'

Stephen sat hunched and despondent.

'How did you know he came here?' he asked at last.

'A Land-Rover went through travelling west, in the last forty-eight hours. We saw its tracks as we came in. It was the same Land-Rover that called for Mr Smith at Bim's Stopover in the middle of the night, I guess. Another of his employees at hand? Flown into Bim's the night before? How much did he dock your pay-packet Stephen, when you told him he'd brought away—from that sucker of a girl at the pub—something that was worth nothing to anybody, *except to that girl?*'

Stephen remained pale and silent.

Through the doorway Kim could see the other two.

Myree reached up to brush away a night wasp that had tangled itself in John's hair.

Kim's heart hardened. It had to harden. That small intimate gesture of Myree's cut her very heart-strings. Also made her blood soar boiling-wards.

'You know something, Stephen?' she said mildly. 'It would be so much easier for me to stack on a show, stamp my foot or burst into tears! Then say—"Stephen *Petso*, let you and me just cut and run." Two vagabonds!' she sighed. 'But I'd rather stay.'

'Okay.' he said looking into his tea-cup. 'So what next?'

'*Kidnap* her. She'd never go if you just *asked*. She'll stick with John till he's taken her out to the sand plain; and he'll take her all right. A twosome according to rules. His precious botanical find comes *first*. I don't know how you'll do it. You'll have to think it out yourself. But please do it.'

'You love him?'

'Of course I do.'

'You know what, Kim?' He was looking at her now. 'In the right kind of a way, *I love you*. I hated this blasted thing that was between us—I mean my being in someone else's pay.'

She smiled across the space at him. It was a bleak smile, but it shone true.

'We're a couple of way-out misfits—our lives behind us full of silly mistakes. Is that it? Me always posing as a sort-of *bratto*. You——' She broke off.

'I guess that's it. We don't conform.'

'Don't be too quiet, Stephen dear. I haven't twisted the noose right round your neck yet. I've something more to ask. Another piece of blackmail——'

'Ask the world, Kim. After that walk of yours—four days and nights through the sand dunes with nothing but a compass and a water-bag—you can have the moon and stars too.'

'*With my hat on my head*. Don't forget that, Stephen,' she smiled, though painfully. 'Dr John Andrews' last and most fear-inspiring command was—*Keep your hat on your head!* And I did. Jolly clever, considering, don't you think?'

'You can laugh about it?'

'It's all over. I'm alive, and I've married Dr John Andrews. What better could I do for myself?'

'Nothing, except get rid of Myree. Well, go ahead. I'll take her off. Heaven knows how—but I'll do it. When my courage falters—— Or Myree, a trussed chicken in the bag, kicks or hollers too much, I'll remember you kept your hat on your head *and beat the sun*. Did you know the sun is more powerful than any other force in the world?'

'There's the other question I have to ask. Remember?'

'Fire away!'

'As we haven't any Bible here you will have to spit your death, *and promise*.'

'Granted.'

'Never—ever—to any living soul—cast a smear-doubt on Ralph Sinclair's doctorate. You heard me, Stephen. The drawings I did for him were only *related* to his topic. They were for reference purposes only. He did all his own drawings for his thesis.'

'Sorry about that one, Kim. It was dirty of me. You knew what I was up to?'

'Buying my loyalty. That's when I first guessed you were up to something. Then came all those questions.'

CHAPTER SEVENTEEN

Outside, the twilight haze of gold and mauve, rose-pink and amethyst, had turned to purple against a wounded sky. Then darkness came on like the slow pulling down of a blind over the western arc.

Footsteps were coming towards the homestead.

Stephen and Kim caught one another's eyes. Solemnly each spat on a forefinger and each made a sign over the heart. A trading of blackmails it was. Stephen would daring-do with Myree; and Kim would never speak of Stephen's past—to anyone.

Only Myree came right into the homestead. John called Stephen out for a short talk.

Kim found herself once again in the role of cook. Stephen and Myree, like themselves, had brought with them a plentiful variety of stores. Myrée made a point of having to jot down at once a few botanical details John had given her. Kim thought this *could* have been an excuse not to play cook. Then again it might not. Myree and John did have important information to exchange. Kim had to be fair about that. Hadn't she had to make duplicate copies of John's notes for Myree? Meantime Myree was ignoring Kim's existence.

Later, when the evening meal was finished and cigarettes were out, Stephen seemed, almost unnaturally to become confident in his role of host.

'I guess you want to take a last look at your specimen cases, John,' he suggested. 'Adjust the thermostats, and all that. Myree and I were here first, so we choose the next chores as ours. We're going out to the trough to wash up. Don't look surprised, Myree! If you really want top marks with the boss you'll shake a hand with the dishes. Kim's done her whack as cook. Besides,' he finished, '*We* haven't been travelling all day. They have!'

Myree's quick mind took less than half a second to jump the hurdle. She saw the point of Stephen's suggestion.

A willing heart and a ready hand! That, of course, would win *any* man! But to the lengths of dish washing——?

She intended to go out to that place where John had found the almost extinct—therefore unique—specimens of *hopwoodi*. And she intended John to take her. She would *please* the man—as from now. The plant was of the same generic origin as some of the plants she was studying herself.

Surprise would make the reference in her thesis worth a mint of gold. She would even get publication. Her name and Dr John Andrews linked together? Oh no, she was in no danger of telling *anyone*, as John well knew. No scientist ever foolishly threw away a chance of success by *talking*.

Myree's thoughts moved on with cold calculation. Out there on the desert fringe—with John—there would be other things to think about too. It was a modern world. It was a see-all and take-all world—permissive, as far as men were concerned. She was an amoral person by her own decision.

As for Kim! Well, poor Kim. It would be her turn to be hindmost again. As *usual*! Personnel had to work with partners, so dear little Kim would have to go back to Base with Stephen!

'Dishes out to the trough first——' Stephen was saying. 'Here—tuck the cutlery under your arm, Myree. I'll bring all the plastic ware. I suppose we'd better wash the billy's bottom. My, oh my! How black can a billy get?'

While the collection of dishes and give-and-take of instructions were going on, Kim sat near the fire with her legs curled under her. She thought it 'fair' that Myree was let in for the washing up.

The temperature was beginning to drop. In two hours it would be fifteen degrees below midday temperature. In four hours it would be very, very cold.

Kim thought of the long night, and the cold hard boards. The sleeping bags and rugs were in the jeep! Perhaps she ought to make things less embarrassing for John by suggesting she slept in the jeep herself?

She would have to wait until Stephen and Myree were

out of the door, and out of earshot. It had only been a vain hope that Stephen could take Myree away *to-night*. Too late now. To-morrow probably! Or the next day——

John, sitting with his back against the wall, had been reading the papers brought out from Base by Stephen. To Kim he seemed preoccupied to the point of not being present at all.

What were their several sleeping arrangements to be? The pantry? The spare room with its hole in the wall? One visitor here and one visitor there? How did she bring the subject up?

Stephen and Myree, cluttered with utensils, had gone through the door. In the stillness before the night wind rose across the desert lands, their voices could be heard as Stephen attempted to give Myree advice at the veranda's edge. Myree—superior and sceptical—was rejecting most of it.

'You'd better see if all's well with your specimens, Myree——' Stephen was saying. 'I put them in the caravan just before dinner when I came out to talk with John. I locked the door too. I have the key here. Let me carry those things. Mind the plastic now——' They had stopped to rearrange their burdens.

'What in the name of fortune were you doing interfering with my collection?' Myree's voice was rising with annoyance. 'The temperature was probably controlled where they were——'

'Sure!' Stephen sounded airy, not at all disturbed. 'Who's to know those prospectors won't come back in the night? Or a kangaroo hop in from the desert to have a munch at your plants? The caravan's the only safe place for them. Specially when it's locked up——'

'They were perfectly safe where I had them!'

They had begun to move on again now, but Stephen's voice came clear and soothing. 'Okay, okay! Let's fix them now. I'll give you a hand. We'll dump this stuff in the trough first, then we'll check if all's well with the caravan. The torch is in the cabin of the utility.'

The voices faded as distance and the corner of the homestead intervened.

Kim, only half listening, stared into the fire coals in the stove. In spite of the echoing sounds of activity outside she had been aware only of the utter stillness inside. It was a long time since John had turned even one page of the paper he was reading.

Kim stole a glance at him—only to meet his eyes straight-on. He was sitting, his back propped against the wall, his long legs stretched before him—looking at her over the top of his paper. In a way that made her heart turn over too. There was something *knowing* in a whimsical kind of way in his eyes.

The paper went down in an untidy sprawl on the floor.

She wanted to blink, but her eyes wouldn't obey.

'Kim——' he said very gently. 'Come over here. This wall will stay warm long after that fire goes out——'

She wanted to shake her head. She wanted to stand on her pride. She was afraid of something smarting behind her eyes that would embarrass her beyond endurance when Stephen and Myree came back into the room.

'I'm beautifully warm just now——' she began. 'I think Stephen has bagged that place against the wall——'

'Damn Stephen!' John said Had she heard right? There was a whole world of emphasis in the very quietness of his voice 'Damn Myree too! I have a hunch they won't be back for a long, long time——'

Kim stared at him. Maybe it was her ears that had gone wrong John was suddenly very free with 'damns'. *One for Myree too!*

In the moment's silence her ears really *did* hear something —a clang followed by a very final bang from outside. A car door being slammed? No, *two* doors surely! The caravan, then the utility?

John too had heard, for he bent his head in a listening way. The queer little smile in his eyes was edging round the corners of his mouth now.

'The wind catching the loose iron on the old outhouse?' Kim asked tentatively Anything to escape the mesmerism with which bent head and all, his eyes were still holding hers.

John was really smiling now. He was enjoying some small joke. Or was he?

'Kim,' he said softly. 'Kim darling.' He held out one hand. 'I want you Because——'

She tilted her head as she looked at his hand. The temptation to go to him was almost beyond endurance. She looked up at his face again.

'Because?' she prompted him.

'Because I need you. Because I want you. Because I love you.'

'But you said—I mean—*what did you say*?'

'Come over here, Kim. Or do I come and get you?'

Slowly, not really believing in magic, she got up from the floor by the stove and went to him. He had said he *loved* her!

She slid down on the floor beside him. His arm went round her. Defeated and at his mercy, yet thankful beyond dreams, she dropped her cheek on his shoulder.

She was too tired. She didn't care any more who came in that gaping hole of a door and saw them. She wanted never to move again from the warm circle of his arm.

She would give in; and take the crumbs. Yet, he had said ——

Her ears were muffled by the pound of her unsure heart. Outside there was a sound for all the world like a car engine. A loud car engine. It pulsed like the rhythm of a car engine speeding up, then rumbling off in the distance. It was mixed up with the noisy beat of her heart.

She could feel John's chin resting on her head, and his other hand stroking her arm.

Suddenly Kim sat up.

'That was the utility going! And taking the caravan with it!' Her voice wobbled as she made this fantastic statement. Yet it was true.

His eyes had in them the kind of light that she never expected to see in any botanist's eyes. Specially not in the eyes of Dr John Andrews.

'*Taking everything with them, including Stephen and Myree*,' he said.

Kim was bolt upright by this time, drawing herself away from him.

'*Stephen's taken Myree?*' She couldn't quite believe in miracles. 'But *how*——?'

'I think Stephen slammed Myree in the back of the caravan with her specimens,' John said gently. 'At least I would guess that from the last of the conversation we overheard.' That maddening flashing smile was there, turning his face into all-heaven. 'Stephen playing the perfect gentleman, would have unlocked the door for her,' he went on. 'Being no gentleman at all—he would have locked it fast behind her——'

'Myree *inside*?' Kim was incredulous.

Then belief came—dawning clear and true like the aurora night lights down in the far south.

It had happened! *They were gone!* Stephen had kept his side of the 'blackmail' bargain!

'But how did you know, John? It was Stephen and I who ——'

'Who plotted it?' John's eyebrows went up quite innocently. 'Stephen never could keep a secret. That's why no one, not even Myree, let him know about *hopwoodi*.'

'Stephen *told* you what I had said when you were talking to him out there before dinner?'

John was enjoying a joke but with a kind-of-kindness that tangled itself in Kim's heart strings.

'He told me the whole plot. I even suggested the first moves for him. Moves such as putting her specimens in the caravan so she'd have to go and check them. Also getting her outside on a washing-up stint——'

'You—*what*?'

This just couldn't be *Dr John Andrews*, the serious brain-box scientist!

Kim was almost shocked, yet beginning in a wonderful way to be wildly happy. It was all right for *her* to be plotting. But not John!

'I didn't think you would ever——' she began. 'I mean, *I* could stoop to things like kidnapping. I've been doing crazy things out of self defence, all my life. I haven't any scruples ——'

He was laughing at her.

'Don't you think a man is entitled to a little self defence too?' he asked.

'Defence from what? Not Myree! Oh no—you are going to give her a job at the Institute by the Mount——'

'I've changed my mind. Some time back! Myree is a brilliant botanist, but much too self-determined. Two of us like that at the Mount would cry havoc, Kim. Pandemonium amongst the potted plants! Imagine it!'

'But you're not . . .' She broke off. The situation was beyond her.

She drew back and looked at him, her brow wrinkled. She was still too nervous of mischance to grasp the invitation in John's face.

He looked so wonderful sitting there—his back against the wall, his long legs stretched out on the dusty, ant-eaten, weather-worn, plank-torn, *heavenly* floor!

'Aren't I what?' he asked, raising his eyebrows as he read her mind. 'Try me out, Kim.'

She was *lost*. She said nothing. She went on looking at him still afraid that the happiness so near might prove only a mirage. Here now—gone in a minute. He actually was capable of doing the artful-awful things she sometimes did herself!

She shook her head.

'You didn't trust me. About that Mr Harold-tycoon-M-Smith——' she said reproachfully. She had her theory about that 'M' initial, but she wouldn't give Stephen away—even to John! She had her side of the blackmail bargain to keep too. Just now her only hurt was because John had not trusted her.

He wasn't smiling any more. He was as serious as if he'd turned one switch off and another on.

'I did not *not* trust you, Kim. My confidence in you as an assistant was absolute. It simply cut me to the quick to think what tricks an unscrupulous man like Smith could have tried on anyone so unworldly as——' He cut short. 'Well, as the kind of girl you are, Kim——' He finished just a little lamely for John.

'What kind of a girl am I?' she asked this ever so carefully for fear he might mention that word 'school girl' again.

He didn't answer her. His eyes watched the shadowy thoughts in her face.

Suddenly he gathered in his long legs and stood up.

'Time this station closed down for the night,' he said abruptly. 'I'm going for the rugs. It's getting colder already.'

She thought he went through the doorway in a *very purposeful* manner.

Kim was beginning to see stars even where there weren't any.

She went out to the trough and finished the dish washing.

Then she washed herself again, and cleaned her teeth twice—just to be sure. She carried the cups and plates, knives and forks, back into the homestead, and tidied them away in a corner. She put the billy-can on the stove ready for the morning. She lowered the wicks of the hurricane lamps a little, then stirred the coals in the stove.

Outside the desert chill was creeping over the land. Her heart was beating somewhat ominously once more. She was anxious all over again because John was a long time outside. Putting his specimens to bed, of course.

She put her beloved hat on the floor by the wall near her. It was part of herself for ever even when she didn't have to *wear* it.

John came in and dropped the rugs in a pile on the floor beside her. She looked at them ruefully.

'John,' she said gently, shaking her head at his absent-mindedness. 'You didn't bring in the sleeping bags. They're under the——'

She caught his eyes.

'Sleeping bags be damned!' he remarked flatly. 'Life in those things would be like living in semi-detached houses. One of us in each——'

Kim sat quite still. Her eyes with their beguiling hint of wonder were very wide.

He dropped down on the rugs beside her. He looked at her for one moment, then held out his arms.

She leaned forward tipping straight into them. Her face was pressed against his shoulder.

'I'm a very determined man,' he said, resting his cheek on her head, holding her warmly to him. 'You need to know about that, my dear, dear Kim. I will have my house the way I want it—*my wife beside me*——' He put his hand under her chin, lifted it and kissed her full on the lips. He took a long, long time about it. Kim could have stayed in that kiss for ever.

'I love you very much, Kim. Ever since the first day I met you—if I'd only acknowledged it then. You were so endearing in that short skirt and those new shoes. Such a haughty little wild-cat. But I can be stubborn too, I'm sorry to say. That makes two of us, doesn't it? But now——'

Kim for the first time in her life, was wordless. *He'd actually liked her all the time?*

He scrambled to his feet, bent over her, then lifted her up in his arms. He set her down again on the rugs, leaning over her. He planted his hands one on either side of her, and smiled into her eyes.

'I'll tell you something else, my darling Kim. I forgot to bring your pyjamas too.'

Kim's eyes widened—just that much. Then, like magic, she too came to life.

With a flip-twist of her quicksilver body she turned and reached for the desert-daubed, earth-brown, hat-ridiculous. She slapped it high on her head, the brim dipping absurdly over one eye.

'Then I'll have *my hat on my head*,' she said. 'Just as you ordered, John. Day and night too!'

She was laughing at him. His eyes smiled back.

Kim had always known it would be heaven in the outback—when she really got there!

That's why she had run away.

[illegible] as minute by minute passed, her fear receded. Something else was taking its place. A sort of muted, mounting
excitement. Her heart could just possibly be beating to the
sound of happiness. . . .

She was married to John. She would make her marriage